Perfect Girl

MICHELE GORMAN

Notting Hill Press
PUBLISHING'S THIRD WAY

Copyright © 2014 Michele Gorman

All characters and events in this publication, other than those clearly in the public domain, are fictitious and any resemblance to real persons, living or dead, is purely coincidental.

All rights reserved. No part of this publication may be reproduced, stored in a retrieval system, or transmitted, in any form or by any means, without the prior permission of the publisher

ISBN: 1501099337
ISBN-13: 978-1501099335

ALSO BY MICHELE GORMAN

The Reluctant Elf
The Curvy Girls Club
Christmas Carol
Bella Summer Takes a Chance
Single in the City (The Expat Diaries: I)
Misfortune Cookie (The Expat Diaries: II)
Twelve Days to Christmas (The Expat Diaries: III)

ABOUT THIS EDITION

Perfect Girl has been written and edited in British English rather than American English, including spelling, grammar and punctuation.

PART ONE

CHAPTER 1

The flashes start as soon as I stumble through the revolving door. Ping, ping, ping. Little white boxes burning across my vision.

'Look here! Hey, this way! Darlin', over here!'

Someone tipped off the media. I could turn away, try to hide my face like the A-listers do, but that'd seem a bit pretentious for someone so far down the popularity alphabet. There are at least a dozen photographers flanking us. I'll have to go down the steps. Even if there was another way out, they'd probably find it. I'm surprised so many are bothering with us. This isn't Boujis and I'm not exactly with Prince Harry.

We're attracting quite a bit of attention now. More and more people are holding their phones up, trying to snatch something worth tweeting. They have no idea who we are. They're just hoping to capture the photo that'll catapult them towards viral Instagram fame.

At least I got to touch up my lipstick before we left. There's nothing worse than those unguarded photos of a woman tumbling from a nightclub with the smudged smile of a psychotic clown. Well, okay, of course there's worse, but I am wearing knickers and my skirt's not too short.

I can see the car now. It's ticking over beside the kerb in a double red zone. Rock Star parking.

As he opens the passenger door (courteous to the end) I think about how far I've come. I can even point to where it started, with Dad's party. Has my life really changed so completely in six months? Time sure does fly.

'Mind your head,' he says as he gently pushes me into the police car. He joins the other Met officer in front as the reporters aim their cameras into the windows and howl like a pack of overexcited hounds.

'Why did you do it, Carol?'

'Are you sorry?'

Over and over they repeat their questions, like there's a simple answer.

At least they don't turn on the lights as we pull away. After all, there's no need to rush now.

CHAPTER 2

Six months earlier...

I feel Ben's lanky body slip into bed behind me. My first thought is, *He's drunk*. My second thought, when he pulls me to him is, *Suck in your tummy*.

Urgh, too late. Palm full of squidge for my boyfriend. It's his own fault, really. He needs fitting with a bell to give me some warning, like Mum did with the cat to stop him killing sparrows in the garden.

'What time is it?' I murmur. Last year the sleep clinic made me take the clock out of my bedroom. Now I just get up to check the one in the kitchen, adding insult to insomnia.

'It's after two, I'm sorry.' He snuggles closer, reeking of gin. I hate gin, but I love him, so things kind of balance out. 'I probably should have called first, but I didn't want to wake you. You did say I could let myself in any time, right?'

True. When I gave him the newly-cut key tied with

pink ribbon six months ago I imagined my bed strewn with rose petals, surprise dinners, my flat redecorated by the *Changing Rooms* team, obvious things like that. He's used it once to let the boiler man in when I couldn't get away from the office.

'You went for a drink after?' Question, not accusation.

'Yeah. We grabbed something for dinner and ended up staying out.' He hesitates. 'I'll have to go back in tomorrow.'

I fizz awake. 'But it's Dad's birthday party tomorrow.'

'I know, I'm sorry,' he says to the back of my head, his face buried in my sheet-frazzled hair. 'You know we're preparing for court. I can't work without the others there. It's a team project.' He grabs my tummy again. This time I'm ready for him. 'I wanted to see you tonight.'

'It's not tonight. It's tomorrow.'

'I wanted to see you tomorrow, too.'

… 'I'm tired, Ben.'

'No ulterior motives, I promise. At least not till I get some sleep first.'

I smile in the dark. 'I'm glad you came over. Though I wish you could come to Dad's tomorrow.'

'Me too. You know I would if I could. I don't want to spend my Sunday working.'

'I know,' I say, pulling his arm around me to hold his hand. 'Like Mum always says, it's the price you pay for your success.'

Lately, though, it's felt like *my* purse being emptied.

* * * * *

My parents' house is bright enough to lure migrating birds off course. In the weak winter twilight, gold and purple metallic bunting reflects flashing strings of fairy lights. Lilac balloons decorate the posts beside the drive and a twenty-foot long banner (*Happy 55th Joel!*) is stretched across the windows at the front. If Dad had his way, he'd hide in his studio till the whole thing blows over. If Mum has hers, we'll be the lead story on *The One Show*.

I stagger towards the front door, still grizzling about my sister's phone call.

'Just a few things to pick up for me, will you please?' Marley had said. 'I'm running late. Have you got a pen?'

Half a dozen Tesco bags rub against my knees. A bargain pack of coat hangers pokes through the flimsy plastic, hitching up the side of my new dress and threatening to run my tights.

The familiar wall of warmth envelops me when I step into the front hall. My parents aren't what you'd call 'jumper people'. For them the perfect ambient temperature hovers around that of the Sahara at midday.

Despite the stress of the past few months, it's good to be home again, even if my eyes are beginning to desiccate.

'Hello, darling!' Mum says as she hugs me. I can hear everyone laughing in the living room. Our neighbours like to hit the bottle early. Mrs McConnell will be Irish step dancing by the time Dad blows out his birthday candles.

'What took you so long? Did you get caught up in traffic?'

Mum steps back, appraising the deep blue jersey

dress and matching suede platform heels I bought for today. Satisfied, she tucks a lock of my thick blonde hair behind my ear. She's always doing that because, she says, I've got too much hair for my face. 'You look lovely, but you've laddered your tights.'

I don't bother saying that this is Marley's fault.

'Where's Dad's cake?' she asks.

'I've only got two hands.' I shift my BlackBerry and keys back to my handbag. 'It's in the car, and I'm late because I had to pick up some things that Marley needed. She should be here soon.'

'She's been here for ages! She's in the kitchen.'

'Then I'm so glad I was able to take the stress out of *her* day.'

'Stop being dramatic. You needed to go to the shop anyway.' She peers over my shoulder. 'Where's Ben?'

'Working. He sends his love, but he'll probably be at the office till late. They're still preparing for that case.'

She nods. Work excuses are the norm in our family. Marley works at the same bank as me, though in another department in a different building. As the investment banking boss's secretary her hours are more regular than mine but she does sometimes get caught up in important meetings (all meetings are important to bankers). And Dad's schedule has always been haphazard.

'Drop the bags upstairs, please, and go get the cake,' Mum says. 'We're all dying to see it.' Her face is flushed with excitement, or possibly heat stroke. Either way, she's beautiful. Tall and regal, her pencil skirt and crisp white blouse accentuates the slim waist she proudly maintains despite having had two children, and her deep auburn updo shows off the diamond and pearl earrings that Dad got her for their thirtieth wedding anniversary last year. My mum, the red-hot stunner of Netherhaven Close.

Upstairs, I can hear the sound of running water coming from the bathroom. The lights are on; the tap is going full-throttle and a half-eaten marmalade sandwich balances on the edge of the bath.

Zoe.

Her room is empty but when I shove open the guest bedroom door it flies closed again with a painful thud. 'Don't come in!' shouts Zoe. 'I'm dressing! Undressing. I'm undressing!'

'Zoe, it's me, open up. Why are you undressing in the guest room?' Carefully, I open the door again. 'You left the tap running in the bathroom.'

'Did I?' she asks vaguely and, I note, fully dressed. 'I was having a sandwich.'

As if that explains the tap. She moves to the window seat in the dark. A lighter flares.

It takes a moment for my eyes to adjust. 'Are you smoking pot?' I say as I flick on the light.

'Turn that off! Don't tell Madame Colbert.'

'As if I would.' I flip the switch. 'When did you develop a drug habit?'

'It is not a drug habit,' she scoffs, making me feel like her grandmother. 'It is no worse than you having a glass of wine.'

'Except that my glass of wine is legal.'

I may as well wag a finger at her and peer over bifocals. Old woman.

'Don't be such a geek. I have only just tried it. I am still deciding if it suits me.'

When she speaks like this it's hard to remember that

when Mum and Dad sent away for their very own foreign student, she wasn't yet completely fluent in English. She came from a village near Toulouse for a three-month stint, charmingly dropped all her h's and made us fall hopelessly in love with her. She's pretty much lived in my old bedroom for the past six years. She goes back to France each year around Christmas, where she gets reacquainted with the family that raised her. Then she returns to England to the family that thinks of her as one of our own.

She turns to blow another stream of smoke, the bulbs outside backlighting her long, dark, candy floss hair, which she likes to pin in a pile atop her head. 'You will not tell?' She sounds much younger than her twenty-one years.

My hug dislodges the sweetly pungent aroma from her grey velvet dress, which Mum will say is too depressing for a party. 'Of course not. But you smell like an Amsterdam coffee shop. Here.' I rummage in my handbag for the little vial of perfume I keep for office emergencies. 'And you'd better clean your teeth before you go downstairs. You know what Mum will say if she thinks you've been smoking. It's bad enough that I do it.'

'Yes, and speaking of that, you should not have your gum.'

I completely forgot to get rid of the Nicorette in the car.

'Do you know you are buzzing?' she asks.

I snatch my BlackBerry from my bag to scroll through the new emails. Just a dozen or so. Not bad for a Sunday.

As Zoe rises from the window seat I say, 'Why

aren't you in your own room?'

'It is too close to the stairs. Madame Colbert might smell something.' She appraises me. 'That doesn't occur to you, I suppose.' She shakes her head. 'I wonder if you have ever done anything wrong in your life.'

I blush at the compliment, then realise as I jog down the stairs to retrieve Dad's cake from the car that she probably means to be insulting.

But she's right. For twenty-six years running in our family drama (now celebrating its thirty-first spectacular year in Greater London), I have reprised the role of The Good Daughter. It's a character I work hard to perfect, and one that means everything to me. My family's compliments are the tokens that top up my self-esteem. I guess most people are the same.

In the kitchen, Mum and Marley are busy piling M&S canapés on to enormous golden serving trays for the waiters I've hired for the day. Granny supervises from her wheelchair. 'Hello, doll,' she says as I kiss her powdery cheek. 'You look gorgeous!'

She always says this, but that's Granny for you. She came to live with us just after I started secondary school. Mum was worried about her being on her own after Granddad died, and didn't trust my Auntie Lou to look after her. I don't blame her. Auntie Lou means well but she can hardly look after her house plants.

Dad had the garage converted into a flat for Granny, all on one level, with a ramp to get into the house through the back. So Marley and I got to grow up with our Granny within wheeling distance.

'Here's the cake!' I announce, opening the bakery box so Granny can see. 'What do you think? Isn't it beautiful?'

'Wow, well done!' Marley says, clapping her manicured hands. 'Jez!' she calls into the hallway when she spots her boyfriend. 'Come and see the cake.'

He ambles in, kissing me hello.

Mum was thrilled when Marley produced Jez for our inspection. She was glad to see my sister finally putting her Cambridge education to good use.

It's a sore subject round the dinner table. Mum thinks being a secretary (even a great one like Marley) is beneath her. A lawyer, doctor or rocket scientist would be more in keeping with our status as the as-yet-undiscovered heirs to the Romanoff dynasty.

But Jez's architect credentials trump even my banking job in the bragging stakes (well-paid *and* creative). He's every mother's dream and she nearly adopted him when she learned that his great uncle had been knighted. Jez told me that this uncle was a sociopath, avoided by the family, but we let Mum enjoy the fact that she's one degree of separation from a Sir.

'Wow, that looks incredible,' says Jez, admiring the cake. 'Can I have a slice?'

Marley shoves him away. 'Not till we sing to Dad! Go, get out. Go talk to Ben.'

Instead, he takes her hand and kisses her. Unlike the rest of us, Jez doesn't always let Marley get her way.

'Ben's not coming,' I tell them. 'He's got to work.'

'Oh, that's a shame!' Marley says, searching my expression with sisterly vigilance for any sign of upset. I keep my smile bright.

'You've done well, Carol,' says Mum, running her expert eye over the confection. 'This is perfect.'

I'm grinning like an idiot. When Mum told me what

she wanted I never imagined finding someone to make it. But after visiting nearly every baker within the M25 to sample their offerings, it was worth it (even the squidgy tummy). As far as show-stoppers go it's even better than the 1920s chocolate fountain that I sourced for Marley's birthday party a few years ago. It might even top Mum and Dad's anniversary entertainment, at least in impact if not effort. You'd have thought I was commissioning Spielberg to direct a feature film about them, not just asking someone to write, direct and shoot a Super 8 film commemorating their thirty years together, with a few interviews of their friends and family and an on-location shoot in Australia where they met.

'I thought you were running late, Marley,' I remind her as I help with the last of the canapés. 'Something about being too stressed to do your own shopping?' She looks about as stressed as our cat after his nap. 'I put the bags in the spare bedroom, by the way. You owe me seventy-five quid.'

'Thanks, you are a star,' she says, digging the money out of her handbag. Marley always keeps a wad of cash to hand, and only uses her cards for important things like shoe investments. Her closets are drool-worthy but she's not a spendthrift. Groomed by our mother, we are women who dress for our success.

'I was running late,' she says. 'That's why I didn't have time to do the shopping. Did you have them use margarine instead of butter in the cake?'

I shake my head, puzzled. Marley's not one to worry about nutrition. She's been blessed with Mum's figure, despite having Dad's appetite. I try not to hate her for her genetic Lotto jackpot.

'Oh, well, it's not really important.'

She purses her lips.

'It's just that margarine would have been a bit healthier for everyone. You know, since Dad's agent had that heart attack. Never mind. I'm sure a slice of cake won't kill him.'

'It's that twenty years of alcoholism that'll kill him,' Granny says, tactful as always. She drives Mum nuts with these outbursts but the doctors say she's not got dementia. Marley and I think she's marvellous.

'Should I run out for some light ice cream at least?'

I've bought enough of the full-fat stuff to send the entire neighbourhood to the emergency room.

'You are going for ice cream?' Zoe says, drifting in on a cloud of my perfume. 'I would like a bowl.' She opens the fridge. 'Will you get me the one I like, with the marshmallows and chocolate?'

'Nobody's going for ice cream,' Mum says. 'Now that we're all here, I want everyone in the sitting room talking to our guests. No hiding in the kitchen like you usually do. Marley, be sure to tell Mrs Latham about your promotion. She was bragging about her son the other day and she cut me off before I could tell her your good news. And Carol, Mr Templeton was asking about you. I'm sure he'd love to know how well you're doing at the bank.'

Our mum holds an Olympic gold medal in bragging. An entire wall in the kitchen is devoted to our awards, from Marley's first Practising Certificate to my Duke of Edinburgh Silver Award. Even worse, she actually shows them to people, like our neighbours will be impressed by my Fire Safety badge.

'And Zoe…' Mum appraises her. 'I do wish you

wouldn't always look like you've dressed for a funeral.'

'Madame Colbert, this is trendy,' Zoe says, wandering toward the granite-topped island where the cake sits. 'Oh, *très jolie*!'

The bakers have captured Dad's garden perfectly, right down to the tiny shovel and clippers lying beside his beloved weather-worn shed. His creaky old wheelbarrow spills over with sugar paste tulips and hyacinths, set upon the path through rose bushes and flowering beds. It looks almost too good to eat. Almost.

Marley wanted us to do a guitar cake to commemorate Dad's career, but Mum was right. The garden is his oasis away from the madness, and a much more fitting way to mark his birthday.

'I think Zoe looks lovely,' I say, slapping her hand as she plays amateur gardener by sticking her finger into the grass. Her heart-shaped face and wide eyes make her look like a naughty pixie.

'What's that smell?' Mum asks, sniffing.

I quickly shuffle closer to Zoe. 'Oh, I'm afraid that's me, Mum. I spilled a bit of perfume on my dress. Sorry, it should air out in a little while.'

Mum puts her hand to her temple. 'Maybe you could borrow one of Zoe's dresses, darling. It really is too strong.'

I nod. 'It's giving me a bit of a headache, too. Come on, Zoe, I need to look in your closet.'

'Hmm? You can help yourself, you know where everything is,' she says, still eying the cake, her Class B offense completely forgotten.

'Come *on*, Zoe. I need your help.' I've got to get her back upstairs before Mum realises that she's the stinky one. 'You need to change,' I tell her, sighing as we mount the stairs. 'And thanks to you, now so do I.'

Dad settles gratefully into his favourite chair after the last of our neighbours stagger home to sleep off the kick of our Moscow Mule recipe. Mom's buzzing with success, having impressed everyone with her offspring's latest feats. And the caterers are clearing up, leaving us wracked with middle-class guilt and at a loose end. We sit in the living room trying not to make eye contact with our servers.

'We have an announcement,' Marley says as Jez grabs her hand. 'As you know, we went away to the country last weekend for our anniversary. Our fifth. What's the gift for a fifth anniversary?'

'It's silverware,' Jez says, smiling.

'And that's appropriate since silver is made into what?' She pauses, possibly just to torture Mum who, I can see, is dying to shout out the punch line. 'Jewellery. And while we were there, Jez proposed. We're getting married!'

Our squeals unsettle the caterers as we rush to hug the nearly-weds, everyone talking at once. Finally, Marley raises her hand when Mum asks if Jez's great uncle will be invited.

'Give us a chance, we've only been engaged a few days! We haven't worked out all the details yet. All we know is that we want a winter wedding. And that we'd love for Carol to be our bridesmaid.'

She takes my hands, with Jez grinning behind her. 'Will you, Carol? Will you be my bridesmaid?'

My eyes well up. I've loved Jez, with or without his sociopathic family member, from the day we met. To think that with all the friends Marley has, she's chosen me!

'Of course I will, thank you. Of course!'

'Fantastic.' She kisses me. 'This is going to be such fun. There are a million things to take care of but I know we can rely on you completely. You did such an incredible job with the party, didn't she, Dad?'

Dad stands up and catches me up in a bear hug as Mum looks on. 'I should have known this was all down to you, Carol. Thank you, my darling girl. I'm sure you did so much beyond what I've even noticed today. You always do. This has been a wonderful day, and it's all thanks to you.'

'Oh, well. We all helped, really. But thank you.'

Dad knows that's a lie but he also knows I don't want the attention on myself. I like my approval whispered in my ear, not shouted for everyone to hear. I'd have made an excellent behind-the-scenes theatre type, maybe the guy who does the lights or writes the music. Then I could sit hidden in the wings revelling in the audience's applause.

'Anyway,' Marley continues, drawing everyone back to her news. Unlike me, she suffers no sensitivity to limelight. 'We've been thinking about churches. Someplace tiny and ancient, in a quaint little village, but with excellent transport links, and of course it has to be close to the reception venue. Wouldn't a stately home be perfect? Maybe you can find one that doesn't charge an arm and a leg. And my dress. We can all go shopping together, but we'll need to make appointments quickly to have time for the fittings. We have to choose rings, and the cake, hotels for the guests. Oh, it's crazy to think we can pull it all together in just a year, but I know you can do it!'

'Of course,' I say weakly, realising what this means for my already meagre allotment of free time. 'Maybe Zoe can help me, since she's not working yet.'

'But I might not be around,' Zoe says, tucking in to another great wodge of cake.

'When might you not be around?' Marley asks.

'When's the wedding?'

'Winter!' Mom and Marley say, trading looks.

'Zoe should concentrate on finding a job,' Mum says. 'It's been nearly a year now.'

'But I've been writing.'

Marley rolls her eyes. 'Poems won't pay your rent.'

I don't want to hear this argument again.

'But I don't need to pay my rent,' Zoe says.

'That's the whole point,' Marley shoots back. 'You live with Mum and Dad!'

Zoe looks baffled by this statement. I hate when they pick on her like this. If she were a deer, she'd have a giant bullseye painted on her side during hunting season.

Marley's objection isn't really about Zoe's employment status, although that does wind her up hilariously. Zoe's parents send a cheque each month to cover her living expenses, and seem happy to do so until she draws a pension.

Marley doesn't think Zoe is particularly smart. She's wrong, though. Dimwits don't become fluent in English in six years. She's possibly just better suited to eighteenth-century novels than boring old real life.

'Are you sure you want to marry into this family?' Dad asks Jez. Outnumbered by eight breasts to none in the house, he's only partly joking.

'It's too late now, isn't it? Come on, Marley, we'd better go. I've got to be in the office early tomorrow.'

Marley hugs me again. 'This is going to be so much fun!'

But my head is spinning. How am I supposed to find the time to plan my sister's wedding when work already sucks sixty hours a week from my life?

MICHELE GORMAN

CHAPTER 3

My eyes are bleary as I wrestle my over-packed gym bag through the revolving doors the next morning. I should really stop kidding myself. That bag gets more mileage on my daily commute than I've had on the treadmill in months.

Despite the early hour, the lobby buzzes with drones. Drones like me.

'Hold the lift, please!' I shout to Ryan, hurrying towards the closing doors.

He avoids my gaze as the lift slams shut.

Welcome to my Monday morning.

'Ryan, didn't you see me in the lobby?' I say a few minutes later as I throw my bag under the desk. The open-plan office is already full, ready for our morning briefing. Even after more than four years, and though I have to speak for less than two minutes, these 7.30 a.m. meetings still make my tummy churn. I always feel like an imposter, waiting for someone to stab his finger at me and say, 'Wait just a minute. You're a twenty-six-year-old engineering graduate. You're not seriously trying to tell us about these investments. What the hell do you know, little girl? Get out!' Then Security will snatch away my coffee and bagel, make me return my subsidised gym pass that I never use and escort me off the premises. And that will end my analyst career.

Most people have nightmares. Not me. I have workmares.

Our department covers an entire floor of the Canary Wharf building, perched above London's Docklands. I'd brag about panoramic views if my desk weren't a three-day trek away from the nearest window. To glimpse the world outside I've got to look over a sea of shouting, cursing traders. It was quite an adjustment after leaving the hushed engineering labs at Cambridge, but once I learned not to venture into the traders' territory when they were restless, it wasn't horrible. Now their colourful perversion of the language is just the background buzz of foul-mouthed bees. It's my job to tell them whether the portfolios they tend are bitter or sweet. And try not to get stung in the process.

'Were you in the lobby?' Ryan says as his computers whir to life. 'Sorry, Colbert, I didn't notice.' He's recently picked up Derrick's irritating habit of using everyone's surname. 'Ready for the big show?'

He's not talking about the morning briefing but the press conference afterwards, and I feel anything but ready for that.

Taking a deep breath, I dial Granny. It's my morning ritual. She thinks it's because I want to check on her and see that she's all right. But really the call is for me. Some people have spin class, yoga or double espresso. I have Granny to kick-start my day and remind me that no matter what crap lies ahead, I've got someone quite wonderful to support me.

'All right, doll?' She says when she answers. 'I watched the most marvellous programme last night. There was a man whose testicle disappeared and one poor woman whose armpits ran like Niagara Falls.'

'*Embarrassing Bodies*?'

'I'll say they were.'

'Did the doctors sort them out?'

'Oh, yes, happy endings all around,' she says.

'Have you had breakfast yet?' I ask, scanning my emails.

'It's more like penance than breakfast. Forgive me, Father, my daughter has sinned. Why do we all have to suffer whenever your mother goes on a diet?'

'Is Dad sharing his secret stash with you?'

When Mum declares the house a fat-free zone, Dad stocks up on contraband that he hides in the studio.

'Yes, and it's a good thing, otherwise I'd starve to death. Have you had your breakfast?'

She asks this every morning. 'I'm just about to. Orange juice and porridge,' I lie. 'Nice and healthy. Don't worry about me, Granny, I'm eating okay.'

'Save your breath, doll, you know I'll always worry about you.'

'I know you will, Granny, and that's why I love you. Talk to you tomorrow, okay?'

As I hang up, Derrick strides into the office, red-faced and shouting on his mobile. So that was thirty seconds of comfortable calm before the storm.

'I don't give two fat fucking rats' pimply arses how many other jobs you've got going. I told your girl the car had to be ready by five-thirty. If it isn't, I guarantee that not one person from this bank will ever use your service again. You'll be out of business in six months.'

Heads swivel across the floor, wondering if the trading desk's heart attack pool might just pay out on our boss this morning. Coronary while on the phone is the odds-on favourite for most of the directors. There's a bonus if the paramedics have to pull him off the loo.

'Yes, that's right, five-thirty,' he continues, calming down.

'Jesus,' he says as he hangs up. 'How hard can it be to detail a Beemer?'

'You'd think they were doing brain surgery, not hoovering an interior,' Ryan says, raising a chuckle from Derrick and rolled eyes from me.

'They're mechanics, not surgeons!' Ryan continues. 'You should still put them out of business, just for making you lose your temper before breakfast. Who do they think they...' His voice follows Derrick's smile, fading away.

'That's not my style.'

'No, no, of course not. I wouldn't either, really,' Ryan mumbles, staring hard at his computer screens.

I'm halfway through my morning bagel, having survived the briefing, when Derrick returns to breathe stale coffee all over me. 'Colbert, go downstairs and wait for everyone. And you.' He points at Ryan. 'Make sure the conference room is set up. Lots of biscuits.'

I start swapping my trainers for a pair of the pumps under my desk, my mouth still full of cream cheese.

'Colbert, I'll go downstairs,' Ryan says when Derrick is out of sight. 'You sort the conference room.'

He just wants to suck up to the journalists, but I nod anyway. At least I'll get to finish breakfast, though my appetite's now gone.

In less than half an hour the trading system that I've built, Green T, is being unveiled to the world's financial press. What started out as a little program I schemed up in my spare time has, after a year's hard work, become the bank's newest hope for riches.

I couldn't care less whether the bank gets rich. Green T is my baby.

By the time we're ready to start, the conference room is standing-room-only. Derrick closes the door and strides to the front of the large room. All trace of his oiky bravado vanishes as he faces the journalists. A few of the women are flushing under his gaze. I suppose he's attractive – late thirties, tall, dark, bespoke-suited and bespectacled. He's got a babyish face and a slightly weak chin. There's definitely a thin patch in that wavy hair. But perhaps I'm just being critical because if his looks actually matched his personality, he'd be slightly less attractive than Shrek.

'Thank you, ladies and gents, for coming this morning. We're extremely proud to share with you our newest ethical trading system: Green T.' He gestures to the projection screen, at the slides that have kept me awake nights. 'You've had the press release explaining the details so I won't bore you with those.'

He pauses to appreciate the ripple of laughter.

'I'll just recap the highlights, and then open up for questions. All right? In simple terms, we've created an IT program that uses the news about a company to predict its share price. We enter the news item, like the company's earnings announcement, or a rival filing for bankruptcy or a change in government policy, and it tells us how much the share price will rise or fall. Then we buy or sell the shares based on the model's prediction. Sounds easy, eh?'

Again, he waits for the chuckles to creep across the room.

'In actual fact, it took nearly a year to build and test. And we believe it's the most accurate predictive trading system in the market. Questions?'

One of the blushing women near the front raises her pen. 'So it's a crystal ball that makes money for you?'

'It makes money for our clients, yes. We've already got several signed up.'

'You're not investing your own funds, then?' she continues.

'The bank's investment is minimal,' he says.

I'm surprised to hear this. As head of our 'prop' (proprietary) trading business, which invests the bank's own money, I figured Derrick would have his greedy little fingers in the Green T pie on the company's behalf, too.

'This is for our clients,' he says. 'Our ethical clients, to be exact. We do what we say on the label: invest in socially responsible companies.'

'How many clients are signed up?' asks a man at the back as the hacks begin to talk amongst themselves.

'Our investment managers are using the program for several clients. We'll be rolling it out fully in the coming weeks.'

'Who developed the program? Was it outsourced?'

I brace myself. This will be the crowning achievement of my short career. Sure, being the centre of attention might be uncomfortable but in just a few minutes, everyone will know that I'm the one who created Green T.

Excitement bubbles up as I think about the warm tide of praise to come. All those late nights, the missed dinners and family occasions and the moments of panic that it wouldn't work have all been for this moment, when I'll be judged worthy by my peers. Me – Carol Colbert of Netherhaven Close, first class graduate of Cambridge University, second-highest rated ethical analyst in London. Worthy.

I just hope they don't ask me awkward questions. Or worse, what if I start babbling trader-speak and confuse the whole room? Must not use acronyms. Must. Not. Use–

'No,' Derrick says. 'We developed the system in-house. It was a group effort. We've got a very clever team. A couple of the guys who worked on it are right here.' He gestures to Ryan and two of our colleagues on the other side of the table.

Ryan sits taller in his chair, accepting the journalists' congratulatory smiles while his sallow, freckled face turns even redder than his hair. The little toad.

Did he spend fifteen-hour days and countless weekends at his computer building each possible scenario? Did he test the system over and over until his eyes crossed? Could he even run the model, let alone build it? No, no, and not even with Bill Gates helping him.

I feel like the pettiest petty thing for wanting to shout that it was me, me, me!

But that's not how this game is played. I'll look absolutely foolish if I do. So I say nothing while the conference grinds on until lunchtime.

By the time the journalists leave I'm wrung out and starving. They fired questions at Ryan but, annoyingly, he bluffed his way through them. I guess he was listening after all when Derrick made me brief him about my system. That figures. The guy is profoundly deaf when I ask for help but when it comes to his own neck his hearing is perfect. It's a medical miracle.

I pull on my coat and hurry to meet Harriet beneath the clocks at Canary Wharf station.

She looks a bit cold when I arrive, shifting from foot to foot as she stares at the January sky threatening snow flurries.

'I'm so sorry I'm late!' I say, kissing my best friend's cheek. 'I didn't bring my BlackBerry into the meeting so I couldn't text. You should have gone inside.' I gesture to the nearby Carluccio's.

'You, not have your BlackBerry? How is that possible?'

'Derrick banned them during the presentation. He knows what we're like. Sorry you had to wait.'

'That's all right. I'm usually the one who holds you up. Besides, I burned at least enough calories from shivering for a panna cotta.'

Harriet has the best approach to the mathematics of dessert of anyone I know.

'How did it go?' she asks when we've found a table in the busy restaurant. Her blonde hair floats on a cloud of static when she takes off her woolly red hat. With our virtually identical thick, straight hair, brown eyes and lanky frames, people often mistake us for sisters. 'Did you have to give the presentation?'

I cringe at the memory. 'No, my boss did all the talking.'

'That's a relief. You hate being the centre of attention.'

'Well, I wouldn't have minded saying something in this case.'

I tell her what happened.

'You can't let him get away with that!' she fumes. 'You've got to say something.'

'To whom, exactly? It's too late. It'd just make me look foolish.'

'He does this to you all the time.'

'Not all the time.'

'Yes, all the time. I don't know why you stay there.'

She's right. I've lost count of the number of times someone else has taken credit for my work. Even so, she knows exactly why I stay there.

It's because of the polar bears. Set adrift on melting ice caps, they haunted my childhood dreams. Then genetically modified wheat stalks became my boogeymen. By the time Al Gore got to me with his inconvenient truth, I'd already applied to Cambridge's environmental engineering course. It never occurred to me that a seventeen-year-old girl from suburban London couldn't singlehandedly reverse global warming and feed the world. I was nothing if not over-confident in my abilities.

By the middle of my Masters dissertation, after two internships that mainly involved making tea for the engineers, reality struck with a painful thump. Unless we could power our future with the mountain of used teabags I'd fished out of the engineer's drinks, I wasn't making a dent in the problem.

But then the banks came to campus searching for engineers and mathematicians for their analyst programmes and I found a different way to approach the problem. Maybe I couldn't invent my way out of an environmental crisis, but I could get a lot of money invested in the companies that did. So I applied.

That means I haven't hung up my green hat. I've just traded it in for a much bigger, well-funded one.

'A single buy recommendation can secure a green company's future,' I tell Harriet, wishing the words back as soon as they leave my mouth. Don't I always make fun of people who spout vacuous marketing-speak? Now I'm the tap, on full flow.

She narrows her brown eyes over a forkful of fettuccine Alfredo.

I knew she wouldn't let me get away with that.

'I stop listening when you start with all that buy-side, sell short, P/E ratio gibberish. I plan bankers' parties; I don't speak their language. If you want to talk about your job using normal people's words, I'll listen.'

'You understand more than you let on.'

She shakes her head. 'No, not really, I just pretend to know what you're talking about so you don't think I'm thick. I did a degree in French, remember? We didn't even use calculators.'

I shrug. 'It's a business full of jargon, that's all. Bankers think it'll convince people they're worth their bonuses.'

'They're worth their bonuses? You're a banker, too,' she points out.

As usual, I bristle at the accusation. 'I'm not really, though. I'm just a research analyst. We're the unglamorous ones who pull all-nighters to make our bosses look good. And I didn't get the bonus, remember?'

Thanks to Green T launching two weeks after bonuses were decided, technically it didn't count in my review. And nobody loves a technicality like a boss trying to keep his wallet closed. I'll have to wait another year to get paid anything for my efforts.

'So you do all the work and Derrick builds his bank account.' She makes a face.

Harriet likes to feel aggrieved on behalf of all us little people who have to fight for the scraps that fall from the master's table. Who doesn't enjoy having a villain around to resent?

'What will you do now that Green T is finished?'

I shrug. 'My regular job. Analysis.'

'What do you actually do with that analysis? I mean, I plan events, so there's an event to show for it.'

'You're asking what I have to show for my twelve-hour days?'

'Exactly. Hang on. Let me get a double espresso before you go on.'

'Maybe just to be safe.' I smile. 'Basically, everything I find out ends up in a research note. Which sounds like something I've scribbled on a scrap of paper, but they can take months to write and run to forty pages. They're research reports that go to our traders and clients. I look at how much money a company makes or loses, check out its competition and keep an eye on innovations in the green energy. That usually means new inventions or technologies.'

'So basically you surf the internet. Got it.'

'And I go to company presentations where they tell us how great they are.'

'Are there biscuits at these presentations?'

'Sometimes. Good biscuits get better results.'

'And if there are cakes?'

'Straight to the top of the recommendation list.'

'I'm with you so far.'

She catches the waiter's eye and orders her espresso.

'Then I write up the research note to tell investors whether their share price is… I mean, how much the company is worth based on how much money it's making, how much it owes in loans, and the technologies it plans to use. I give the notes to the traders.' I shrug. 'And that's it.'

'So you pass notes to people sitting at the next desk.' She smiles. 'Children do that.'

'And now you know why I work with such infantile men.'

'Still, I'd take your job over mine,' she says. 'I'm going to murder someone soon and then my twenties will be completely ruined by parole curfews.'

'Can't you tell yourself it's just a job and keep the homicidal thoughts at bay?'

'Could you?' she asks, shrugging when I shake my head. 'Has Derrick been a wanker in general lately, or dare I hope it was just today?'

'He gets more vile by the day. He bullied the car detailing man this morning. Do you know this already?'

If you want to know anything about anyone, anywhere, at any time, ask Harriet. Gossip always seems to know where to find her.

'How would I know it?'

'In the nicest possible way, Harriet, you're like the madam of Canary Wharf. Minus the sex, obviously. You hear everything.'

'Thanks for reminding me about the lack of sex, but no, I hadn't heard about Derrick. Not that I'm surprised.'

'So at least I'm not the only one he bullies.'

'Bullies are cowards. He'd leave you alone if you stood up to him. Someone should report him to HR.'

'You are joking. That'd be like chumming the waters with the body parts of analysts. You know how all this works.' I sigh, thinking again about how my face had burned as Ryan took credit for my work.

Now that the Green T project is finished, I notice its absence, like the ringing silence after leaving a concert. It's back to my usual job, distilling reams of information into a single judgment on a company. It's a lot of responsibility. When I first joined I'd asked Derrick, 'What if I'm wrong?'

'We'll fire you,' he'd said.

I make sure I'm never wrong.

At 4.30 Derrick saunters over to our desks. 'Ready?' he asks Ryan.

'Just one more minute, okay?' he says, concentrating on his screen.

'The Bolly won't wait, my son.' Derrick claps him on the back. 'Tell the others, will you? I'll meet you in the lobby in five.'

He notices me listening.

'It's just a little drink, Colbert. And you won't exactly fit in at Browns. Best that you stay here and do your job.'

I don't bother pointing out that they could celebrate the Green T launch in a venue not filled with stripping women. 'You're leaving now? What about your car?'

He shrugs. 'I'll pick it up tomorrow. See you later.'

'Wait up!' Ryan says, grabbing his coat. 'Later, Colbert. Don't work too hard.'

The office empties of colleagues, a train of young

men wafting testosterone and the confident air of Those Who Have Been Chosen.

Minutes later, my BlackBerry buzzes on my desk. Grinning, I answer Marley's call. She probably wants to congratulate me on the launch.

'Carol, I'm not interrupting anything am I?'

'No, no, the conference finished just before lun–'

'Good, good. This is an unbelievably exciting day!' she trills.

'I know, it was so much work but it'll be worth it.'

'Of course it will be. That's why I'm calling. Remember that gorgeous house we took Mum to visit on Mother's Day last year? The one in Hampshire?'

I wait, wondering what a stately home has to do with my trading program.

'I just got off the phone with the events manager there and they have one Saturday in December available for a wedding. Can you believe it?'

So the call isn't to congratulate me.

'Great.'

'The thing is, I need you to go see it. We can't let someone snatch it from under our noses when it's so perfect.'

'When do you expect me to go?'

'There's another couple interested who've already seen it, and two more couples are going tomorrow. If we don't get in there tomorrow, one of them might book it before we've seen it. I'd go but I'll be tied up in meetings with Karl all day.'

Karl is her boss, whom I'm forbidden to even think about. It's a long story, and not the kind with a happy ending. Suffice to say that we had an interlude for a few months which ended when he ran away faster than

Michael Johnson at two hundred metres. I never did get an explanation.

'You can do it, can't you?' she continues. 'Please say you can.'

'It's short notice, Marley. My boss isn't expecting me to take the day off to visit stately homes.'

'But it wouldn't be the whole day, not at all. It'll be a couple of hours at most. You could go at the latest possible moment. He won't even know you're gone. Please say you can go, Carol, please? Please? It's just the perfect place and if we don't get it, I'll always look back and wonder if my wedding was second best. It would absolutely mean the world to me if you could check it out. I'm depending on you. Please say you can go.'

Of course I want to help Marley, but this is banking. We don't take unscheduled time off with our boss's blessing unless it's for something really important like paying women to lap dance. Derrick won't be pleased about me leaving the office for something as trivial as my sister's happiness.

But if I don't go, and someone else books the venue, Marley might not get her dream wedding. That's more important than Derrick's annoyance. And if he gets really irate I can always double down on my heart attack bet.

'Okay. Of course, I can go. I'll take photos on my phone.'

'Thank you so much, I love you!'

'I love you, too.'

And despite the bollocking I'm going to get from Derrick, I want to help my sister.

'Here's the woman's number,' she says as I hurry to

scribble it on the edge of an old company prospectus. 'She's probably gone now but you can call her first thing in the morning to arrange a time to see the ballroom. And the chapel too. It's on the grounds. How perfect is that? She said it's a bit tricky to get there from the station, so you'll want to take a cab. Maybe collect the driver's card in case we need to arrange for people to get from the village to the venue on the day. On the day!' she squeals. 'I'm getting married!'

I laugh as I hang up. Then I wonder how I'm going to break the news to Derrick.

CHAPTER 4

Zack comes by, as usual, on his way home.

'It's 6.01 already?' I say as he hovers by my desk. He gets to leave the IT department at the same time every night. Lucky sod.

'Time flies. Do you have to stay late?'

I don't bother reminding him that around here, 6 p.m. is early, not late. 'A while longer.'

'Sure you don't want to go out to celebrate the launch?'

'That's really kind, but I've got a lot to do before I can go.'

'Are you going to eat something?'

Zack appointed himself as my digestive system monitor long ago. Granted, sometimes I do get through the day without having lunch, which gives him all the justification he needs to stay vigilant.

'I suppose,' I say. 'I'll probably order noodles later.'

'Why don't you order them now, and I'll eat with you?'

'Well, erm...'

'Great. Order me the sweet and sour chicken, please, and fried won tons.' He digs a twenty pound note out of his wallet. 'I'll be right back.'

I shake my head. 'You eat terribly.'

'Luckily, nobody's asked me yet to model for Abercrombie & Fitch.' He pats the little belly protruding from his otherwise slim frame. 'I'll be back in a bit.'

It's no use stopping him. In the four years we've known each other, I've only won a handful of arguments. He gets his way through sheer good-natured reasonableness, which doesn't even give me the satisfaction of resenting him.

Zack is definitely my best friend at the bank. Not that it's a hotly contested title. My colleagues have all the warmth of piranhas at a pool party.

Zack and I sat next to each other on the new hire induction course, where they gave us our access cards and explained what to do in case of fire drills. They didn't teach us anything useful, though, like how to keep from crying when shouted at by a trader, or that blowjob screen savers were a normal part of office culture. These things I quickly learned on my own.

Zack's gone for about twenty minutes before I hear the clanking of bottles. 'Zack, we're not allowed to have alcohol on the floor since the champagne incident.'

Each Friday afternoon the beer cart comes around to reward thirsty traders, but one afternoon last month it was stocked with champagne after an especially good week. Things got out of hand and, fuelled by bubbly, some of the traders emailed obscene photos (even by their low standards) to all the bank heads. They used fake accounts from their own computers so it took about ten minutes for Zack to trace the emails and report back to our irate chairman, who was sharpening the guillotine. He probably hoped to behead someone expendable in the operations department but the traders would have had to murder an old lady in cold blood, on film, and be unrepentant, and then lose the bank millions, before anyone would kill those golden geese.

'It's just a beer, Carol.'

He waves a bottle of Leffe Blonde.

'My favourite.' I smile, pushing one of the warm delivery bags towards him. 'Here's your order.'

'Thanks. Are you going to eat now?'

'I'll work a bit first.'

'Your noodles will get cold.'

'That's why Percy Spencer invented the microwave.'

It's trivia like this that make engineering graduates useful at pub quizzes, if useless at small talk.

'Have a seat if you want, but I really do need to get some work done.' I pull Ryan's chair over. 'Do you have an opener?'

He holds up his keys. 'I was a Scout. Always prepared. Cheers. Congratulations on Green T's launch. You should be proud of yourself.'

He's absently thumbing through the stacks of papers on my desk. He's always doing that. One day I'll wedge a few tampons in there and teach him to mind his own business. 'Those are confidential.'

'Carol, I can see every keystroke you make. Nothing is confidential to me.'

'That's a bit creepy.'

He sits back, smiling. 'Your secrets are safe. So you are going to celebrate properly, right? Is Ben taking you somewhere nice?'

He runs his hand through his always-messy and usually-too-long dark hair. He does that whenever he suspects he's about to be lied to. His hair sometimes goes mad when he talks to the traders. *Did you spill anything on the laptop before the screen went blank? Are you sure?*

'I'll give him a call in a bit,' I say. 'What are you doing tonight?'

He ignores my question. 'Hasn't he planned anything for you?' he asks, hand in his hair again.

I shrug. Ben can be a great planner, and exceedingly romantic. For our one-year anniversary he organised a balloon ride because I'd once said I couldn't imagine anything better than watching the Great Migration across the Serengeti from that vantage point. 'It's not Africa,' he'd said, pointing at the M25 below us. 'But look, it's the Great London Easter Exodus. And it is romantic, because we're together. I love you, Carol.'

We'd kissed like teenagers and if it weren't for the balloon pilot with us, we'd probably now be members of the thousand foot high club.

'I'm sure we'll do something later,' I tell Zack. 'Listen, I'm sorry to chuck you out but I've got a lot to get through if I'm going to leave at a reasonable hour.'

'That's okay,' he says, collecting his dinner. 'There's a football match on tonight anyway. Don't work too late, okay? You deserve at least one evening of fun after all the work you've put in.'

'Thanks, Zack, and thanks for the beer. See you tomorrow.'

I watch him stroll to the lift before going back to my screens, sipping my beer.

It's after eight by the time I shut down my computers and ring Ben. Most of the other analysts have left for home (those who weren't already stuffing five pound notes into Eastern European G-strings).

I stare across the open-plan office, my eyes itchy and sore. Computer monitors pepper my vista – plastic and glass, hard-edged, uninviting and indispensable. Each trader has six that connect him to the world's news feeds. An electrical hum reverberates through the walls. There's nothing inviting about the floor. Even the artwork that HR optimistically hung to cheer the place up is cool and impersonal.

I'm about to hang up when Ben finally answers.

'Can we meet for a drink?' I ask.

'Sure, darling,' he shouts over the background din. 'I'm out now with a couple of others anyway. Why don't you meet us?'

'Okay, I'll leave here in five minutes,' I say, shrugging into my smoking jacket and checking my bag for a lighter.

Smoking Jacket. That sounds a bit posh, doesn't it? Very pipe-and-slippers eighteenth-century stately home. It's really just a very pretty, cast-off coat that keeps the chill out when I smoke by the bins. If Sgt. Pepper had been a twenty-six-year-old woman, it's exactly the kind of thing he'd wear – deep green velvet with a nipped-in waist and black braiding on the collar and cuffs. I wore it everywhere when I first got it but as fickle fashion moved on, eventually I relegated it to the back of the closet. Then, one afternoon, Harriet casually mentioned that she could smell the smoke on me. How mortifying. The green coat re-emerged to hang on the rack between my desk and Ryan's. It never goes beyond the smoking area at the back of the building.

Despite the coat I shiver in the January evening. I'm not exactly oozing glamour as I stand alone beside the goods entrance, but I enjoy the warm stream of smoke that fills my lungs. I know it's a terrible, deadly habit, and I will quit. Eventually. Especially since Ben did it (and is being a bit of a self-righteous knob about the whole thing).

It only takes a moment upstairs to eliminate all traces of my filthy habit before hurrying to the Tube, and Ben.

He and his friends are at their usual pub, the Hope and Anchor. It's where we met, just around the corner from his office in Holborn.

I'd clocked him that night as soon as Harriet and I arrived. Who wouldn't? He's about ten miles beyond gorgeous, from his incredible ice-blue eyes to his thick longish blonde mop and open, utterly charming smile. He thinks his cheekbones and sharp jawline make his face look too feminine, but there's nothing feminine about Ben. He's the kind of bloke that guys want to be friends with.

As I push open the pub's door I see him standing near the bar with his colleagues. He smiles as soon as he sees me, making my heart skip. I take him in in a glance – perfectly at ease in his dark grey suit, his hair just long enough to be cool without looking unprofessional, and my, oh my, those eyes.

'Darling, help us settle a bet,' he says, kissing me hello. 'What's the longest river in the world?'

'The Nile?'

'Thank you,' he says, kissing me again. 'Pay up, gentlemen.'

When his colleagues protest, Ben grasps my shoulders and looks into my eyes. 'Carol. Are you absolutely sure?'

I stare between three expectant faces. They've played this game for a few months now, since one of their law firm partners said using smartphones to settle pub disagreements was cheating. Call me Carol Googlebert. 'I'm sure. The Nile is the longest river and the Amazon is the biggest.'

'You know you can't argue with Carol when she's absolutely sure. She's a genius,' Ben says, smirking as I shoot him a warning look. Mum never lets me forget that I do, in fact, have a high IQ. On paper, anyway. Whenever I do something stupid, Harriet wants those tests re-sat.

Some men have a thing for blondes, or big boobs or plump lips. Ben loves smart women. Which is lucky because I don't have big boobs or plump lips. It's also lucky because my intelligence won't sag or go grey.

'How was your presentation?' Ben's colleague asks, handing me a glass of Pinot Grigio. 'Wasn't today the big day?'

Trust Jim to remember. All of Ben's colleagues are friendly, but Jim is the kind of guy you instantly know you can trust. That's also why Ben likes him so much. It's nice to have another dolphin around when you're swimming with sharks.

'It was, thanks,' I tell him. 'It went okay. The conference was packed but I didn't have to say anything.'

'Which is good, right?'

'Carol hates being the centre of attention, don't you?' Ben says.

We've had this talk a lot. As a trainee barrister, Ben can't understand why I don't like being singled out for attention. I've tried to explain it to him, but it never sounds right when I do.

I vividly remember the last time I enjoyed the glare of the public eye. I was seven when Mum entered me into the school's Stage Two spelling bee. We practised for weeks together, and I was pretty sure of myself when I got through to the final round. As I stood there with the other three finalists, the whole auditorium erupted in applause and I felt a dizzying wave of approval wash over me. Mum clapped her hands off. I couldn't imagine feeling happier.

Then came my words in the final. E-v-e-r-y-o-n-e. The audience (everyone!) cheered. T-o-m-o-r-r-o-w. I guessed on the m's and r's, and got them right. Mum could hardly contain herself. When the moderator said the final word, I flashed my newly-budded grown-up teeth at the audience. Incidentally, a few years later those teeth would be painfully wrenched into place by braces. I didn't know that then, but I did know how to spell the next word. N-o-u-g-h-t-y.

No, I'm sorry, said the moderator. *The word is naughty. N-a-u-g-h-t-y.*

The air left the room. I'd failed. In front of everyone, I'd failed. What must Mum think?

I searched for her in the audience. There was effort behind her smile when our eyes met. Stiff upper lip, better luck next time. But I saw the disappointment there.

Now I'll take my praise whispered in my ear.

'Definitely,' I say to Jim. 'I'm much happier in the background.'

Ben snakes his arm around my waist. 'Glad it went well today.'

But it hadn't gone well. I told him that when I called after lunch. Maybe I wasn't clear enough. Or maybe he wasn't really listening.

When we were first together, no detail about my life was too small to catch Ben's interest. He's one of those people who make you feel like you're the most interesting person in the room. He wanted to know what I had for lunch, whether I'd avoided the rain on the way home, if I'd found the nail polish I wanted to go with the sandals I planned to wear for the weekend. At times he was a little too attentive. He remembered all the nonsense I uttered too, even my post-weekend self-improvement vows. But other than being reminded that I hadn't done yoga/given up chocolate/sorted out my bank statements, things were nearly perfect. Our worlds revolved around each other in a way that made me feel wonderfully loved. I've missed that feeling since his stupid case began.

He can't give me too many details because of client confidentiality. Not that it ever stops me from blabbing the bank's secrets to him, but then our clients aren't abused wives and children like his are.

More than a year into his training contract, he's working day and night, all in the hope of being made next year. Which sounds like he's trying out for the Mafia.

Sometimes I think being in 'the family' would be easier.

Later, after one last drink, we walk hand in hand to the Tube.

'Why don't you come back to mine?' I suggest, suggestively I hope. I badly need a… well, let's just call it a cuddle.

'I'm dead on my feet. I should head home before I fall over.'

'We could just sleep,' I say, unconvincingly. 'We don't have to, you know…'

He kisses me tenderly. 'I'd love to, Carol, but I'm exhausted. If you were in bed with me it'd be too tempting not to, you know… Why don't you come over tomorrow and I'll make us dinner?'

I bite down my frustration. 'Sure. Okay. I'll bring the wine.'

My cuddle can wait a day. I'll probably need more comforting tomorrow anyway after facing Derrick.

CHAPTER 5

'I'll come with you to Marley's mansion,' Harriet says as we stand in the queue for coffee the next morning. The café is heaving with the tired, the agitated and the late for work. Whether secretary or CEO, Pret a Manger clerk or management consultant, there's no pulling rank here. Everyone has to wait their turn. 'I do plan events, remember?'

'Yes, but for bankers,' I point out.

'Don't judge me just because my clientele demands open bars and busty waitresses. My talents are under-utilised, that's all. Didn't I always throw the best parties at school?'

She did, and thank God she'd caught me crying in the girls' loo during freshers' week, or I'd have been miserable for four years. It had only taken me a few days to realise that I wasn't going to have the university experience Marley had bragged about. Well, what did I expect, signing up for engineering?

But Harriet took one look at my blotchy, tear-stained face, pretended not to notice the snot bubbles, and pulled me into her new world with a group of girls who were smart, silly and fun and neither knew nor cared what fluid mechanics was. I did become friendly with my fellow engineers, too, but the girls were my salvation.

'So what time do we need to be there?' she asked.

'I'm not sure yet. Hopefully it won't be till after six.'

I don't remember it being a very big stately home. Mum only took forever there because she kept turning over the decorative pieces on the mantelpieces to see if she'd correctly guessed the luxury brand. Without the label-spotting, it shouldn't take more than an hour to whip around it. I can still be back in time for a late dinner with Ben. 'If it's earlier, Derrick will kill me.'

Within ten minutes of arriving at the office I know that Derrick is definitely going to kill me. The woman I phoned says I have to be in Hampshire by 5 p.m. to see the house because another couple already has the later appointment. When I suggested joining them on the tour she acted like I'd offered to bathe with them. 'We take our guests' privacy very seriously,' she'd snapped.

It's no use dragging things out with Derrick. He'll make me suffer no matter when I bring it up.

I'm waiting for him to finish his discussion with Ryan about the ideal woman's cup size. Unsurprisingly, their ideals align in double letters. Derrick loves holding conversations like this over the low partition at the side of my desk. That way he can talk across me and get two audiences, one willing and one captive, for the price of one.

'Derrick, if you've got a minute,' I say as he cups his imaginary breasts. 'I have an appointment that I can't miss.'

He waits.

'I'll need to leave at three. I can take a half-day holiday.'

He leans further over my desk. Coffee breath, incoming! 'Colbert, you know the protocol. Fill in the form and give it to that fat woman in HR who gets off on paperwork. If your schedule is clear, I'll sign it and you can have your holiday.'

'I'd love to, but there's not time for that. I need to go at three today.'

'And you couldn't have given us, your team–' he gestures around the room, '–the courtesy of a little more warning?'

I fight the urge to apologise. I'll lose the game completely if I do. Ryan has done it loads of times, and it's earned him nothing but contempt. Being an ingratiating little weasel, he can't help himself. 'No, Derrick, it only came up last night.'

He shrugs. 'You can't go.'

'But I have to.'

'Why? Is it medical? Can we guess? Let's guess. Ryan, what do you think? Colbert has a medical condition. What might it be? Sexual? Do you even have sex, Colbert? I can't imagine. Wait, let me try.'

The lie flicks through my mind. Something potentially terminal. No. He'll make me spell out the gruesome details. And then he'll want to see scans as evidence. If I do manage to produce something, they'll end up on the wall in the kitchen with a colourful explanation. 'No, nothing medical. It's personal.'

'I see. Are we having trouble at home? You can tell me.'

I can see that Ryan is enjoying this immensely. 'Nothing like that. I've got to do something for my family today. I'll make up the time.'

'And what about your briefing for the traders this afternoon?'

'What briefing?'

'The one I was going to have you do with the traders. This afternoon.'

'Can't I do it tomorrow?'

'Colbert. You don't expect everyone to work around your schedule, do you? Do you?' His voice starts to rise. 'Just because you want to fuck off to have tea with your mother, or whatever girly shit you've got planned. Isn't that a little selfish?'

'Please, Derrick. I'll make it up.' I can hear my voice wavering.

'Yes, you will. In fact, I'll tell you just how you'll make it up. Since poor Ryan now has to do the briefing today, you can go with Joe to lunch tomorrow. He's seeing your favourite client.'

Derrick's eyes narrow with glee.

My heart sinks to my knees.

'But you said I could go to lunch,' Ryan whines, shooting me a dirty look. As if I'm happy with this turn of events. 'Why does she get to go?'

'Because she has a much nicer arse than you do.' Derrick leans in still further. I can feel his breath coming in warm, odorific waves. 'Make sure you wear something to show it off. You know he's an arse man.' He stands up straight again. 'You can go today. I hope you appreciate that.'

He waits.

'Well, Colbert? Don't you have something to say?'

'Thanks,' I say in a small voice, already dreading lunch tomorrow.

You may suspect by now that I suffer from some kind of incurable mental illness that keeps me working for Derrick. The truth is that there are lots of reasons and as many trade-offs. At first, I didn't really believe my colleagues were as bad as they seemed. By the time I realised that they were worse, I was six months into a job that felt right for me. I also knew I was right for the job since, for all his shouting, Derrick can't deny that I'm his best analyst. And, most importantly, I'm getting millions invested in green energy, which must have saved some polar bears by now.

Of course I don't enjoy working in a place that makes the website menarebetterthanwomen.com look like an ode to feminist thought. But as much as I despise the company I keep, I love the work I do, and so far I've been able to separate one from the other. Besides, I'm not about to be chased off by a bunch of breast-obsessed mouth-breathers who aren't as good at their jobs as I am at mine.

It's just before five when Harriet and I arrive at the house in Hampshire. As the taxi crunches along the private road, under ancient bare-branched chestnut trees, I know it's exactly what Marley is looking for. We sweep around a bend and into the circular gravel drive at the front of the house. In the twilight it's as stunning as I remember, even though the enormous expanse of grass leading up to the creamy stone façade is yellowing from the harsh winter. I imagine Marley hiring gardeners to paint it green. Then I imagine me out there with the paintbrush on the night before the wedding.

'This is gorgeous!' Harriet says as I pay the taxi driver. 'What's not to love?'

'You know my sister. That's exactly what we're here to find out.'

I'm Marley's eyes and ears. Which means I'm also about to be her proxy pain in the neck.

'Thanks for coming, Harriet. There's a lot riding on this.'

'You mean just because you're choosing your sister's wedding venue and if anything goes wrong it will be totally your fault?'

'Well, when you put it like that, I don't know why I'm worried.'

I take a deep breath and push open the ancient, iron-studded reception door. A large fireplace is merry with crackling flames and a row of wellies stands near the entrance. A thin young man waits behind the deeply polished oak reception desk, his dark suit impeccable and his thinning hair tidy.

'Good afternoon, how may I help you?' he asks in an unusually deep voice.

When I tell him about our appointment he nods before speaking quietly into the phone. 'Mrs Thatcher is coming.'

Sure enough, within seconds we hear clicking heels approach from the flagstone-floored hall. She'd intimidated me on the phone. I'm afraid of what she'll do to me in person.

'I am Mrs Thatcher,' proclaims the white-haired woman. Like her namesake, this is someone unaccustomed to objections. I bet she'll be a blast to plan a wedding with. 'How very nice to meet you.'

She extends her hand. On her finger sparkles a jewel I may have seen in the Tower of London.

The oak-panelled hall is imposing and lined with austere, oil-painted ancestors. An enormous staircase with flora-carved newel posts dominates the room, winding its way to the floors above. Its wide, shallow steps will make the perfect backdrop for wedding photos. Mrs Thatcher no doubt knows this when she stops to make sure we admire it. She explains that the original building has stood on the spot since the sixteenth century, built with riches bestowed on the family by Queen Elizabeth I. That'll suit Mum and Marley down to the ground.

Mum drooled over the house when we came here last year. Even Dad, who's not one for ostentation, enjoyed himself. He was most impressed with the gardens, and the cakes in the orangery café. Dad has rarely met a cake he didn't like.

I worry sometimes about his health. He might spend every weekend mowing and weeding, trimming and digging (when Mum isn't making him take her shopping). But a lifetime of gigs and touring with his band must have taken their toll. He's not exactly Keith Richards, but Dad's jazz career still meant years of late nights, smoky bars and takeaways.

He could be one of those thin fat people the newspapers like to frighten us about. As if we don't have enough on our minds, what with expanding waistlines and orange peel thighs. Now our organs might be secretly obese?

'We are not simply a wedding venue,' Mrs Thatcher says as Harriet and I gawp at the sumptuous drapes and the silk-upholstered furniture that nestles beside the open fires in each room.

How I'd love to come to a house like this with Ben after his case finishes. We can curl up together on the sofa to read the weekend papers, reciting interesting bits to each other and sparking lovely, rambling conversations. Maybe we'll bring a board game or two. We'll sip tea and eat bucketloads of clotted cream on scones in the afternoon, perhaps go for a gentle walk around the grounds to work up our appetites for a gourmet dinner. Then, late in the evening, full of champagne and love, we'll retire to our carved four-poster bed where we'll eventually fall asleep in each other's arms.

'We are your wedding partners,' Mrs Thatcher continues, pulling my thoughts out of that nice warm bed. 'Once we have our instructions, you can confidently leave everything to us to create your perfect day.'

I guffaw at the very idea that Marley would ever be hands-off in her planning (by which I mean my planning).

Mrs Thatcher glares at me. 'Did you have a question, Miss Colbert?'

'No, Mrs Thatcher,' I say, feeling like I've been ticked off by the headmistress for chewing gum. 'I'm just delighted to be here. It's beautiful.'

She nods, mollified. 'We've hosted some of the most elegant weddings in the country.'

Which leads nicely to my first question. 'I'm not surprised. You've probably seen royalty here?'

She is tight-lipped, only nodding once.

'Anyone I might have heard of?'

'Miss Colbert, I'm sure you appreciate that our clientele very much expects our complete discretion.'

'Of course, of course. It's just that, well, you see, it's my mother.'

Mrs Thatcher waits for more. But how am I supposed to explain about Mum? Famous marriages are a highly valued currency, and one she plans to spend when it comes to her eldest daughter's wedding venue. There's Mrs Latham to impress, after all.

Mum wasn't always so attuned to the weeklies' social pages. Lord knows Granny isn't one for airs and graces and Dad thinks chocolate digestives are too fancy for every day, so it didn't come from him either. At least not directly. But his parents were wealthy and while I know that wasn't why Mum married him (she didn't find out till after the wedding), it probably seemed like a nice bonus when they were newly-weds living above the pub. It's one thing to sling drinks, helping to get your husband's jazz career off the ground and wondering how on earth it'll ever get any better. It's quite another to know the love of your life will have a fortune one day, whether he ever produces a successful note of music or not.

That was the idea, anyway, but Dad didn't inherit any of Granny Colbert's money when she died. He loved his parents but never wanted their cash. By the time Granny shuffled off this mortal coil, his career was taking off and we were living comfortably. So it all went to Aunt Margaret, who now lives in the manner to which Mum feels accustomed. Mum's not overly fond of her sister-in-law.

'This is such a gorgeous house,' Harriet says, stepping smoothly into my silence. 'And it will be perfect for the wedding. But Carol's Mum has looked at several beautiful venues. And while we absolutely love it here, it's her Mum who'll make the final decision. I'm sure you understand.'

She smiles engagingly through her lie.

'I just know that hearing about the fine pedigree her daughter would be following will convince her that this is the venue to choose. Maybe you could just tell us about one wedding? Perhaps one that was covered by The Telegraph or Harper's anyway? It wouldn't be indiscreet then, would it, since it's not a secret.'

Will she buy Harriet's flattery?

No, it doesn't look like she's giving an inch.

Harriet turns to me. 'Carol,' she says, sotto voce but certainly loud enough for Mrs Thatcher to hear. 'I think this is so much nicer than Woodclare Castle, don't you? I don't know why your Mum thinks that's more elegant. Just because Princess Katarina of Moldovia had her wedding there, I guess.'

An inelegant noise escapes from Mrs Thatcher. 'I suppose if you want opulence, then Woodclare Castle may be more appropriate. Our clientele tend to be English, Miss Colbert, who naturally prefer understated elegance. Our own Lady Sophie was married here in 2008. The princes were in attendance and it was beautiful.'

'I'm sure it was perfect!' I say. 'How could it not be? Just look at this house! Can we please see the chapel?'

As Mrs Thatcher leads us to the grounds I give Harriet a thumbs-up. Not being intimately acquainted with the royal family, I'll look up Lady Sophie when I get back, and perhaps embellish a bit to Mum. Who's to say the princes weren't William and Harry?

The chapel is ancient, and beautiful in its near-dereliction. Faded murals of the Ascension decorate white-stuccoed walls and the flagstone floor is worn away down the centre aisle. Imagine the feet that have trod that aisle. Oliver Cromwell might have nipped in to pray for a boost during the Civil War. Mum'll just love that.

'Marley will want to know how long the aisle is,' I tell Harriet. 'Her entrance needs to be grand.'

'Then this is your chance to walk down the aisle!' she says. 'Wait a sec. Let me get to the front so I can watch.'

'Don't, you'll make me self-conscious.'

'You'll have to do it one day, Carol. Maybe soon. Now's your chance to get used to it. Do you want music? I'll hum you in.'

As she begins humming 'Here Comes the Bride', my mind flicks to Ben. What would it feel like to walk through the church, past all our friends and family, to stand beside him on our wedding day? Of course I've thought about marrying him, but only in a silly, doodle-your-new-surname-in-your-notebook way. I'm too young to get married.

But Harriet is right. At some point he might ask me. Will I say yes? Six months ago I wouldn't have thought twice. Does that mean I'm thinking twice today?

No, of course not. It's normal for a couple to settle into their relationship after a while, for the first thrill of love to dim ever so slightly. I just hope his case finishes soon so he can concentrate a bit more on his priorities.

As I reach Harriet at the altar, this wish settles uncomfortably on my shoulders.

'Twenty-seven steps. That's probably long enough,

even if Marley wants a cathedral-length train.' I turn to Mrs Thatcher. 'Do you know how many guests the chapel can seat?'

'Eighty-six.'

That could be a problem. Our family is small, just us two girls, Mum and Dad, Granny and a few aunties and cousins. But Marley and Jez have a lot of friends.

I check my watch. Time is ticking and we still need to see the reception room itself. And one more thing. As we make our way back to the house I ask to use the loo in the ballroom.

'You may use this one,' she says, gesturing to the cloakroom by the main hall staircase.

'Is that the one we'd use at the reception?'

'No. The event lavatories are off the corridor beside the ballroom itself.'

That's what I was afraid of.

'I'd like to see them, please.'

'I can assure you, all of our facilities are impeccable.'

'It's not that. It's… well...' I'm going to have to tell her. And then she'll think my sister is insane. Which is a bit true. 'My sister dislikes mixer taps.'

That's an understatement.

'I'm sorry, but I'll need to check.'

'They are traditional British taps.'

'Perfect. I'll just need a photo.'

I wait for her to unlock the loos, sure that she'll reject our application on the grounds that we're social-climbing bathroom fixture nuts.

It's after six by the time we shake hands and say our goodbyes, and I'm dying for a cigarette.

Lately, I've really started to wish I didn't smoke.

How nice it must be not to worry about your next nicotine hit. On regular workdays, lighting up seems normal. Ben hardly ever stays over, so I can puff at leisure fresh from the shower, and there are enough breaks in the day to shrug into my smoking jacket for a quick cigarette beside the rubbish bins.

Right now, though, as much as I need the hit, smoking just seems like an inconvenience. I quickly suck down two cigarettes at the front of the station, flapping my coat to air it out. I won't have time to go home to change before seeing Ben.

Once Harriet and I settle into our seats, I text Marley so she can call Mrs Thatcher first thing in the morning with her credit card details. Then I call Ben. It'll be after eight by the time I get to his flat for dinner.

'Hi, darling,' he says when he picks up. 'How was your day?'

'Good. I'm just on the train now.'

'On the train? Where?'

'I told you I had to come out to see a venue for Marley this afternoon. Remember? I told you last night.'

'Oh, that's right,' he says vaguely. 'Is it nice?'

'It's beautiful. She'll love it. What a relief. It's the first one we've looked at. Unfortunately, it ran on longer than I expected so I won't be back till a bit later. I'm sorry, is that okay?'

'It's fine. In fact, I've got a lot to do here anyway. Why don't we have dinner tomorrow night instead?'

I hesitate. 'I was looking forward to tonight.'

'I know, but isn't it better to have a relaxing evening together when we're not rushing to make time for each other?'

'I guess so.'

My cuddle is becoming a fast-moving target.

'Tomorrow, I promise. What would you like for dinner? I'll pick everything up at lunchtime.'

'You choose something. I don't mind.'

'All right, I'll get something nice. And I'll make you chocolate fondant for pudding. How does that sound?'

'It sounds like an offer I can't refuse. I'll talk to you later then. Good luck getting your work done.'

'Thanks. Have a good trip back into London. I'll talk to you tomorrow. Bye bye.'

Harriet glances up from her magazine. 'He's cancelled on you?'

She's an unapologetic eavesdropper, as any good friend would be.

'No, he didn't cancel. He just postponed rather than have me rush over there when we get back. It's fine. We can have a relaxing dinner tomorrow instead.'

I don't add that I'll also now get to make up for lost cigarettes when I get back to my flat.

'Is it really fine?'

She's watching me carefully.

Harriet doesn't love Ben as much as I do. That's my fault, really. I never should have told her what he said after she went out with an intern from his office. But she never should have given that guy the time of day. And she certainly never should have been so obsessed with him when he stopped calling. But Ben also should never have called her Stalkerella.

'I really don't mind,' I say. 'I've got that client lunch tomorrow. I'll get an early night.'

'You're more forgiving than I'd be. Of course, I'd probably be a big pushover too if it meant having sex eventually.'

'I'm not a pushover!'

'I'm sorry, I didn't mean to upset you. You're not a pushover. You just, erm, accommodate everyone.'

'It's called being nice.'

'Some people call it being a pushover, but if you're happy then who am I to argue? I'm hardly a dating expert.'

She stares out the window, watching my reflection against the dark sky outside. 'Seriously. When was the last time I had a date?'

I think for a moment. 'That guy you met on the train from Glasgow? Whatever happened to him?'

'You mean after he left my flat with my pearl necklace? I'm not sure. Oddly, he didn't think to keep in touch.'

'That's right. The police never found anything out?'

'No. They pretty much said it was my fault for letting a stranger I'd met on a train into my flat.'

'Well, you can't fault their logic. At least you didn't give him your car keys this time. Speaking of which, did that insurance claim ever go through?'

She shakes her head.

Harriet is the unluckiest women I've ever known when it comes to love. She already had a diary full of dastardly bastardly boys when we met at university. Since then, she's graduated to full-size ring binders to log her love woes. Most of the men she dates aren't thieves, so she's held on to most of her worldly belongings. It's her self-esteem the others tend to walk away with.

I just don't get it. Despite Ben's unkind moniker, Harriet is no more stalky than the rest of us. She might even be slightly more normal. And while none of us is one hundred per cent honest with our friends when they ask what's wrong with them, in Harriet's case, it really isn't her. Or at least, it isn't something within her that makes men run. The problem is that she is the worst judge of men in the history of womankind. Which she already knows. But how do you change something like that?

'That was last Christmas,' Harriet muses. 'Has it really been over a year since I've even kissed a man?'

'You've just been busy.'

At least when she's not dating I don't need to worry about getting a panicked call from the boot of her car.

'You're kind, but I've been hard-up. Face it, Carol, I need help.' She takes a deep breath. 'I think it's time I tried the internet. I'm never going to meet anyone at work–'

'Because you loathe them?'

'I'd rather volunteer for conjugal visits at Broadmoor prison. So, I was thinking I could put a profile up online and see who's out there. Lots of women in my office are doing it and their dates haven't all been horrible. It might be good to spread the net a bit wider, don't you think?'

Her big brown eyes are hopeful but fear grips my heart. What percentage of men are psychos? One per cent? Five? Ten? And yet she unerringly finds every single one in her physical proximity.

I dread to think what she'll find online.

'Why don't you let me help?' I say. 'We could fill out your profile together and have a look at who's out there. It would be fun. I'll come over one night when you're free.'

'Really? But you've already got so much on.'

I wave away her objection, true as it is.

'Okay, then, that's a great idea,' she says. 'And I'll buy the wine. Lots of wine. Thanks, Carol.'

As we settle back in our seats to continue the journey in companionable silence, I wonder how I'll squeeze guardianship of Harriet's love life into my schedule.

MICHELE GORMAN

CHAPTER 6

It isn't till I've left for work the next morning that I realise Marley hasn't called back. It's not like her to miss the chance to profit from my efforts. She must really be busy.

Derrick is laughing with Ryan over the top of my desk as I throw my gym bag underneath. 'Honest to God, she sucked like a Hoover.'

I flip on my computers and shoot him a dirty look.

'It's not polite to eavesdrop, Colbert.'

'It's not eavesdropping when you're talking in a normal voice,' I remind him. 'That's called not being able to avoid listening.'

'What's got your knickers in a bunch this morning?' he asks. 'Did you get up on the wrong side of someone else's bed?'

I ignore him. Sometimes, if you play dead, he gets bored and goes away.

'Speaking of knickers, are you ready for lunch today?'

This isn't going to be one of those days.

'I'm ready.'

'Good. After the briefing, be sure to tell Joe you're going in place of Ryan.'

Ryan glares at me.

'You didn't tell Joe yet?' I whisper. This is bad. Very bad.

'I thought I'd let you give him the good news. After the briefing. Oh, and Colbert,' he says, peering over the desk. 'Nice dress.'

I suppress a shudder, though I recognise this is just his usual power trip. The men are just as sexually harassing to each other as they are to me. It's to the point now that I'd worry if they weren't accusing each other of gay sex or bestiality. I've grown rhinoceros-thick skin since working here.

That doesn't mean I wasn't shocked the first time a colleague called me a c*nt. Okay, I was more than shocked. I cried in the loos. I couldn't imagine how I'd ever face that trader again. But when I emerged, puffy-eyed but composed, he was back at my desk within minutes to carry on a perfectly normal, c*nt-free conversation. As if nothing had happened. And then I realised: in his mind nothing had happened.

Over the next days and weeks my ears were alert to their language, and I heard it over and over again. Traders were c*nts. Football players were c*nts. Stale sandwiches and cold cups of coffee were c*nts. Unsettling as it sounds to the uninitiated, traders lack the filters that most normal people have. When you're in their world, you live by their rules.

So that's what I've done. I've become a master at stamping down my emotions. If they can't see them, they can't use them against me.

Of course their behaviour isn't acceptable. HR has very clear rules about harassment and bullying, just like every other company. The difference is that nobody enforces it here. It may be one of the last strongholds of the unreconstructed man, along with construction sites and the cabs of delivery vans. They aren't going to change until and unless they have to. So every time Derrick tells me my arse looks fat or asks what new sexual positions I've tried at the weekend, I take a deep breath and ignore him. He can only hurt me if I let him.

Besides, why should I be scared off when nobody else is? If a coward like Ryan can handle it, so can I.

His actions, however, are harder to ignore but again I have no means to fight them. If I go to HR to make a formal complaint about him giving credit for Green T to the others, for example, he'll certainly find some excuse to fire me. Which will mean giving up the bonus I've worked hard all year to earn. I'm not about to let the fifteen-hour days, working weekends, sleepless nights and forgone social life go to waste. Just one more year and at least my bank account will have something to show for it.

As bad luck would have it, Joe is at his desk after the briefing. So there's no chance of scribbling a note and hiding in the loos.

'Morning,' I say cheerily.

He grunts, efficiently setting the tone for what's coming.

Joe and I had a pretty good relationship before Green T launched. He's 'my' trader, which means he buys and sells shares in many of the companies I analyse. It's my job to read all the news as soon as I wake, so that I can tell him how our companies' shares will trade that day. One oil spill or hurricane can send the markets into a panic. He needs me. Unfortunately, lately he doesn't want me.

We're an unhappy couple stuck in a loveless marriage.

'Derrick says I have to go with you today to lunch.'

I wait, wondering if he'll smile. Joe is a cheeky chap from Epsom but speaks like he's come straight from an East London market stall. Despite his suspiciously false accent, the others like him, though they rip him apart for having gone to university. Funny how some people's idea of affection often looks a lot like abuse.

Joe doesn't take his eyes from his screens. 'No fucking way.'

I steel myself. I can't take no for an answer. If Joe doesn't let me go, I'll have to trail him to the restaurant. 'Derrick says I have to. I haven't got any choice.'

'Maybe not, but I do. You can't come.'

He looks up, challenging me to disagree.

'Joe, please? The client likes me and–' I lower my voice. 'And I can tell him why Green T isn't for him. I'll convince him not to use it.'

Derrick will fire me on the spot if he hears me say this. But he'll torment me if I don't go to lunch with Joe.

To think I get to have all this fun before 8 a.m.

He blows out his cheeks. He's been looking haggard lately. They all party pretty hard, and alcohol is the mildest of their vices. I hope he's not sniffing away his weekends like some of the others do. Joe is one of the okay guys. 'I don't care what you do,' he says. 'Tag along if you want to. But you better not say one fucking nice word about that piece of shit system.'

That's the problem between me and Joe. He isn't a big fan of automated trading systems. Why would he be? If enough clients invest their money through an IT program instead of their brokers and traders, then the writing is on the wall. Traders know it and they aren't going down without a fight.

Our taxi ride to the restaurant for lunch passes in silence. I try a few times to make conversation, until Joe asks me to shut up because he's got a headache. That gives me plenty of time to quietly contemplate the horror awaiting me in the restaurant.

I've met the client twice before, once at a conference and once at a dinner. If William Hogarth had been alive to paint him today, he'd have captured huge, moist, flaccid lips on a red-veined face that suggests too many glasses of wine at lunch. Watery grey eyes and pale lashes that contradict the sparse dark hair on his head, and a girth that would keep cannibals fed for weeks. He wouldn't, however, have the palette to convey this man's impact on the other senses. He smells. Pits *and* mouth. Jabba the Hut would make a more appealing lunch companion.

This isn't the first time I've been wheeled out as client bait but thankfully, as a quantitative analyst (meaning I am officially a geek), I don't have to do it as often as some of the other women in the bank. It's an open secret that banks hire gorgeous young women to work in other teams like Capital Introductions. Ostensibly, they're investment matchmakers, sent out with clients to get them to buy the bank's latest offerings. In reality, they're served up with glasses of champagne to greedy fund managers in the hope that they'll charm their way into his portfolio.

The client, Trevor, is waiting for us in the restaurant's bar. He downs his large gin and tonic as we approach.

'Joe, good to see you. And Carol, what a lovely surprise. Yes, lovely indeed.'

I stick my hand out to greet him, but he pulls me close. As his blubbery lips linger on my cheek, I get a whiff of his breakfast. And probably a bit of last night's dinner, too, given the amount of gunk between his nicotine-stained teeth. 'It's delightful to see you again, my dear.'

Trevor is probably a bit younger than he looks, maybe around fifty. His manners are old-school and repulsive in turns. But he's an important client and richer than the Queen, so I can't drive a fork into his hand, no matter what he says.

'After you, my dear,' he says as the waitress leads us to our table. I know his gesture has less to do with chivalry than lechery. He's staring at my arse.

The restaurant, overlooking the Thames, is full of men and women in suits. Joe and Trevor get straight down to business. It's always a race against the gin and tonics with Trevor, who doesn't like pesky business details interrupting his drunken fun.

Since some of his biggest investments are with my clients, he asks me several questions, and for those moments I feel like an analyst, not a woman. It's welcome respite.

I love this part of my job. When I get to talk strategy, the rest of the day-to-day crap seems worth it.

All around us, business is being conducted over

expensive bottles of wine and three-course lunches while the black-clad waiters pretend not to overhear confidential conversations.

The first few times I was let 'off the lead' to join a trader for a client lunch, I was nearly sick with nerves. Sure, I'd researched the companies for more than a year. I knew them inside and out. But I was going to have to prove that. Hundred quid bottles of wine and Michelin star food were small compensation for being the performing monkey. I'd have been much happier eating a Pret a Manger sandwich at my desk.

These days I'm less nervous, and even able to focus beyond our table. You know the feeling when you're abroad and see other tourists? I mean obvious ones – sandals with socks, necks hung with cameras or those sun-scalded beer-bellied families. Don't you feel a little bit smug? I know I do. I like the idea that they stick out and I blend in. It's totally untrue, of course. At the very same moment that I'm judging that sunburnt trainer-clad couple in matching fleeces, a local is judging me. I'm very aware of this sensation as I eye the other diners.

At the table behind Trevor sit three men, the youngest in his twenties. His twitchy laughter and the way he keeps checking his notebook give him away as the analyst. The fact that he *has* a notebook gives him away. The two older men talk with the ease of a married couple doing their best to ignore their offspring. Then the older of the two calls the waiter over and begins speaking French to him. The waiter patiently nods as the man gestures to the wine list. When the waiter answers in French, the man's expression slips from self-important to self-conscious.

The waiter repeats his answer, in English, smiles and recedes. 'Couldn't understand his bloody accent,' blusters the man. 'He's not from Paris.'

He laughs at the waiter's substandard heritage.

The other man has one eye on his client and the other on his BlackBerry, which insistently dings for his attention. In fact, the restaurant is alive with chirping, singing, bonging, buzzing phones. Several diners are talking on them, their hands held over their mouths like they're spreading state secrets. They're probably investment bankers who create a lot of the investments that we sell. Their projects all have big, macho code names like Jedi or Lord of the Rings. Nobody wants to be Steel Magnolias. Having to remember which banker is Gandalf and which is Bilbo Baggins is almost as hard as working on the deals themselves.

As I watch the bankers, I know they're watching us, too. They see a fat aging client in a two thousand pound suit being sucked up to by a fast-talking trader. And they see me for what I am: a young bit of eye-candy, the after-dinner mint presented with the bill. We're all actors in the same parody.

I don't have to say very much as we eat, aside from making sure I rubbish Green T enough to put Trevor off. The waiter pours the last of the second bottle of wine as our client brags about his latest purchase: a hundred-and-thirty-foot yacht being delivered to St Tropez next weekend.

'Come down,' he says to Joe. 'Catch a bit of winter sun. There'll be a bunch of us. It might be a bit chilly for the D.O.s, but very nice for us.'

He pokes his tongue out to lick along his sweaty upper lip.

D.O.s are Deck Ornaments. He's talking about the women supplied as accessories with the delivery of a large yacht. Yacht brokers arrange for the lovely leggy models to be on deck for the amusement of the yacht's new captain. All over the Mediterranean, beautiful women accessorise rich, ugly men.

'Two come as standard,' Trevor continues once he's got his tongue back in his mouth. 'And they'll be beauties. One blonde and one brunette.'

'What, no redhead to complete the set?' Joe jokes.

'I'm not a fan of ginger minge.'

I suppress a shudder. The very thought of that man being anywhere near a woman's…

I doubt Joe will go to St Tropez. He talks a good game but he actually seems to quite like his wife. I've never heard him linked with prostitutes like a lot of the other traders. Strippers, yes, hookers, no.

When the bill comes, Joe slaps down his credit card. I'm just beginning to hope I'll get off lightly when Trevor says, 'It's a shame to go back to the office on a day like this. Let's have another bottle.'

'I'd love to, Trev, but I've got to meet another client at four,' says Joe. 'We should probably head back.'

'But Carol can stay, can't she?' He reaches over to tickle the back of my hand with his meaty thumb. It takes all my willpower not to move my hand. Frozen in a half-smile, caught between my revulsion and the need to keep my job, I stare at Joe.

'I'm sure she'd love to, Trevor. This has been really nice, thanks again for having lunch with us. But she'll have to be at the same client meeting. It was arranged weeks ago. I'm sorry, Carol, I'd let you get out of it but I need you.'

I nod in as disappointed a manner as possible, shrugging at Trevor. I don't mean to mime like Marcel Marceau. I just don't trust my voice not to betray my relief.

We say our goodbyes and hail two taxis on the approach to Blackfriars Bridge. Trevor pulls me into a hug that smells of day-old shirt. I fight not to gag as he pushes his corpulent tummy into me. At least his precipitous overhang means there's no chance of accidentally feeling an erection.

'Carol, my dear, it's always such a pleasure to see you. We should meet again soon.'

'Ah, yes, sure, I'm sure we will.' I disentangle myself from his sweaty grasp and duck into the taxi with Joe.

Once we're safely away, my heart rate returns to normal. It's naïve to think that men like Trevor are an anomaly. There are too many yachts in the South of France with D.O.s to believe that.

'Thanks, Joe. I don't think I could have managed any more time with him.'

'He's a disgusting fucker, isn't he?' He laughs, running his hand over his short-cropped hair. 'Even I wouldn't leave you to a pervy arsehole like that. My standards are low, but I do have them.'

And I'm grateful for whatever low standards he has.

I let myself into Ben's flat just as the rain starts pelting down. 'Hello? Anyone home?'

It's always best to check whether Ben's flatmate is home. He's not likely to be sitting alone in the dark, but I once surprised him just as he was exiting the shower. Luckily he was wearing a towel but neither of us wants to repeat the experience.

Thanks to my parents' forward planning, I don't have to worry about naked flatmates of my own. A decade ago, Mum and Dad invested in a small two-bedroom flat in the unfashionable end of Dalston so that Marley and I would have a place to live when we took our places in London's workforce. Since Marley moved out to live with Jez, I've had the place to myself.

It would be nice for Ben to take more advantage of that. His flat is comfortable, and his flatmate's consulting job means we rarely see him, but I always feel like a guest here. Ben's bedroom décor is twenty-first century single man and we don't spend enough time together in the flat to feel like it could be ours in any way. If we'd spent any time at all in my flat, I'd make sure it was couple-friendly.

That makes it sound like I want to live with Ben, doesn't it? All right, fine, yes, I do. Very much. Maybe I'm not ready to march down the aisle, but I can see myself pledging half my closet space to him. And after what he said last week, about how much easier it would be if we lived in the same place, he seems to be thinking along the same lines. I hope so, because I'm going to ask him about it when the time is right.

It's a risk, I know. If I spook him, he can't be unspooked. But I know he loves me, so I just have to stop being such a coward.

I find a vase for the vivid orange rose and gerbera daisy bouquet that I impulsively bought on the way to the Tube. The fridge shows no sign of Ben's flatmate. When he's in town he likes to keep at least a week's worth of half-eaten takeaway in there. I'm not one to throw takeaway stones, given how often I slurp noodles at my desk. But I do love homemade food best. Mum taught us to cook and bake as part of her attempt to round us for life. Mum is a great believer in rounding. We also had to learn musical instruments. Thanks to her we could have toured as a family like the Von Trapps, pedalling our meagre talents and baked goods.

I hear the key in the lock. 'Is that you, Ben?'

'Yep. God, it's awful out there. I'm glad we don't have to go out again tonight.'

He strides into the kitchen where I'm cutting some melon to wrap with prosciutto. 'These are for you.' He pulls a bouquet from behind his back just as he spies the vase on the table. 'Oh, you got flowers already.'

'Yes, but I got them for you, not for me. Thank you for mine. I'll just find another vase. I'm sure you've got something here.'

I busy myself opening cabinets to hide my embarrassment. Way to scupper a lovely gesture, eh?

'There, the jug'll do. I'll leave them in the wrapping because I want to take them home with me so I can enjoy them. They're really beautiful. In fact, they're my favourites.'

I'm babbling. Shut up, Carol.

'Glass of wine?' He opens the bottle.

'Yes, please. Now, how can I help? Do you need a sous chef?' I wind my arms around his waist and kiss him. To hell with the ham and melon. I'm thinking about a different kind of starter.

'No, I can handle everything.' He holds up M&S bags. 'Misters Marks and Spencer have kindly taken care of the hard work. Twenty minutes from packet to table.'

I don't want to sound ungrateful, and it isn't that I

don't like slow-cooked lamb and, yes, there they are, chocolate fondants just like he promised. But when someone says he's cooking for you, it seems reasonable to assume there'll be some cooking involved. 'I could have cooked something,' I say.

'Why would you do that? It's my turn to cook. Carol, is something wrong?'

'No, nothing at all. This will be lovely. Here, let me help you, erm, open the packages.'

As we pierce clear plastic and read heating directions, I start telling Ben about lunch.

But his phone cuts me off mid-sentence. 'Sorry, Carol, but that's Jim. I need to take it.'

'Sure, no problem,' I say to his retreating back. I'm used to half-spoken conversations. He'll be on the call a while.

Lately I've stopped smoking around Ben, at first out of respect for his attempt to quit, but now out of fear of his judgment. But I'm dying for a cigarette. I slip into one of his coats from the peg in the hall and let myself out.

Standing under the eaves to shelter from the rain, as soon as I hold the smoke in my mouth for that second before inhaling, I feel myself relax. Tension escapes as I exhale into the chilly night. I've never meditated but imagine the feeling is similar. I'm getting closer to the decision to quit, and that makes every cigarette all the better.

I feel guilty as I shrug out of his coat, but I'm an expert at covering my tracks. I nip to the loo to brush my teeth and spritz my hair. Nobody needs to be the wiser.

By the time Ben finishes his call I've worked my way

through half the melon. 'I hope you don't mind, I was hungry,' I say. 'It's pretty tasty for being out of season.'

'That's fine, I'm glad you started. I'm sorry I had to take the call.' He puts his arms around me and pulls me to him. 'No more interruptions tonight.'

'I have an idea,' I say, kissing him deeply. 'We can always microwave dinner later, if you've got any other ideas now.'

'I like your thinking. Tom will be back later from Germany. Let's take advantage of the empty flat while we can. In fact…' He cocks his head towards the kitchen table. 'What do you say?'

'I say let's go in the bedroom.'

'Carol, Carol, Carol, where's the impetuous girl I fell in love with? We used to do it everywhere, every way. Remember? God, I do.'

'Then let's go in the bedroom and replay some of our greatest hits.'

He walks me down the hall from behind, one hand stroking my breast as he kisses my neck.

Later, as we lay together in a tangle of sheets, Ben says, 'I've been thinking. Do you want to go away for the weekend? Somewhere very grand. I could do it this weekend. What do you say? You deserve some pampering.'

'I'd love to!' I kiss him again, wondering about the chances of another starter before dinner.

Then I hear the front door slam. 'Hey, something smells great!' Tom shouts.

Ben sits up, smiling regretfully. 'So much for the romance. He'll know we're in here. Is there enough to share, do you think?'

'You mean dinner, right? Not–' I gesture to myself.

'This?'

He laughs.

'Yes, I'm sure there's enough. But you'll have to split your fondant with him. I want a whole one.'

The important thing is that we're going away together this weekend. Who cares if I have to share my romantic evening with my boyfriend's flatmate?

CHAPTER 7

I get home from work the next night still reeling from the afternoon's trader briefing. I know Zack was just trying to help, but he was so not helpful. I chuck my keys in the bowl in the hall, tripping over the rubbish bag I forgot to put out before I left. Shrugging out of my coat and kicking off my shoes, I wander into the living room.

With my head so full of work, I don't notice the light on until Zoe pops up over the back of the sofa. 'Welcome home!' she cries. 'Would you like a glass of wine?' She lifts the bottle from the table.

'Jesus, you nearly gave me a heart attack! What are you doing here?'

'I'm welcoming you home?'

'I don't mean literally, Zoe. I mean, why are you here instead of at home?'

'Your Mum gave me the key. I have moved out. Wine?'

'Does that mean you're moving in here?'

She nods, smiling.

I sigh, slumping down next to her. 'Give me a glass, please. What happened?'

'Well, you know how Madame Colbert is always saying I should stand on my own two feet? She thinks I should stand here.'

'You're standing on your own two feet in my flat?'

'It is your family's flat, no?'

Oui. When Mum and Dad bought it for us, it was with the understanding that we could live here whenever we needed to, no questions asked. Mum might have even used the words 'two feet' and 'standing' over the years. Since we'd effectively adopted Zoe, that promise seems to extend to her as well, so I can't blame her for taking Mum at her word. I just wish her timing was a bit better. I'm thinking of Ben.

Not that he'll necessarily object to living with Zoe, but it does take some of the romance out of the whole moving-in-together thing. Now how am I supposed to ask him?

'Was there something specific that, erm, encouraged you to decide to move in today? Something that couldn't wait till, for example, after a phone call to tell me you were coming?'

Her eyes fill with tears. 'Do you not want me here?'

'Of course I do! Sweetheart, come here.' I hug her close. As if I could chuck her out. First of all it'd break her fragile little heart, and that would break my heart. Secondly, what kind of person would I be if I did something like that? Selfish, that's what kind. And I don't ever want to be called selfish again, especially by my family. I heard enough of that over the years to make sure it's no longer a charge they can level at me.

'It'll be wonderful to have you for a flatmate,' I tell Zoe, shaking away those memories. 'I'll just need to clear out the second bedroom to make some room for your things. I'm sure I can find somewhere to store everything. Maybe hire a storage unit,' I say to myself.

'There is no rush. Do it whenever you can. I have already moved the clothes from my closet into yours.'

Her closet? She's already claimed her room.

'It is a bit squashy but they fit. You do have fast broadband, right? I have a blog and I will need to be online a lot.'

I look around. 'Did you bring your computer?'

Mum got Zoe a computer in her last year at school. It's not that Zoe's own parents wouldn't have paid for it, but Mum wanted to give her something for her birthday that she'd love. I would never accuse Mum of trying to buy Zoe's affections. Let's just say she likes to make periodic payments.

'No. I will not rely on Madame Colbert for anything. I can use yours if that is all right. I have all my documents on my zip drive, so I can keep writing just like normal. You know what?' She twirls a lock of her dark hair. 'Leaving home was very distressing. I would not be surprised if I suffer separation anxiety. It is important for me to get back into my normal routine as if nothing has happened.'

'I don't blame you.' I hug her again. 'Make yourself at home and I'll fix us something for dinner.'

'Thanks, Carol, you are *superbe*!' She settles back down under the blanket on the sofa with a contented sigh.

I wish I felt as comfortable with the turn of events. I grab my mobile on the way to the kitchen.

'Hello?' trills Mum.

'Mum? It's Carol. Zoe is here.'

'I know, darling. She left us a poem.'

Only Zoe would write a leaving-home poem. 'Did you have an argument or something?'

'Oh, nothing more than usual. Between you and me, she's not been easy to live with lately. Marley and I've been talking and we think the time has come for her to spread her wings. She hasn't tried very hard to find a job, and that's our fault, really. What incentive has she got when we're taking care of her? It's best for her to stay with you. I know you'll be a good influence. Maybe you could even find her a job at your bank.'

It's not the first time she's brought this up. And it's not the first time I've objected. 'It's not my bank, Mum. And I can't imagine Zoe wanting to work there.' A poet in a bank? They'd destroy her.

'Well, we don't always get what we want in life. Zoe needs to start a career and that will be easier when she's already living in London.'

'I don't know, Mum. I mean, she's not exactly a city girl.'

Zoe moved from a village outside Toulouse to our leafy suburban neighbourhood. It was a shock when I first moved to London, and I have both feet on the ground. Zoe hovers about a foot in the air. I can't imagine her coping well.

'I'm worried about her here, Mum.'

'Oh, we're not worried at all, darling. You're there to look after her.'

So now I'm my Gallic sister's keeper. I sigh dramatically.

Mum ignores me.

'Fine. I'll talk to you tomorrow.'

'Bye, darling, have fun!'

The fridge holds two onions, some eggs, broccoli and a bit of hard cheese. I feel like a contestant on *Ready Steady Cook* as I slice the onions and grate the cheese. I could order something for delivery, but Zoe deserves a home-cooked meal, no matter how slapdash, on her first night in her new flat.

My phone rings just as the onions have started to sweat.

'Hi, Zack.'

'Hey, Carol. Listen, I wanted to apologise again for today. I had no idea they'd be such dicks. I was only trying to help.'

I sigh as the afternoon's meeting comes flooding back. 'I know you were. Don't worry about it. Besides, at least now everyone knows I was the architect.'

Carol's Kiss. That's what the traders are now calling Green T, thanks to Zack's 'help'. As in the kiss of death.

Derrick made me give everyone a practical demonstration today. I might be able to build a complex computer system, but I couldn't get the projector to work properly, which was why Zack was in the conference room as I started to explain how Green T works. The traders were being rude as usual, and the noise level was getting a bit hard to talk over. Zack finally got fed up and shouted something along the lines of 'You could give Carol a little respect after she worked a year on the system. If it wasn't for her, it wouldn't even exist.'

I don't know who started making kissy face noises but it took about ten seconds before the whole room was puckering up and calling Green T Carol's Kiss.

'I'm sure it'll blow over soon,' I say to Zack.

'Well, anyway, I think I owe you at least a drink to make up for it. Tomorrow night?'

'I can't. I'm meeting Harriet after work. Maybe next week?'

'It's a date. Again, Carol, I'm so sorry.'

As I hang up and stir the onions, my thoughts turn to Harriet. It's been a long time since we've hung out together like we used to. After we graduated and first came to London, we had a few local friends but relied on each other for most of our entertainment.

Lately, I've started to feel pulled in so many different directions that there isn't even space for me in my own life. While technically working on Harriet's dating profile isn't my life, at least it'll be a night out with my best friend.

Zoe and I finish off the bottle of wine and tuck in to our broccoli, onion and cheese omelettes while she tells me about her latest poems. I don't usually know what she's talking about, but her poetry makes her very happy, and that's enough. Pleasantly tipsy, I'm in a fine mood by the time Ben rings.

'Hi, Ben! Guess what? Zoe's here.'

Permanently, I don't add.

'Oh, that's nice. Say hello to her for me. Sorry I didn't call you back earlier. It's just been a crazy day.'

He sounds tired. 'Never mind, you're calling now. Hang on, let me go in the other room and you can tell me about your day.'

'I'd love to, but it's got to be a quick call. Everyone is still here. It's going to be another late one. Did you find somewhere nice for us to go this weekend?'

'Oh, I didn't realise I was supposed to do that. I thought you were going to look.'

It's not my imagination. He did ask me to go away for the weekend.

'I'm sorry but I haven't got time. You know how busy I am.' His exasperation starts to dampen my mood. 'If you want to go, you'll need to do a tiny bit of research to find somewhere. It won't take very long. Just pick a nice one that we can get to by train. I'd rather not have to drive. You'll let me know when you've booked?'

'Erm, yes, okay. I can have a look tonight.'

'Great, thanks. It's going to be so nice to get away. Just make sure they've got WiFi there, okay? I might have to answer a few emails. We'll talk tomorrow, okay, sweetheart? Have fun with Zoe. Bye-bye.'

Zoe has migrated to the laptop while she waited for me to finish my call. 'Just checking my blog stats.'

I sit beside her. 'Show me this blog you've got.'

'Here, look. It is where I post my poems. I've called it The Read Poet's Society.'

'Does anybody read them?'

She looks hurt. 'I have twenty thousand hits a month.'

'That sounds like a lot. I didn't realise so many people were interested in poetry. If you've got such a big readership, maybe you'd like to publish them some day.'

'I have published them. They are all here.' She scrolls down the substantial list.

'I mean for money. Since you love it so much, wouldn't it be nice to be able to do it for a living?'

She shakes her head. 'You sound like Madame

Colbert. I do not want to make money from something that I do for love. That would defeat the whole point of doing it.'

Of course. How silly of me. 'Will you be finished soon? I just need the laptop for a little while.'

'I will just check facebook quickly. And twitter. Then it is all yours.'

I go to the kitchen to clean up our dirty dishes and kill some time till Zoe is finished with my laptop.

CHAPTER 8

Harriet and I meet under the clock after work the next night. I can see she's merry by the glow in her cheeks. Also, it's nearly eight and she never works past six, so she must have been doing something for two hours, and it wasn't exercise. She favours Sauvignon Blanc over spin class.

'Been killing time at the Horny and Shallow? That's not your style.'

After work the Corney & Barrow is packed with women who like their dates to come with six-figure salaries, and men who need six figures to attract a date.

She rolls her eyes as we walk together towards the station. 'I'm narrowing my horizons. I saw your boss there. He really is a wanker.'

'I'm surprised you could tell in a room full of them. What made him stand out? Offering to judge the barmaid's nipples? Lighting cigarettes with twenty-pound notes?' I'd love to say that these are the fanciful musings of a disgruntled employee, but I speak from experience.

'He probably would have if the bartenders weren't all men and smoking wasn't banned indoors. He was just being himself, braying with the other traders.'

'So just a normal night out.' I might get brief pangs of jealousy when my colleagues trundle off to the latest bar with Derrick, or get wined and dined on the company account, but that's only because I know that enforced camaraderie helps around bonus time. When I remember that the experience would be utterly, excruciatingly, three-hours-I'd-never-get-back painful, I'm glad to pore over my spreadsheets instead.

'Are you ready to find online love?' I ask when Harriet lets us into her flat.

A stranger would think she'd been burgled, but she just prefers her chaos to my 'sterile' (read: perfectly stylish) flat. Harriet's place may look like a jumble sale but at least it's not dirty, thanks to a very tolerant cleaner who painstakingly restores the place to disorder after cleaning beneath the clutter each week.

'Am I ready? I've been dying to do it!' Her eyes are shining like she's got a fever.

'Well, just don't build up your hopes too much. There are probably a lot of weirdos on dating websites.' And she's likely to attract every sodding one of them.

'That's why you're helping me,' she calls over her shoulder as she runs the obstacle course to the kitchen for wine. 'You're my filter. I won't make a move without your say-so.'

She sets a bottle of red on the table. 'Here, I thought we could start with these sites.'

Her handwritten list goes halfway down the page.

'Are you going for some kind of dating record?'

'Well, I want to cover my bases, don't I? I figure this way I'll get a nice selection of dates.'

I doubt there's anything nice about what she'll get from that list, but I won't burst her bubble. Harriet could find love in amongst the flotsam and jetsam. And I'm that tool that skims the dead leaves and insects out of the pool so that she can dive into the clean water. I just hope she won't have to hold her breath for too long.

'First of all, you cannot sign up to Uniformdating.com. You don't wear a uniform.'

'But I like uniforms,' she says. 'And I've worn a uniform before.'

'McDonalds doesn't count.' She only worked there for a month before getting fired for giving away French fries to boys she fancied. 'You should probably stick to a couple of sites and see what happens. You don't want to be overwhelmed by messages.'

She totally will be. Harriet's a catch, whichever way you look at it. Not only is she smart and fun, she's also funny and pretty. 'Have you thought about what you want your profile to say?'

She nods, pulling up a Word document and a photo of her wearing a strappy sundress at the beach. I took that when we went to Majorca together last year. It was an all-inclusive resort full of German families who woke before dawn to stake their claims on the poolside chairs. We spent the week happily sitting on the sand at the edge of the beautiful little cove beside the hotel.

'I don't want to come across as too serious,' she says. 'So I thought I'd say I'm up for a good time and let's see where we go from there. How's this?'

As I read the paragraphs, I can see I've got my work

cut out. 'You don't need these sites at all, Harriet. You could just put up a few photos in phone boxes around Central London. You'll get the same result. Think about it. You can't tell blokes you're just up for a good time. You'll have a queue around the block looking for a shag buddy. Is that what you want?'

'It's been over a year, Carol.' She crosses her eyes, grimacing.

'Fine, it's probably exactly what you want. But you've waited this long. You may as well find someone worth spending time with out of bed too, right? Let's tone down the good-time girl wording. Just try being yourself. And I wouldn't put a photo on there. What happens if a colleague finds out you're on the site?'

She thinks for a moment. 'They'd probably announce it in the next conference just to see me cry in public. Right. So, no photo.'

'You can always send one privately if you hit it off with someone and it gets to the I'll-show-you-mine-if-you-show-me-yours stage.'

Redrafting her profile is like writing a sexual CV. With cover letter.

Marley calls while we're debating whether Harriet should be a party planner (fun but too frivolous?) or events coordinator (more accurate but possibly boring).

'Carol, I've been meaning to call you all day!' Marley says.

'I haven't had any missed calls. Did you book the venue?'

'I said I've been *meaning* to call. Anyway, luckily I didn't book it.'

'Why is that lucky? I thought it was perfect.'

She makes that noise she does when Mum

aggravates her, like the sudden release of air when you push the valve on a bicycle tyre. 'It's not perfect. Did you see the ballroom? It's green.'

'It's a lovely pale green, yes.'

'Green? With my skin tone? I'll come up all sallow in the photos. I need blue, cream or white.'

'I see.' I vividly remember the website's photos. There were loads of the green ballroom. Which she could have seen from the comfort of her office chair and saved me traipsing to Hampshire to make a personal inspection.

'Have you talked to Zoe?' she asks. 'She flooded the bath this morning. I said I'd tell you so you wouldn't get angry with her.'

'So I can get angry with you?'

'You know you never get angry with me. Besides, it doesn't sound like anything serious. It'll dry out eventually. But you'd better apologise to Mrs Gaynor. It went through her kitchen ceiling.'

Mrs Gaynor threatens to call the police for disturbing the peace if I walk on my floor with shoes on. I'm going to have to bake something for her to make up for Zoe's flood.

'Anyway, now I've broken the news, so don't be too hard on her. You know how sensitive she is. I'll keep looking for options for the wedding and let you know, 'kay?'

''kay,' I say, ending the call.

We've finished the wine by the time Harriet hits the 'update' button and her profile goes live.

'Now what do we do?' she asks.

'Drink more wine?'

The computer pings just as she gets up for another bottle. 'I've got a message!'

'Don't be too excited. It's probably just a confirmation that your profile is live.'

I can see I'm going to have to do a lot of calming over the next few weeks. I'll just add Dating Whisperer to my job description.

But it's not a confirmation email. It's from a real live man. *Hi, your gorgeous!* It reads. *Interested?*

'He's got bad grammar,' I say.

'Don't be such a snob. Maybe he's in a hurry. Or on his phone.'

'Maybe he can't spell and is a moron.'

'He said in-ter-es-ted. Four syllables. At least he didn't say whatcha think, or use textspeak. There's no photo, though.'

His lack of photo sets alarm bells ringing, even though I've just advised Harriet to do the same thing. That's different. Harriet isn't hiding anything horrible. 'Click on his name. It's hyperlinked. It should take you to his profile. There might be pictures there.'

We stare at the screen. 'Oh.'

Judging by the two photos on his profile, Harriet has caught the eye of a fifty-something Vauxhall Corsa enthusiast with a hearty appetite.

'Do you mind bald men?' I ask, scrutinising the grainy photos.

'Not in theory, no, but taking the whole package into consideration… hmm.'

'Agreed. Are you sure you don't want to narrow your parameters a bit?'

When we filled out the 'perfect match' questionnaire Harriet checked nearly every box. That's commendable when you're recruiting for a job, but I doubt she really thinks she'll have much in common with a 50+ separated school leaver living in Manchester who's a born-again Christian twenty-a-day smoking tattoo lover.

'You might want to limit your age range and geography, for example? Twenty-one *is* probably a bit too young when you think about it. And realistically you're not going to be hopping on the train to Leeds for a date, are you? There must be enough men to choose from in Greater London.'

She nods. 'You're right. Let's see that questionnaire again.'

We work through it together, sticking to a reasonable range of attributes for the perfect potential partner. Which makes me wonder: how would I fill out such a survey? It isn't easy to think hypothetically because Ben keeps popping into my head, but I suppose my *perfect* boyfriend would be around my age, living on his own in London with a job he loves. He'd be smart, ambitious, funny, tall, fit, adorable, sexy and kind. He'd also be impulsively romantic and amazingly supportive. So, basically, he'd be Ben. Well, he'd be Ben before his case took up his every waking hour. I really can't complain, though. It's not like I'd ever want to trade places with Harriet.

Her PC has been pinging while we reworked her questionnaire, and the new batch isn't wholly terrible. Two more over 50s have slipped through before we changed parameters, but there's one more message.

SweetyPetey16's very handsome face grins at us. 'What do you think?' I ask her.

'Should we email him now and see when he wants

to meet?!'

This is exactly why I'm here. 'At least read his profile first. Petey asked you "How You Doin'?" That could be the sum total of his conversational skills.'

'With biceps like that I'm not fussed about his conversational skills,' she says.

But a cursory glance tells us his biceps aren't his only assets. At twenty-eight, he lives in Croydon, has a good job and a soft spot for snow sports. 'I guess he's okay to email,' I say. 'He's not obviously insane.'

'How do you know that?'

'Well, he hasn't talked about his ex in his profile, or mentioned medication or therapy or included any sad quotes about loving and losing or dancing like nobody's watching.'

I'm teasing, of course, but Harriet is nodding like I've just given her the secret to eternal youth.

'Right, no medication or exes or cheesy quotes. What else?' she says.

My heart sinks. Even after so many disasters, she's still got no idea how to spot the most obvious man-flaws. How is this possible for such a smart girl?

'All right. Please don't email anyone back till I've had a look at their profile, okay? I can at least vet them to begin with.'

Her expression crumbles. 'But you won't be there in person to see if they're psycho. God, Carol, what am I thinking? I haven't been too unhappy, you know, this past year. Sure, it's been lonely, but at least I haven't had to live with the daily dating drama. I wish you could go on my dates and see if they're okay.'

Thoughtfully, she sips her wine, then starts to smile.

I don't like the way she's looking at me. 'Harriet,' I

say as her grin widens. 'What is going on in that daft head of yours?'

'You could be there to help me judge,' she says.

'You're not seriously suggesting that I go on your dates with you.'

'Not with me. It would never work if we were both there.'

'*For* you?'

'Well, we do look alike,' she says. 'The guys would never know. Most men couldn't pick a woman out of an identity parade after sleeping with them. They'd never be able to tell us apart after just one date, and you could suss them out in about an hour. It could be the perfect solution.'

It's a crazy idea (though she's probably got a point about the identity parade). But then again, letting her back out into the dating scene without adult supervision is crazy, too. And that may have more dire consequences. I can't believe I'm even thinking about this.

'It won't work,' I say.

'But why not? People mix us up all the time. You've said yourself that if you'd had half an hour with my dates you'd have known they were insane. You've got good judgment, Carol, and I completely trust you.'

'What about Ben?'

'Well, all right, you haven't always got good judgment, but he isn't a complete wanker all the time–'

'I meant, what am I supposed to tell Ben about going out on dates?'

She looks mortified at her slip-up. 'Do you see? Do you see what bad judgment I've got? You wouldn't have to tell him anything, would you? He's always working late. A drink wouldn't take more than half an hour. One hour, tops. He'd never know.'

Sadly, I know that's true. Besides, I wouldn't be dating other men. I'd be helping my best friend avoid psychopaths. 'All right, I'll do it. But you have to show me every email you send, and those you receive back, so that I know what I'm supposed to say. If they seem worth a date, I'll tell you everything we talked about. Okay? Now, let's email SweetyPetey16 before I change my mind.'

I must be soft in the head.

CHAPTER 9

Ben doesn't need to know that I'm recycling Marley's rejected wedding venue for our romantic weekend. Sure, I wanted to search online for the ideal retreat but between Zoe running her poetry empire from my laptop, and helping Harriet avoid London's psychopaths and working late, there just wasn't time.

If I choose my words carefully, I won't even need to lie about it and my reputation as magic-fixer-of-everything will be safe for a while longer.

'Isn't this beautiful?' I say when we've paid the taxi driver. Our feet crunch on the gravel drive as we make our way to the imposing front door. The grandeur of the place is enhanced by the light blanket of snow covering the grounds. Warm light glows from the tall windows and smoke wafts from the chimneys into the crisp, still air. It's fairy-tale perfect.

Ben puts his arm around me, pulling me into a deep kiss. 'You're beautiful, and it's perfect, as always. Of course it is. Do they have a spa?'

As if Marley would have considered a venue without one. I tell him, yes, there's a spa.

'Then let's have a late dinner and get massages first.'

'Oh, well, you go ahead if you want. I'll probably just relax in front of the fire.'

As if I'd like to be stripped naked to let a stranger paw me.

'Hello again,' says the slender desk clerk with the deep voice. 'Welcome back.'

'Oh, erm, hi.' So much for the ruse. I rush to explain to Ben before his imagination runs away with him. 'I was here earlier, remember? To check out the hotel for Marley's wedding?'

He nods, probably relieved that I'm not having illicit liaisons at country house hotels.

At least the clerk has the good grace to realise he's made a blunder. Blowing a guest's cover must fall outside Mrs Thatcher's rules on discretion. I glare at him to let him know he'd better suck up to me for the rest of the weekend.

'Where's the spa, please?' Ben asks the clerk. 'I'll just go check for appointments. Are you sure you don't want a massage too?'

I feel a twinge of annoyance that he's rushing off like this. Isn't the whole point of spending a romantic weekend together to spend it together?

'You've got the whole weekend. Why don't we relax now and you can get a massage tomorrow, or Sunday?'

'Right, Carol, we've got the whole weekend. Don't you want me to be nice and relaxed for it? You know how much fun we have when we're relaxed.'

I can't stay annoyed when he grins wickedly like that. And he did suggest we get massaged together. I'm being silly. 'You go ahead and I'll go up to the room. I should check my emails anyway. Maybe I'll have a bubble bath.'

'You? You hate baths.'

'Maybe I'll have a bubble shower.' I kiss him lightly and follow the clerk upstairs to the room.

It's as gorgeous as I imagined. The giant four-poster bed is hung with brocade and there's a sandstone fireplace that I can nearly stand up in. The huge windows overlook the sweeping snow-covered driveway and lawn. I'm nearly tempted to draw a bath when I see the claw-foot tub, but then I remember how much I hate stewing in my own juices.

Instead, I shower and, donning a fluffy white terrycloth robe, curl up on the bed to check my emails. Derrick wasn't happy about my leaving early today and sure enough, there's an email from him telling me I have to be in at 5.30 a.m. on Monday morning to talk to Hong Kong. I'm not surprised. There's always a stiff penalty for our transgressions.

At least the fallout from Zack's 'help' hasn't been too bad. The traders are still making kissy noises around me but they're not overtly hostile. They have short attention spans when there's no cash involved.

The door opens minutes later, sending me scrambling off the bed. 'Oh, it's you,' I say to Ben.

'Who were you expecting?'

'Nobody. I thought you were having a massage.'

He sighs. 'They're booked up. We should have rung ahead.'

He means I should have rung ahead. 'Can you book for tomorrow or Sunday?'

'I did, tomorrow morning at nine. Did you have a

nice shower?'

'Wonderful,' I say, stretching on the bed again. 'This is beautiful, isn't it?'

He nods, grinning. 'Absolutely gorgeous from where I'm standing. We've got at least an hour before we can go down for dinner. What shall we do in the meantime?' He sits on the bed.

'We could watch the news,' I say, smiling.

'I was thinking of something a bit more interactive.'

'Wii?'

He shakes his head, unbuttoning his shirt.

I yank back the duvet, patting the soft smooth cotton sheets beneath. 'Well, why don't you come over here and we'll figure something out together?'

We're a bit drunk at dinner thanks to the champagne that Ben ordered. We've toasted our way through most of the bottle – to our weekend away, and the Green T launch, and the hopefully swift end to his court case. As I sit in the formal dining room giggling with my boyfriend, I realise that it's been a long time since we've been this light-hearted. We should make more of an effort to enjoy each other, I think as he tops up our glasses. Otherwise we'll turn into the kind of old couples who are sitting around us. Some look bored. A few wear overtly hostile expressions. I wonder how we look to them. Do they think we're in love? We must at least give off a comfortably together vibe. Do we look married? Or living together? Or just dating from separate abodes. That's really what we are, after all. He's not exactly beating down my door to move in.

'I've been thinking,' I say before I can chicken out. 'About our living situation.'

Ben stares at me but I can't stop now.

'You mentioned that it would be nice to spend more time together, so I wondered what you think about making it more official.'

Something in his expression tightens. 'Official?'

'I don't mean getting married or anything like that!' Maybe this isn't such an appetising dinner topic after all. 'I just mean spending more time together. Officially. Like maybe at night?'

Why can't I just say what I mean?

'Carol, you know I'd love to spend all my time with you but it's hard with my job right now. I'm working such long hours and I can't really plan anything in advance. Even though I'd love to.'

'I don't mean having more dates, Ben. That'd just put pressure on us and we don't want that. I mean, maybe it'd be easier if, after work, even after long days, we see each other afterwards. We could do that if we were going home to the same flat.'

There. I said it. I search his expression for any encouraging signs.

Suddenly he lights up.

'I would love that!' he says, grasping for my hand. His smile is one of pure joy.

'You would?' Excitement bubbles up within me.

'Absolutely. We should live together. It makes total sense. Then we wouldn't have to plan when we can be together because we'll see each other every day.'

I didn't expect it to be this easy. But why not? We've been in sync since we met. Neither of us chased the other, or thought things were moving too fast. I never had to wonder where we were going because, with Ben, it was obvious. He told me he loved me first and I told him right back. It was incredibly exciting. It's incredibly exciting now.

'So, do you want to move in with me, or should I move in with you?' I ask as he strokes my hand. I'm already rearranging his bedroom furniture. 'Well, Zoe's at my place. On the other hand, your flatmate is hardly ever home, and maybe he wouldn't mind. I'd pay part of the rent, of course.'

But when he shakes his head my excitement dims. 'I think I should move in to yours when Zoe leaves. That way, we'll have the flat to ourselves. How long do you think she'll be there?'

Suddenly our romantic plans seem a long way off. 'I really don't know. Mum says she can stay as long as she wants. That's the deal with the flat. We siblings can live there whenever we need to.'

'But she's not really your sibling. And she doesn't need to live there. She's got a family in France. Or she could move back in with your parents. Can't you move her along?'

'Well, I'm not sure.'

I'm not sure I'd want to do that anyway. It's not fair to Zoe, who I do love like a sister.

'I guess maybe we'll have to wait and see,' I murmur. 'Although it might make sense to move in together anyway, as an interim measure until Zoe leaves. It's not ideal but at least we'd be together.'

'Me, live with two women?!' He laughs. 'You'd gang up on me with your potpourri and candles and your coordinated periods.'

He's right. Just having to accommodate our bathroom schedules would send him over the edge. He'd have a breakdown after having to dig our hair out of the drain or navigate the veil of bras drying on the shower rail. Men are fragile creatures.

'Well, then, why don't I move in with you?' I try to sound nonchalant as I say this, as if it's just occurred to me. 'I could handle the odd video game or flatmate's occasional sneaky fart. Besides, he's hardly ever there. It'd be like having the place to ourselves.'

Ben probably wouldn't fart in front of me.

'Nah,' he says. 'If we're going to do it, we should do it right. Zoe can't stay forever and when she goes, I'll move in.' He drains his glass. 'More champagne?'

'No, thanks, I've had enough.'

So we're going to live together. One day. I should be elated at the prospect, not resentful that Zoe is standing in our way. This isn't the satisfying outcome I'd imagined when the conversation started.

'To our living together. Eventually,' Ben says, raising his glass. 'It just goes to show that there's a first time for everything. For me, at least. Of course, you've already lived with someone.'

He makes his usual face.

'That was a long time ago,' I say, not wanting to go over it again.

But Skate pops into my head, as annoyingly happy and carefree as ever. He's got a habit of turning up where he's not wanted, even four years after we last saw each other.

We were childhood best friends, neighbours above the pub where Mum and Dad lived before Dad's jazz career took off. By the time we went to university we'd figured out that it would be quite nice to go out with one's best friend. Even from different cities we managed to hold on to the drama-free, easy-going relationship we'd always had. We moved into a tiny London flat together when we graduated. Sure, I loved Skate (with all my heart, if you must know), but my relationship with Ben is so much better. First of all, Skate was generally away with the fairies on his Greenpeace missions when we were supposedly living together. Ben hates fairies and I know we'll come home to each other every night. Secondly, Ben and I are well-suited. Skate and I were about as opposite as you can get and still be in the human race. Ben and I have the same outlook on work and life; we want the same things and we understand each other. Besides, Ben wants to live with me. So this is completely different.

Although it's barely ten o'clock, most of the other guests have left the restaurant by the time we sign for the bill. Hand in hand we climb the wide staircase to our room. Ben kicks off his shoes, throws himself on the bed and opens his laptop.

'What did you think of the food?' I ask.

'It was good.'

'It was a bit stiff down there, though, don't you think? Not exactly a buzzing scene.'

Everyone spoke in a whisper and Ben was the only man without a jacket.

'Mmm.' He starts typing.

The thing I love about Ben is how committed he can be to whatever he's doing. But it's also the thing that drives me nuts. I can tell that he's no longer with me under the brocade canopy. He's with his colleagues now, and he won't be back tonight.

So much for dissecting the evening and dishing on the clientele. Sighing, I dig my BlackBerry out of my bag and scroll through my own emails.

It's not even light yet and I'm dying for a cigarette. I managed to get to sleep last night despite the craving, but it's refreshed from a good sleep and stronger than ever. Ben continues to snore as I gently roll off the bed and dress.

Downstairs, dishes clatter in the kitchen as the staff prepares for breakfast. I make sure to smile at them all as we meet in the corridor. I may not always be the world's most emotionally attuned woman but I can empathise with an early start to work – the alarm pulling you from sleep as if being lifted from drying concrete, the disorientating fuzz as your eyes tell you it's still night-time, wondering if you're ever going to catch up on the hours you've lost, and the tear-inducing fact lodged somewhere in your hippocampus reminding you that the scientists say that catching up is impossible. I pass a few of the waiters from dinner but I don't see any other guests as I make my way to the lawn.

The first inhalation hits the back of my throat with welcome warmth. Even before the nicotine works its magic I feel myself relax. That's when I realise I'm tense. At 6 a.m.? I shake my head, inhaling deeply again. Clearly I'm not over last night yet. In goes another hit of smoke.

It's not that Ben was on his laptop till the wee hours (though he was), or that my attempts to cajole him into conversation failed (they did), or even that I wanted to fool around again (I didn't). The irksome fact, the smoke-this-butt-down-to-the-filter fact was that last night was no different than any other night that Ben and I have spent together in the last six months. Yet we were in a stately home! We'd drunk champagne. We'd had sex with the lights on, for crying out loud. Surely that called for a sense of occasion. At least it did for me.

'Carol?'

Ben is standing shirtless at our open bedroom window.

I'm busted.

'Ben, what are you doing up so early?'

'What are you doing smoking?' asks my holier-than-thou boyfriend who, until a few months ago, would use the dying ember of his old cigarette to light his new one.

'I'm not smoking.'

'Carol, I can see you. I had laser surgery, remember? No glasses anymore. You are smoking.'

'No, technically I was smoking. I've finished now. You should go back inside. You'll catch your death.'

'It's your own health you should be worried about.'

He slams the window.

I could drag this out, maybe even until after breakfast, but it's no use. At 7 a.m. or 7 p.m., he's going to want to make an issue of it. Sighing, I make my way to our room.

He's back in bed, allegedly sleeping, when I let myself in. As I clean my teeth I think about the early days. We used to share a cigarette in bed together after sex. It felt very intimate and even a little bit French. We talked till the early hours, often about silly things, but over time we revealed the important bits, the bits we didn't want other people to know. The bits you have to trust the other person to share. These days we rarely even share a pudding.

His body is toasty warm as I press myself behind him.

'Jesus, your hands are freezing!' he says. 'And you stink of smoke.'

Well, good morning to you too. 'I brushed my teeth, and used mouthwash.'

'It doesn't matter. It's in your hair. It's disgusting.'

'You didn't think it was so disgusting when you were a smoker.'

'That's because my senses were dulled. Just like yours are now.'

As a matter of fact my sense of indignation feels pretty sharp. 'You know what, Ben? I'm sorry that I'm a smoker, but you knew that about me when you met me. We were both smokers and it didn't bother you. It's not my fault that it bothers you now. You changed the rules because you stopped, so now I have to as well? I can't always be perfect, you know.'

But even as I say this, I know that's not true. I can be perfect. I have been for most of my life. Sure, there were a few wobbles along the way – the horrible spelling bee, the below-par SAT score in Year 2 (which was never repeated) and the Silver Duke of Edinburgh Award (why not Gold?) – but I've generally done everything I set out to do, in school, work and life. I can stop smoking if I really want to. It's the one bone of contention between us. So what's stopping me?

'I'll try,' I say to his warm, smooth back. 'I promise that I really will try.'

He rolls over and envelops me in his arms. 'I don't mean to be hard on you. It's just because I care. I very much want you to quit for your own good.'

'I know you do. Let me go wash my hair quickly and

we can have breakfast together before your massage.'

The water pours scalding from the shower head, exactly as I like it. As it washes over me I really do feel like I can do this, once and for all. Henceforth, I will be Carol Colbert: non-smoker.

CHAPTER 10

'Who put these on my desk?' The cigarette packet's siren call grows louder.

'Who frickin' put these on my desk?!'

I don't dare touch it in case I don't let go until it's just a crumpled bit of cardboard and smoking butt ends.

'For Christ's sake, Colbert,' Ryan says, throwing my smoking jacket at me. 'Why don't you just smoke them? You've been a complete bitch for weeks. Do us all a favour.'

'It hasn't been weeks.'

It's been eleven days and five hours. And I'm a bitch? This is coming from someone who just last week used his brother's confession about his job fears to trade against him. On a floor where our boss threatens to crush people daily and sexually harasses most of his staff. Yet they get called aggressive achievers.

Not that I'm really surprised by the hypocrisy. My consensus-building has always been called appeasement, standing up for myself means I must be pre-menstrual, and flexibility is irrational flip-flopping (generally also blamed on PMT).

'Do yourself a favour and stay out of my business,' I mutter to his hunched back. I tip the packet into the bin where it sits, shiny and new, with whole cigarettes inside. That won't do.

Ryan's smile is triumphant as I dig into the bin to retrieve the packet.

'You don't win,' I say, tipping the cigarettes into my hand. The lovely scent of fresh tobacco tickles my nose as I grind them into bits.

'Hey, that cost me seven quid,' he says. 'Waste of money, Colbert, when you could be relaxing outside.'

But relaxing means relapsing, and that's the last thing I want, not now that I'm over the worst of it.

Buoyed by my own tenacity, I'd managed the rest of the country house weekend without a cigarette. I'm sure it's due to extreme control freakery that I feel such joy when I set my mind to sorting something out. In that way I'm just like Mum. There's a thrill in the determination to do it, then doing everything it takes and not deviating even one millimetre until the job is done. Definitely freakery.

It wasn't too bad on the Saturday. Ben and I loosened right up once the smoking issue was behind us. We did throw ourselves on a squishy sofa in front of the fire with the weekend papers, just like I'd imagined. He had a lot of calls to make but I couldn't really complain (out loud anyway) since my BlackBerry chirruped most of the time.

By Sunday, though, the cravings had dug in their claws and wouldn't let go. Scenes played through my mind as if I'd broken up with a lover, not stubbed out my last filthy butt. It wasn't just that I very badly wanted to smoke. I got physical withdrawal symptoms. By Monday my throat was sore. By mid-week I was so backed up that I resorted to Granny's tried-and-tested prune juice remedy, which had alarmingly successful results. They don't highlight that on the NHS Smokefree pamphlets, do they?

The physical symptoms seem to have abated, except for a big spot on my chin which is probably unrelated. But after more than a week (eleven days, five hours and three minutes) I'd roll and smoke Ryan, after shredding him into little pieces first. Even my short fuse has a short fuse.

That might explain why the new intern is approaching my desk as if sent to disarm a roadside IED.

'Hi, Stephan.'

'Is now a good time? I could come back.'

'Try coming back in a month,' Ryan mutters.

'No, no, it's fine,' I say. 'I'm training you this morning, aren't I?'

He nods eagerly, straightening his suit jacket. I can't help but grin, remembering my own first day when I'd walked into the maelstrom of noise and movement. Cajoling, swearing traders shouted into their phones and at each other over their screens. The analysts darted everywhere, doing their masters' bidding. I had a moment of pure panic as I stood there clutching my coffee. It was going to be too much – too much noise, too much to remember. Too much pressure. When Derrick showed me around, my unease intensified. He kept firing information at me – what each trader covered, daily call and meeting schedules – and I knew he expected me to perfectly recall each detail. He kept saying 'Are you following me?'

I could only hope I wasn't lying when I said yes.

I got the chance to find out within hours. 'Read these,' he'd said, throwing a pile of reports on my desk. 'Let's meet in an hour and you can tell me what you think of the company.'

An hour?! In engineering, projects were measured in months and years. I dove into the reports, skim-reading the headlines and titles of the tables and graphs. I took pages of notes, carrying them into the loo instead of stopping for a break. It was a baptism by fire. Little did I know it wasn't a fire drill. This was how our business worked all the time.

The nervous poo cramps started just as I'd approached Derrick's office. Tough luck, intestines, I thought. My will is stronger than you today. You'll have to wait till I'm done.

Ignoring the impatient growls emanating from my trousers, I launched into my analysis of the company that Derrick had chosen as my proving ground. His face wasn't confidence-inducing. I didn't realise then that his expression is permanently set at disdain. He didn't let me talk for long, though. He never keeps quiet when he thinks he knows best.

'You say their projection shows profitability in two years, but what if the government's renewable energy funding bill is pushed back?'

'Erm, I didn't read anything about that,' I say, shuffling the stack he'd given me.

Smugness lit his face. 'It's not in there.'

Then how was I supposed to know about it?

Osmosis? It was like being given a maths textbook to study and then being asked to write about Picasso in the exam.

I tried to remember the company's funding structure. 'Well, I guess that since most of its funding comes from private sources – the endowment and also long-term bank loans – then a delay in government funding won't have as big an impact on them as it might on other companies. In fact, it's probably worth checking how reliant their competitors are on that bill. They might actually have a comparative advantage if there's a delay.'

Derrick narrowed his eyes, but said nothing. He leaned back in his chair, put his hands behind his head and flashed me his moist armpits.

'Not half bad, Colbert,' he finally said. At that point I realised I'd been holding my breath. He nodded. 'Not fucking half bad.'

Faint praise indeed, but I leapt on it. It was official. I wasn't fucking half bad.

I've spent the last four years trying to top that.

I won't continue the cycle of abuse with Stephan. He'll be lashed half to death by the others anyway.

'Let's introduce you to Joe,' I say, leading the way to the traders' desks. 'He's my trader.'

I always try to gauge their moods before approaching. Not that I'd rely on my intuition alone. I'm up at 5 a.m. each morning to read all the news that could impact our sector. It's my job to digest it over my breakfast and regurgitate it into the traders' gullets at the morning meeting. One natural disaster and everyone's morning goes to hell. But the weather reports were clear last night.

'Joe, this is Stephan, our new intern.' I don't need to add that Stephan's dad is an important client. Everyone got that memo before he started.

Joe ignores us for a few seconds while he finishes typing, then swivels in his chair. 'Nice to meet you, Stephan,' he says, extending his hand. 'Welcome.'

'Thanks, Joe, I'm really happy to be here. I'll be working really–'

But Joe swings back around to his screen as his phone chirps. 'This is Joe. Yeah, yeah, hell no!'

'How do you know if they're on the phone?' Stephan asks as we creep away. 'With those headsets…'

'It's hard to tell, I know. Sometimes it's a client, sometimes it's just voices in their heads. I generally wait a few seconds to see if they say anything. If not, I just start talking. They'll tell me to shut up or ignore me if they're on a call. You get a sense for it after a while, but you probably won't have to talk to them much. You'll mostly be doing analysis with us.'

He looks relieved to hear this. In fact, he looks like a scared sixteen-year-old. An angry razor burn trails down his cheek, inflaming the acne scattered there. He probably shaved off some trendy stubble this morning, not realising how his skin would resent the assault. I can see the tiny hole in his earlobe. He probably took that out around the same time he lost the stubble, maybe on his own initiative but probably on the advice of his father. A bunch of bracelets circle one skinny wrist – strings tied by friends and rubbery ones for the causes he supports. I know if I ask him he'd tell me all about the reasons he wears them. His huge brown eyes will shine with sincerity. Suddenly I feel protective of this boy.

'What do you want to get out of your time here?' I ask him as he wheels his chair to my desk.

'I'd like to know how everything works,' he says.

'Do you want to go into banking?'

I catch his look of uncertainty before he says, 'It's a great opportunity and the bank has an excellent reputation. I feel like my qualifications and aptitudes—'

I hold up my hand. 'I'm not interviewing you, Stephan, so you don't have to impress me with your answer. And if I were you, I'd just be myself and answer honestly if someone around here asks you something. These guys have a nose for bullshit like you can't even imagine. Just be yourself.'

His narrow shoulders drop a few inches as he relaxes. 'Okay, thanks. Actually, I'd just like to see how everything works.' He shrugs. 'I like details.'

'Well, then you're definitely in the right place. Why don't I show you Green T?'

We work companionably together, going through the mechanics behind the trading system. Stephan wasn't kidding when he said he likes detail. He asks all the right questions and is clearly a very smart guy. He should do okay here, but I'm still going to keep an eye out for him.

'Hey, Stephan,' Ryan calls over his desk as the end of the day nears. 'Want to come out for a drink with the other guys?'

He makes this sound casual but I know he's been practising the question, trying to imitate a real human being.

'Yeah, sure, thanks.' He turns to me. 'Are you coming?'

'Colbert can't come,' Ryan says gleefully.

'Don't be uncharitable,' says Derrick, striding over. 'Colbert is very welcome. In fact, I insist she comes.'

Stephan looks pleased, but then he doesn't know Derrick like I do.

'That's all right,' I say. 'I don't need to go.'

'No, come on, Carol, it'll be fun,' Stephan says, not helping at all.

'Yeah, come on, Carol, it'll be fun,' Derrick mimics.

'I'm so sorry, Carol, I had no idea,' Stephan whispers as the bouncer waves us in.

'It's okay. Let's call it your lesson for today.'

Why should he assume that *drinks with the guys* means a night at the strip club? He's not yet fluent in trader-speak.

As far as strip clubs go, it's not too bad. Except for the naked women writhing on stage it could be any nightclub. There's an art deco vibe, with its geometric railings, ornately corniced golden ceiling and the wall sconces that cast flattering light all around. Mirrors cover every wall but the purple booths jar with the rest of the interior. Not that the clientele are much interested in the soft furnishings.

A hostess leads us to one of the large booths where I'm sandwiched between Stephan and Derrick. 'Bolly all around,' Derrick shouts, not bothering to ask us what we'd like. 'We're celebrating. Hey, mate, just in time,' he says as Joe approaches the booth. 'Ryan, push over and let Joe sit down. No,' he says when Ryan scootches along the booth. 'Get out and let him sit. You sit on the end.'

Ryan reddens as he gets up to let Joe take his place. There's clearly not room for him to sit again, which

Derrick can see. He's left hovering over the table like the unwanted guest he's become and, while I generally have no pity for the little jerk, his unease gains my sympathy. I catch his eye and smile. He sticks two fingers up.

I'm surprised to see a few (fully clothed) women here. There's a group of four, who must be on a girls' night out, at a booth near the front. If all this goes horribly wrong, I'll go hover over them like Ryan is doing to us and beg them to make some room.

Once the champagne arrives Derrick raises his glass. 'We've signed eight more clients to Green T, well done to everyone.'

Eight more clients! At this rate there'll soon be billions flowing into my companies for research. *This* is why I joined the bank. It's the reason I get up at 5 a.m. each morning and why I put up with all the bullshit. Hang in there, polar bears, we might just find a way out of this mess yet.

Joe looks like he could eat a bear for lunch. I avoid his glare and guiltily meet Stephan's raised glass with a clink.

'It looks like a great system!' Stephan says, oblivious to the sudden tension. 'I've been having a look with Carol today and it's very impressive.'

He just looks confused when I kick him under the table. I can't blame him. He doesn't know that the less said about Green T around the traders, the better. Derrick just can't help himself. If there's something to brag about, he's going to do it, and he's backing Green T with everything he's got. Why wouldn't he? Each new client ratchets up his bonus pot. He can afford to make a few enemies out of old friends. He'll just buy new ones with his giant year-end cheque.

'Fuck Green T,' Joe mutters. 'And fuck Carol for making it.'

'Aw, Joe, now don't be a dick,' Derrick says. 'You've got to embrace progress, mate, not be frightened of it. Besides, none of your clients are signed up, so what are you bitching about?'

'I don't want to talk about it,' he says. 'Mark my words, that system is no good.'

He stares morosely at the woman on stage.

'Fine by me,' Derrick says, suddenly distracted by a voluptuous black-haired woman in a red thong. 'Jesus, will you look at that arse? I could rest my cigar on that.'

I hope that's not a euphemism.

'Colbert, what do you think of that arse?'

'It's a nice arse, Derrick,' I say, careful to keep my voice devoid of any emotion.

'Does she turn you on?'

I sigh. 'No, Derrick, she doesn't turn me on.'

'I'll bet she does.' He lifts his finger, drawing the waitress straight to the table. 'Darling, we'd like a dance please, if that beautiful girl is free?' He points her out, sending the waitress hurrying to tell our private entertainment the good news.

It looks like my basement-level expectations for tonight are about to plummet to Middle Earth.

Stephan looks very sorry he asked me to come. I smile reassuringly through gritted teeth. The way I see it, I've got two choices. I could challenge this objectification of women and stomp off in a huff. But this would seem an odd time to stand up for women's rights after putting up with moderate sexual harassment for years. Besides, I wouldn't be fooling anybody.

They'll know it's just mortified embarrassment driving me away.

So, I haven't really got two choices, have I? Not unless I want this round in the Humiliations Stakes to go to Derrick.

Derrick watches me carefully as the woman approaches. One tiny lapse in expression, or a hint of dread in my eyes and I'm finished. I won't give him that satisfaction.

'You want a sexy dance?' she says to him, staring deeply into his eyes.

'Not me. My friend here. Is that okay?'

She shrugs. 'Sure.'

'Here, Colbert,' he says, shifting out of the booth. 'You should sit on the end.'

I do as I'm told. He doesn't intimidate me.

'I'm Cinnamon,' the woman purrs as she thrusts her chest in my face. Her breasts are magnificent, if technologically enhanced. But it's her face I keep staring at (and not just out of courtesy). Her make-up is so flawless that she looks airbrushed. She's drawn on the most perfect liquid liner I've ever seen. Even the women at the Laura Mercier counter in Harrods don't do as good a job.

'Are you ready for me?' She makes this sound like sex in vocal form, but I think she's actually asking if I'm all right with this. I nod.

For a split second we look into each other's eyes, and we're just two women making the best of a bad situation. I wonder if she's as uncomfortable as I am.

She doesn't seem to be, judging by the way she starts grinding away in my lap. When she wags her cigar-supporting arse at me, all I can think is that she must spend a fortune on waxing.

Then she flips around, whipping my face with her long straight hair. At least her glossy tresses are shielding me from my colleagues. If I catch anyone's eye right now, I'm going to lose my nerve and bolt for the door. When she begins undulating her breasts toward my face, Derrick can no longer contain himself.

'That is hot, Colbert. Are you getting turned on? Oh, my god, I'm getting hard.'

Jesus. The very thought of by boss's erection makes me queasy. Thankfully, Cinnamon is just wrapping up her show with a bit of squeezy cleavage and some more flinging hair.

I thank her politely. Mum would be proud of my manners.

'Are you okay?' Stephan asks quietly once Derrick and Joe start bickering with each other over football. Ryan has finally given up hovering over us and gone to hover near the stage. I bet he's collecting fantasies for his at-home-alone-sock-time later.

'Me? Oh, yes, I'm fine. Another drink?'

Of course I'm not fine. I can't shake the sickening feeling in the pit of my tummy. 'Excuse me a minute,' I say as my BlackBerry goes. 'It's my sister.'

'Where are you?' Marley asks as I pick up. 'I can hardly hear you.'

'Oh, just at a bar with some colleagues. Hang on, let me go outside where it's quieter.'

I pull my coat around me as the cold February night buffets my clammy skin. I want a long shower when I get home. 'What's up?'

'I don't know what I'm going to do. I really need your help.'

'Of course. But what's wrong?'

'Jez's mother wants children at the wedding! Can you believe it? Children, at my perfect wedding.'

'Who's got children?' Jez is an only child.

'His cousin has two girls, so they're not even closely related to Jez. Carol, you've got to talk to his mum and make her see sense. I can't have a bunch of brats running around ruining my wedding.'

'Well, in fairness to the cousins, Marley, they may not be brats at all.'

'But I don't want them there! We've got to manage her expectations now before it's too late. Please, Carol, will you call her for me?'

'Why don't you talk to her yourself? She likes you.'

'Yeah, right. And she'll love me after I tell her that her family isn't welcome at her son's wedding.'

She's got a point. 'Then why can't Jez do it? She couldn't hate her own son.'

'Imagine what Jez'll think if I say I don't want his family attending our wedding. He'll jump to the conclusion that I hate children. Which I definitely do not. In fact, I love them. I definitely want them some day.'

Sure she does. As long as they don't interfere with her party planning.

'It's got to come from someone outside the family,' she continues. 'I mean, not from Jez or me. She really likes you. If you mentioned that it's going to be a grown-up sort of event, I'm sure she'll be happy to tell the cousin to leave them at home. You will, won't you? You've got to meet with her anyway about the wedding to get her input. You could slip it in over tea or something.'

Yes, because I have all the time in the world for tea parties. Honestly, Marley should know better by now. Actually, she does know better. She's just pushing her luck, though she is right about one thing. Getting Jez involved won't help matters. He's a great guy but he's not known for his tact. He'd only tell his mum that Marley is behind the request, and then she'll be mad at my sister for the snub and for getting Jez to do her dirty work.

'Fine, send me her email and I'll find a weekend to meet to go over her wedding ideas. You owe me big-time for this, Marley. Just remember that.'

'Of course! Anything you want, just ask. Thank you so much. I'm sorry I've kept you from your friends. Go back inside.'

'Nah, I was about to leave anyway. I promised Zoe I'd read some of her poetry tonight.'

'Don't stretch yourself too thin, Carol. I'll talk to you later.'

'Uh-huh. Talk to you later.'

I'm stretched so thin that I'm not even Carol-shaped any more.

CHAPTER 11

I'm still not Carol-shaped a few nights later. I'm Harriet-shaped, and I'm running late for her date.

With my make-up in place, lipstick slicked on (in Harriet's colour) and my all-black ensemble spotless, I know she was right. If we stood together in matching outfits, with our hair done the same way, most strangers (and all men) would have a hard time telling us apart. One well-coordinated blonde is as good as another.

It's a bit of a risk meeting in Canary Wharf given that SweetyPetey16 could be a psycho stalker-type person. But I need to run back to work afterwards so I'm not travelling far. And if he is a psycho stalker-type person, the security guards around here can take him down.

But there's been no hint of weirdness so far, and he and Harriet have been emailing for nearly two weeks. It's always possible that he'll be a shocker in person. I find that a lot in my job. I know the analysts at the other banks through their research notes and emails. They're intelligent, well-balanced and even sometimes funny. Or so it seems till you meet them. Some make Ryan look personable in comparison. So I haven't let Harriet get her hopes up too much.

And yet, I'm a little excited to meet him. It's not often you get to have a date with absolutely no consequences. It's like getting to eat an entire chocolate cake and not having to work off the calories. If he's nice and we hit it off, I'll pass a pleasant hour with someone who wants to go out with me. I mean, Harriet, of course. If he's a toad, then I'll walk away and won't ever have to deal with him again.

I'm glad we agreed on a way to spot each other, because the pub is jammed. I resisted the temptation to suggest a rose in his lapel and red umbrella for me. Instead, I've got my paperback clutched to my chest. In a world of kindles, tablets, i-this and berry-that, such an old-fashioned gesture should make me easy enough to spot.

He's carrying *The Guardian*, which sticks out like a liberal's thumb in this *FT*-reading crowd. He's at a small table by the window and first impressions are good. He's got all his hair (thick, brown, trendy cut), as advertised in his profile photos, and deep blue eyes. He's really quite good-looking.

'Harriet?' he says as I reach the table. My smile falters for just a second before I remember the ruse.

'Yes, hello, Pete.'

When he stands up I have to wonder where the rest of him is. Unless he's standing in a hole, he's not even close to six feet tall. It's a good thing Harriet and I are only five seven.

'I took the liberty of ordering a bottle. You said you like red.'

He pours me a brimming glass of Cabernet.

I daren't be too picky given that my main criterion for Harriet's next boyfriend is lack of insanity. It's just that, if I were to be picky, I'd prefer for Pete to have a voice that didn't sound like he'd been sucking on helium balloons under the table.

'Thanks very much,' I say, accepting the glass. 'Did you find your way here all right?'

He works over in West London for a software sales company. Zack hasn't heard of it but there are probably loads of them around, and I can't really expect my friend to know them all just because he works in IT.

'Oh, yes, I've been to Canary Wharf before. On dates, actually.' He grins shyly as he says this and I forgive him his lack of stature. 'That isn't a problem, is it?'

'Oh, no, not at all. We're all on the internet these days, right? Everybody's doing it.' I sound like my mother. Those zany kids and their new-fangled ways.

'You're very pretty,' he says.

'Erm, thanks. So, how was work today?' It's such a humdrum question but he's been in daily contact with Harriet so I know all about the big contract he's been working on and his review coming up and a lot of detail about what he eats for lunch.

'Very, very pretty.'

'Yeah, thanks.'

'Have you been with many men, Harriet?'

'Have I…?'

'You know, have you had many boyfriends. Any

long-term, serious relationships?'

I swig my wine and think back to Harriet's dating record. It's a charge sheet of misdemeanours and felonies. 'No, nothing very long term.'

'Oh? Why do you think that is?'

Straight in there. I have to admire his candour, if not the predicament he's now put me in. If I'm honest and say that it's because the men were all psycho, he's not likely to believe me, is he? I wouldn't have believed it if I hadn't been there to pick up the pieces (and soak them in wine). 'We wanted different things from the relationships.'

That was true. Harriet wanted a boyfriend. Her dates wanted her car, her pearls, her blind devotion and, in one case, someone to call mummy in bed.

'What about you?' I ask to stave off further analysis. 'Any serious relationships?'

'A few. I went out with one woman for three years, but that was a while ago now. I've been happily dating for the past year or so.' He fiddles with the stem of his glass. 'To be honest, I'll be very happy to settle down with the right woman, when I find her.'

This is promising. Harriet's men are usually unavailable in some way. They're emotionally stunted or geographically unsuitable or incarcerated (though that was just one guy and we did believe he was innocent). We know Pete lives inside the M25. I glance at his ankles for electronic tags.

'Tired of playing the field?' I ask.

He nods. 'It is nice meeting different people but I'm ready for more than just dates. Not that I'm unhappy with my life! I go out a lot with my friends, have a laugh, take some drugs. You know, the usual.'

From hero to zero in one sentence. 'Drugs are usual?'

He shrugs. 'Aren't they? Everybody does them, right?'

'I guess.' Harriet's smoked pot. I must remember that Pete isn't auditioning for the part of my boyfriend.

'Do you like drugs?' he asks. 'Weed, ecstasy, Rohypnol?'

Did I hear him correctly? 'The date rape drug?'

'It isn't always rape,' he says quietly.

Oh, really? When, exactly, is rape not rape? I'm not sure if I'm more shocked by his statement or the fact that he's just told me that he drugs women for fun. He's not reading his audience very well.

At best, this guy's a waste of time. At worst he should be under police investigation. My gut is telling me to leave but it's like watching extreme breast enlargement surgery on telly. I want to see how it ends.

'I take it too, you see,' he says by way of explanation. 'Not a whole pill, obviously. But a quarter is nice. Like Valium. You should try it some time.'

'I don't really do drugs, but thanks.' I wish I could stop my face from pinching up when I say this. It's not cool.

'Fair enough. Are you uptight about anything else?'

'I'm not uptight!'

'Well, you're not relaxed. I can see that and I've just met you. Is it because of your job, do you think? Or have you always been like this?'

'Just because I'm not taking ecstasy every weekend, doesn't mean I'm uptight.'

'I'm sorry, Harriet, I didn't mean to insult you. I was just curious about how your boundaries were formed.'

Oh, right, I'm Harriet. Not that it matters at this point. I won't be setting my friend up with some roofie-popping weirdo who speaks like his testicles haven't descended.

I pick up my glass to finish my wine before remembering who bought it for me. 'Well, thanks for the wine. This has been interesting but I've got to get back to work.'

He laughs. 'I think you work too much.' He leans in and kisses my cheek. 'Well, it was nice meeting you.'

'Yeah, thanks.' I grab my coat and try not to run for the door.

When I get back to the office I'm googling the symptoms of Rohypnol. If I nod off at my desk, I'm having him arrested as soon as I wake up.

* * * * *

My favourite days at the bank are when Zack and I go to lunch together. I don't usually have the time to stop for a proper meal but today I'm making a special effort. When you've had a date like I've had, you've got to share it with someone.

I told Harriet last night, of course. She was initially disappointed not to have a second date, on account of Pete's full head of hair and encouraging emails. But she agrees that it's best not to start a relationship with someone who's so casual about sexual assault. I know she'll bounce back easily and forget all about him in a few days.

Not me. I plan to trot him out as a cautionary tale to every single person I know. Starting with Zack.

'You should have him taken off that dating site,' he

says, after listening politely to my story. 'Who knows what he's doing to other women. Can you report him?'

'We did already. But he'll just pop up somewhere else, like a sexually harassing penny. Honestly, Zack, the men out there.'

'Oh, you're only looking at half the equation. The women are just as insane, believe me. Maybe more so.'

'Ha, no way. I know lots of normal women.'

He stares at me. 'Who, Harriet? The stalker?'

'Once! That only happened once.'

'She's got you going on dates for her, Carol. That's not the behaviour of a normal woman.'

I assume he's talking about Harriet's behaviour rather than mine. 'It's to protect her from psycho men, but you have a point. What about Marley? She's normal.'

'You mean your sister who expects you to be her personal servant? Who rings you every day with another terrible crisis like what shade of green her wedding napkins should be? That woman is so high-maintenance that a Maserati mechanic couldn't keep her running.'

'You're exaggerating, and Marley can't have green napkins at her wedding. The colour clashes with her complexion.'

We both laugh.

'I know she's difficult but she's my sister. I've always looked out for her, even though I'm the youngest. That's my role in the family.'

'Don't you ever get sick of it?'

I can't answer his question because it's not that simple. 'They count on me, and I love doing things for them.'

It's not the first time a well-meaning friend has questioned this. And I never find the right words to explain what it means to me. It's just who I am, like being clever or sporty or musically inclined. Being the best daughter or sister or girlfriend is what makes me *me*. I'm very proud of that person, and I like her.

Everyone's family helps form them. We're the valleys in the landscape carved and shaped by the glaciers of family dynamics. I was just like most other ten-year-olds until the summer that Mum got ill. There's nothing like the prospect of losing a parent to make you want to be a very good girl.

Marley didn't share my point of view. She got angry and sullen, went on strike when it came to chores and homework and, frankly, needed a good slap most of the time. Dad was so upset about Mum's cancer that I couldn't let my sister add to his stress. So I covered for her.

Then Mum needed surgery and chemo and a peaceful, well-run house while she recovered. I made sure that happened.

In true Mum fashion she put the whole episode behind her once she got the all-clear, but by then my role as family fixer was rock solid.

Zack doesn't know any of this. Not many people do.

'You're too accommodating with everyone, Carol,' Zack continues. 'Even at work. You're one of the best analysts there. You don't have to take shite from anyone, especially Derrick.'

At the mention of his name, memories of the strip club resurface. Memories of letting a woman get paid to humiliate me. I shouldn't have sat there and taken it. I don't know what I should have done instead, but not that. I didn't win. Derrick did. He managed to exploit two women for the price of one lap dance. I'm disappointed with myself but I won't tell Zack this. If I did, I'd only have to tell him what happened.

'You should do what you want to do,' he continues.

'But I am doing what I want to do. Besides, who would I be if I wasn't this?' That's the question I always come back to. It's not that I believe my own hype. God, far from it. My flaws are painfully obvious to me and sometimes I feel like a fraud when I hear praise. But I crave it. Every time someone tells me I'm the best, the greatest, the most (fill in the blank), it adds a little more strength to my foundations, and I'm grateful. This is who I am.

'Ben doesn't mind you going on dates?' he asks, sipping his espresso as his hand goes to his hair. He's so predictable.

'If you must know, I haven't told him. Oh, don't pretend to be shocked. I just don't want to upset him for no reason. It's really not that different from being Harriet's wingman on a night out.'

'Just be careful. If he finds out later, it'll look like you're being sneaky. It won't matter what the truth is. I'd mention it to him if I were you.'

'It's our anniversary next weekend. Maybe I'll slip it in over a romantic glass of champagne.'

'You could make it into a parlour game. Give him clues to follow. Surprise! Cheers, darling.'

'You know, that's not a bad idea.'

'Carol, I'm only joking. What are you going to do, play betrayal charades? First word, sounds like heating.'

'I'm not heating! No, I mean a treasure hunt for our anniversary. I've been trying to think of something special to do. I could lead him to all the places we went together when we first went out. That would be fun, right?'

'Why isn't he thinking of something to do?' Hand in hair again.

'Well, I'm sure he is. This can be in addition to whatever he's got planned.'

I'm already thinking about how to do it. What a great idea!

When my BlackBerry pings I realise I haven't looked at it in nearly an hour. That's some kind of record.

Harriet's been typing in capital letters. It's never a good sign. I scan the forwarded message from Squeaky Pete.

Dear Harriet,

Since we've been emailing a lot I thought I should get in touch after last night. I took the time to meet you and yet I feel like you were judging me about the whole drug thing. I didn't appreciate that. I was open with you but felt like you're a very closed, uptight person. If you open up and have some fun you might find it easier to meet people.

I'm sorry but I don't think I want to be with someone like you.

Take care,
Pete

We've been rejected by the drug-addled sex pest?!

'Everything okay?' Zack asks, eying the thunder in my expression.

'Here, read this.'

'The guy's got balls,' he says when he finishes. 'Harriet will respond, right?'

I shake my head. 'I will. Are you ready to go? I've got an email to draft.'

My fingers fly across the keyboard.

Hi Harriet, please email this exactly as it is to Pete. God, what a twat. We'll find much better prospects than him! xoxo C

Pete,

    Thanks for taking time from your busy schedule drugging women to meet me last night. With so many potential dates to molest I'm honoured that you've spent time with me. I'm sure your mother tells you that you're quite a catch but I'm afraid I'd rather suffer complete rectal prolapse than be in the same room with a deluded and potentially psychotic person like you.

    Oh, and by the way, just to help you with your vocabulary: rape is always rape.

    If you find that you're banned from the dating site, there's no need to thank me.

    Don't contact me again,
    Harriet

Harriet's email pings back moments later. *You are beyond awesome, Carol! Please write all my emails for me (kidding, kidding ☺) Hxx*

CHAPTER 12

'Whatcha doing?' Zack says, peering over my shoulder at my screens.

'God, Zack, you know I hate it when you sneak up on me like that!'

'I wasn't sneaking. Ryan saw me. You were too engrossed in your spreadsheets to notice.'

'He's right,' Ryan says without taking his eyes off his own screen. 'He wasn't sneaking. And you were talking to yourself again.'

'I just came up to show you something,' Zack says, ignoring Ryan. 'Go on YouTube.'

'I don't really have time to watch *Family Guy*, you know.'

'Trust me, it's not *Family Guy*. Now type in Bernard Smith Green T.'

Bernard Smith is our president and CEO. I smile. 'What is it?'

'Click on the link. Here.' He hands me my headset. 'It's about a minute in.'

Bernard is standing behind the podium at an investor's conference. Waffle waffle waffle, piffle, piffle. Then... 'Over a year ago in Sustainable Investments, we began developing our showcase trading platform, Green T. Some of the cleverest minds in the business conceived and developed it, and the result is the first predictive trading system in the green investment space. It's been phenomenally successful for our clients. That's why our customers trust us. It's because we're constantly looking for ways to enhance value for them. For us, innovation isn't an empty phrase, or a concept we read about other people doing. It's what drives our business. It's what we're known for. And it's what you expect from us. Thank you.'

Zack's grinning like a mad thing. 'How does it feel to be the cleverest mind in the business?'

'I'm sorry, I don't understand you. You'll have to use bigger words.'

'Sorry, I speak in binary languages only.'

'Speaking of which, can I save that video?'

'I'll make you a copy. You can play it for Derrick at your next review. Seriously, Carol, if Bernard Smith is talking about your system to investors, it's big. Congratulations. The bastards can't take anything away from you now. I'll see you for lunch later?'

'I can't. I'm sitting with Stephan today and I'll have to leave on time tonight to go to my parents' for dinner. I'll just grab a sandwich in a bit. Thanks for showing me the video, though.'

'No worries. Actually, there was one more thing.' He looks uncharacteristically shy. 'I'm having a thing two weeks from tomorrow for my birthday. It's just drinks but I wondered if you can come?'

'I'd love to! Just let me check my diary, okay? Can I tell you for sure later?'

'Yeah, that's fine, like I said it's just drinks. Nothing formal. See you later.' He waves over his shoulder and ambles toward the lifts. My bearer of brilliant news.

Stephan arrives exactly on time for our session. I'll be sorry to see him go when his internship finishes, though I'm sure he'll be invited to apply for a job when he graduates.

'I've got a few questions about Green T,' he says, perching stiffly on the extra chair. 'If that's all right?'

'Of course! You're here to learn.'

'Yes, well, the thing is, I don't understand why I'm not getting the same results when I run the mock-up. I mean, I spent most of the weekend trying, but I must be doing something wrong. Could we run through an example together?'

It's hard not to ruffle his hair and make Gran's aren't-you-sweet face. 'Hang on, let me get us some tea first. Milk, no sugar, right?'

Our teas are long gone by the time I give up trying to make the model spit out the correct data. Stephan's right. The pretend computer program that I made for him isn't mirroring Green T.

'I'm sure there's a logical explanation,' I tell him. 'It's probably just a ghost in the machine. I'll have a closer look and let you know, and in the meantime, why don't you finish those reports for Ryan?'

As he leaves, I smile with all the confidence I can muster. I'll have to get Zack to create another copy of the live trading system for us to use. It's one more thing for my to-do list.

Jez's mother, Isabel, rings just as I spot Ben waiting for me in front of the Tube station. I hold my finger up in a wait-a-minute gesture just as he does the same thing. He's on the phone, too. This is love in the twenty-first century.

'Hi, Isabel.'

We've talked a lot since I broke the news over tea that her own relatives aren't welcome at her son's wedding. I can't really blame her for refusing to take no for an answer. I wonder what her angle will be today. 'Is everything okay?'

'Oh, yes, fine, thanks. Well, no, actually, not really. I've just had another email from Susie about bringing the girls to the wedding. She says Little Philippa was heartbroken not to get to go to the Royal Wedding until Susie explained that it was just for Will and Kate's friends and family. So naturally she's been looking forward to seeing Jez being married and I don't know what to tell her.'

'Why don't we arrange a Skype linkup for the ceremony and the girls can dial in? It'll be like they're there. Listen, Isabel, I'm in a bit of a rush. Could we maybe talk more tomorrow?'

'Oh, no, there's no need. I know you're busy. I'll tell Susie about Skype. Thanks, Carol!' She rings off, no doubt already thinking up another excuse.

We're late getting to my parents' house. Just as I got Jez's mum off the phone, Ben took another call, and then another as I pointed at my watch and made empty threats to leave him standing in front of my parents' Tube station.

Zoe is cooking tonight and her efforts fill the air with a rich, meaty aroma.

'*Zut alors*, Zoe, that smells amazing!' Ben kisses her cheek as she rolls her eyes. He always trots out that old chestnut when he sees her. She always pretends to be amused by his mildly xenophobic stereotyping.

'Thank you, Ben. It's coq au vin. I'll teach you how to make it if you want. It's very easy. You too, Carol.'

I hug her. 'I don't need to learn how to cook, Zoe, when you already cook for me. In fact, I could probably stand to eat salads a bit more often. Your food is making me fat.'

Even our downstairs neighbour, Mrs Gaynor (owner of the ceiling that Zoe's bath rained through), has been won over by Zoe's treats. That woman has hardly said a civil word to me since I moved in, yet the other day I caught her waving at Zoe.

Zoe hugs me back. 'You're perfect as you are, *ma chérie.*'

Is it any wonder we love her?

'Dinner will be ready soon. Would you please see if Monsieur Colbert is ready to come inside? Jez and Marley are in the living room, Ben, if you want to say hi.'

'In other words, get out of the kitchen?'

'Please go away,' she says, opening the oven to release another delicious blast of dinner smells.

I can hear Dad's guitar as I walk along the back garden path to his studio. I recognise snippets of the melody, but he's arranging it differently. The little light beside the door is unlit, so I know it's safe to go in. He had the light installed after Marley and I ruined one too many recordings with our boisterous arrival.

I don't knock, but quietly open the door and peek in. I like to watch Dad play. He gets a faraway look, and his face settles into a concentrated stillness as his fingers fly over the strings.

He looks up as the last notes die away. 'Hello, sweetheart. Have you been there long?'

I shake my head. 'Only a few minutes. That's pretty. Does it have a name?'

'Not yet. I'm just playing around. Is dinner ready?'

'Nearly. Marley and Jez are here. Do you want to come in now?'

He stands up, stretching his back before setting his guitar on its stand alongside the others.

'Your mother and Marley started speaking in wedding so I thought it best to come out here. They'll tell me when they need my chequebook.'

We walk together back to the house, following the sound of laughter. Jez is telling everyone about a client he's been fighting with and I can see that Ben is dying to jump in with his own story. When I sit on the arm of his chair he turns his face up for a kiss.

'Aw, aren't you sweet?' Marley says, clearly high on romance. 'Speaking of sweet, what are you doing for your anniversary?'

I shoot her a warning look to shut her up, or she'll ruin my treasure hunt surprise. She makes a sieve look watertight when it comes to keeping secrets.

Ben shrugs. 'That's miles off.'

Marley nods. 'Well, I suppose you solicitors are used to working on tight timelines, so three days probably does seem miles off.'

'We're not really big on set dates for things,' says Ben, suddenly grinning. 'Are we, babe? Like Valentine's

Day. Why go out of your way on one day, when you should do it every day?'

'As long as you do,' Marley murmurs.

'Okay!' Jez says, standing up. 'Dinner's probably ready now. Come on, sweetheart, let's go see if Zoe needs help.' He rushes Marley from the room before she can follow up her line of discussion.

Zoe has outdone herself, and we gorge on the richly flavoured, fragrant chicken and wine. Marley once suggested that Zoe try doing something productive with her love of food. That sent Zoe into a week-long fit of poetic outpouring about the joys of the perfect fondant potato. It wasn't worth mentioning that Marley had meant finding work serving food rather than writing about it.

'Can you get drunk from this, Zoe?' Gran asks, forking in the last of her chicken.

'I don't think so,' I say. 'The alcohol burns off when it cooks. Why, Gran, are you feeling tipsy?'

She shakes her head. 'Unfortunately not. Pour me a wee glass of wine, will you please?'

Mum snatches the bottle from my reach. 'You shouldn't be drinking with your medication.'

'Oh, Eleanor, I wish you'd lighten up and let me have some fun. It's not like I'm driving.' She leans over the arm of her wheelchair to whisper to me. 'You'll get me to my room safely, won't you, doll?'

'You can count on it, Gran.'

'Then pour me a glass of wine, Eleanor.'

I try to hide my smirk, but Mum sees me. 'I wish you wouldn't encourage her,' she says. 'I do my best to make sure she stays healthy. At her age–'

'At my age I can do whatever the hell I want to,' Gran says. 'It's one benefit of getting old. The only other time you get to do that is at your wedding. Right, Marley?'

'Definitely, Gran! And that reminds me. Carol, I'll definitely want flowers in my hair. Will you please find me someone who can make silk ones to match my dress?'

'You've found a dress? Where? What does it look like?'

'No, no, not yet. You have to help me, remember? I just want to have someone in mind for the flowers for when I do find the dress.'

'But how am I supposed to find someone who can make flowers for a dress you don't have yet?'

Marley waves her fork. 'I'm just asking you to start looking, that's all, so that we have some options for when the time comes. You're the researcher. It'll take you two minutes to find someone.'

'It's just that I haven't really got a lot of spare time at the moment…'

'Well, neither do I, Carol. Karl has me working like a dog. But that's fine, if you're too busy to be my bridesmaid.'

Maybe it's the strain of the last few weeks, or the fact that our second anniversary seems to be news to Ben. Or maybe Gran is right and the chicken is alcoholic, but suddenly I feel my heart begin to race.

'This may come as a surprise to you, Marley, but I have a life too, and it's pretty hectic at the moment. I don't really have time right now to research your hair flowers for a wedding that's more than six months away.'

The table goes silent. Marley stares at me with her mouth open. Then her lip starts to quiver.

'Fine. I'll do it all myself, then. I just thought you'd want to help because you're my sister. I'm sorry I'm putting you out with my demands.'

Jez rubs her back as tears slide down her cheeks.

'Carol, what has gotten into you?!' Mum finally says. 'Please tell me what's so urgent in your life that you can't take five minutes to help your sister. You know she'd do the same for you.'

I feel the fight leave me as quickly as it came. Marley is right. It'll only take me a few minutes. And it'll keep Mum off my back. I hate when she looks at me like that.

'Fine, I can have a look tonight when I get home. Is everybody finished? I'll clear the plates.'

'Thanks, Carol,' Marley says, smiling again. 'I love you.'

'I know,' I say, as I carry the stacked plates into the kitchen to wash up.

MICHELE GORMAN

CHAPTER 13

Of course, Mum was right. It took only an hour to find a few websites where Marley can order hand-made silk flowers for her hair, once she finds her dress. Not that we're likely to do that before the end of the next decade. We've been in and out of three of London's best wedding dress shops and plied with enough champagne to resurrect Marie Antoinette, but Marley's perfect dress eludes her. It's taking all my willpower not to shout *Just buy that one* every time she steps gingerly from the fitting room with that look on her face.

'I'm just not sure about the neckline,' she says as she emerges in a cloud of tulle.

'I thought you wanted a sweetheart neckline?' Mum asks. 'Didn't you decide on that already?' She looks as worried as I feel that we've backtracked on even this small accomplishment. If we lose ground now, we'll be revisiting the sequins versus pearl debate before you know it.

'This is much harder than I thought!' says Marley. 'If

I choose the wrong dress, you know I'll just hate it and have to change it later. At least I know exactly what I want you to wear, Carol.'

'You do? What've you got in mind?'

'I saw a beautiful Herve Leger bandage dress. You are planning to go to the gym before my wedding, right?'

'Are you saying I'm fat?' I tease.

I'm fooling no one by hauling my gym kit into work every day but it's an expected part of the banker's uniform, along with the BlackBerry, customised suit jacket lining and air of superiority.

Marley looks horrified. 'No, not at all. But those dresses are unforgiving so you may have to do some work, that's all. I was thinking a muted colour like taupe or mocha. That way you'll make the perfect backdrop for my dress… If I ever find it.'

A taupe bandage dress. If I didn't know better, I'd think she was trying to make me look awful. 'Why not take a break?' I suggest, instead of telling her what I think of her choice. 'You must have tried on forty dresses already.' Forty-two, actually. I know this because I've been counting. 'Come, have some champagne. You're the bride and you're hardly drinking.'

'Let me just get out of this dress.'

As she minces back to the fitting room, I sneak a glance at my BlackBerry.

'Do not check that thing,' Mum warns.

'I'm not checking it. I'm just seeing what time it is. You know I need to leave by two.'

She rearranges the scarf on her neck, which has shifted one degree off-kilter. 'This is your sister's day,

Carol. We're here for her today.'

'It's also my anniversary, Mum. I've got plans and I can't be late. I have to be at the salon for two-thirty.'

Her face softens as her romantic heart overrules her censorious head. 'Has Ben planned something special?'

'I'm sure he has, but so have I.' I'm grinning like crazy at the brilliance of my idea. 'I'm leading him on a treasure hunt, Mum, to all the special places we've been on dates together. We'll end up in the pub where we met. Then we can go on from there to whatever he's planned.'

Marley pads across the thick-pile white carpet and throws herself on the leather sofa (white, of course – wedding dress shopping is like being trapped inside a series of very expensive marshmallows). 'What are we talking about?'

'Carol's anniversary surprise for Ben,' Mum says, taking a sip of her champagne. 'It sounds like fun, sweetheart.'

'Oh, yes!' Marley claps her hands. 'The treasure hunt is today, isn't it? Are you excited? I'm excited and I'm not even going!'

I nod. 'I've got a lot to do beforehand, though, so I have to leave by two, if that's okay.'

'Of course it's okay!' she says, like I'm insane for thinking she might be reluctant to loosen her grip on proceedings. This, from my sister who had me disinvite her future cousins from her wedding because they won't match the decor. 'It's your anniversary. Does he suspect anything?'

'No, I don't think so.'

'Good,' says Mum. 'It's best to keep men on a need-to-know basis.'

'Is that the secret to a happy relationship?' Marley asks Mum, who considers her question before answering.

'The secret to a happy relationship is feeling that the person you're with loves you for exactly who you are.'

Marley smiles. 'Jez thinks I'm perfect.'

'Then you're in the right relationship.'

Does Ben think I'm perfect? Sometimes I feel like I couldn't be less perfect in his eyes. If it's not the smoking (yes, I'm smoking again), then it's the nagging. If I'm not nagging, then I'm too demanding. If not demanding, then I'm too aloof. It's like a balancing act when I don't know where the centre of gravity is supposed to be.

But today will be perfect. Definitely.

'Do you think Jez is perfect?' I ask.

'Nearly perfect,' says Marley. 'Though he still doesn't put the loo seat down. That's trainable, right, Mum?'

Mum squeezes my sister's narrow shoulders. 'Sometimes, sweetheart, it's best to choose our battles carefully. You can always just get a flat with two loos.'

My hair is smooth and swingy as I hurry from the salon to the Tube bound for Ben's flat. I know he's still at the office because he hasn't called yet. He works most Saturdays now. With all the delaying tactics by both sets of lawyers, the trial that was supposed to end months ago hasn't even begun yet.

I let myself into the silent hallway. 'Anyone home?' I need to be sure his flatmate isn't roaming around in his underwear.

There's no one home, which makes me wonder why

I'm creeping towards the bedroom. I feel a bit naughty being here. It's the first time I've been in Ben's flat without his knowledge. Is that weird after two years together?

His bedroom door is closed. I always leave mine open at home. It's not like a closed door (or a locked one) would keep Zoe from taking what she liked anyway.

When I push open the door, a stale blast of air hits me. The window is tightly shut, along with the curtains. The bed is unmade and Ben seems to have shed his clothes on to the floor every night like a commuting snake. If I leave the clue in here, he probably won't find it until Christmas.

Boys are feral when left on their own.

BlackBerry says I'll have just enough time to tidy up quickly and still plant all the clues around the city. It only takes me a few minutes to fluff up the duvet and straighten it on the bed, plump the pillows and sweep all the clothes from the floor into the clothes hamper. Which does beg the question: Why can't Ben do this? There's probably a very complex genetic answer involving Y chromosomes.

Carefully, I prop up the clue with a pair of socks behind it.

Go to the square where we first tried The Vermonster together. Ask for The Vermonster for two and you'll get your next clue.

The trail of red rose petals does look a bit naff, and if Ben's flatmate gets home first he might wonder why they're trailing from the front door, but it's best to be obvious about the clues. Sometimes you can beat a man over the head with a proverbial cricket bat and he'll still wonder what the score is.

Leicester Square is busy with late afternoon tourists. Catching a whiff of the candied nut vendor makes my mouth water. I'm tempted to buy a cone full to munch as I go along, but if I really am destined for a bandage dress, as Marley threatened, then every nut will show.

I'm nervous as I push open the ice cream shop door, and feel like a bit of a prat as I approach the counter. Two beautiful young Muslim girls, their hair swathed in black hijabs, excitedly point out their favourite choices.

It was much more crowded the night Ben and I first came in. We were a bit tipsy, fresh from dinner in nearby Chinatown. Despite the chilly March night we'd sat at one of the little tables out front, and were too lost in our conversation to notice anyone else. It was probably our third or fourth date, and it would be the first night we spent together. Every time I looked at him my tummy flipped like a Russian gymnast.

'I know I'm supposed to play it cool, Carol, and be all aloof,' he'd said. 'But I don't want to.' He guided my lips to his while our ice creams melted in their bowls. 'I want to spend all my time with you. I'm sorry that's not very cool.'

'I don't care if it's uncool. That's exactly the way I feel, too.'

For the first time I felt completely safe, and able to show my feelings. Ben wouldn't hurt me. It was one of those nights that will remain lodged in my memory.

'Are you ready to order or are you still deciding?' The handsome young teen smiles patiently, holding up his ice cream scoop. The memory of our date pops and I realise I've been standing alone in the shop, staring at the server's crotch through the display glass.

'Oh, yes, hi... I wondered if you could do me a favour? It's my anniversary and I'm setting up a treasure hunt for my boyfriend. We came here on one of our first dates. When he comes in, he's going to order the Vermonster for two. This is his photo.' I flash my BlackBerry at him. 'Can you give him this piece of paper when he comes in?'

The boy grins, taking the folded paper. 'Sure. That's very cool. He's a lucky guy.'

'Thanks. I think so!'

'Hey. What's the next clue? Can I read it?'

'Won't you read it anyway when I leave?'

He shrugs. 'I thought I might as well ask first.'

'It says, *We crucified What Makes You Beautiful. Go to the venue and the bartender will point you in One Direction.*'

'And that'll mean something to him?'

'I hope so. Thanks, he should be here soon!'

The boy waves me off before tending to the customers that come in as I leave.

Lucky Voice isn't too far away, but I hurry anyway. For all I know, Ben could be right behind me. I'm dying to call him but don't want to make him suspicious. His solicitor's mind would know something is up.

Just walking into the karaoke bar again sends a shiver up my spine. Who enjoys these places? Certainly not anyone who wants to impress her new boyfriend, unless she happens to be Adele.

Ben's boss organised the night out when Ben and I came here, and Ben couldn't imagine a better occasion to introduce his colleagues to his tone-deaf girlfriend. 'They'll love you,' he'd said.

'Yes, but they'd love me over dinner and drinks too, without a microphone.'

'C'mon, this is more fun,' said my show-offy boyfriend, leading me into the venue with his arm comfortably around my shoulder.

To my horror, Lucky Voice wasn't even a karaoke bar in the traditional sense, where the 'act' standing on stage can hope that the audience is too drunk and rowdy to listen to her. Ben led me to a small sound-proofed room where his colleagues were already adding their favourite songs to the playlist. It was my worst nightmare.

'Everyone, this is Carol,' he shouted above their excited chatter.

Eight pairs of eyes swung in my direction. 'H– hi, everyone.'

They all smiled their greetings, but one slender young man broke away from the rest. 'Hey, Carol,' he said. I recognised him from the night Ben and I met. He had a kind face. 'I'm Jim. We've heard a lot about you lately.'

I smiled. They were about to hear a lot *of* me. I felt like apologising in advance.

The only two other women then came over to introduce themselves. 'Do you do this often?' I asked.

'No way!' said Amy, the paralegal who I'd heard a lot about already. She'd started with Ben and was some kind of wunderkind. 'We've never come here before.' Her open smile and wide eyes tempted me to like her, but I was reserving judgment until I knew she had no interest in my new boyfriend.

'But you've come here before, Amy,' the other, older woman said. 'Amy's practically a professional singer.' She looked as glum as I felt at this news. 'It was her idea to come.'

Amy nodded happily. 'Well, this is more interesting than standing around in a pub getting drunk, isn't it? Carol, what song will you sing?'

'Me? Oh, I'll leave the singing to you, if that's all right. I'm just a guest tonight.'

But they wouldn't let me off until I'd added one song to the list. Then all I could do was hope for a technical malfunction, fire alarm or city-wide power cut.

Ben swooped up behind me, kissing me on the ear, as Amy took the microphone. 'Having fun?'

'Your colleagues are nice.'

'They're great. I'm glad you like them.'

'Wow, Amy can sing.'

'Yeah, she sang in the choir at uni.'

'I'm a bit intimidated.'

'You shouldn't be. You're ten times better than Amy.'

'You haven't heard me sing.'

'I'm not talking about your singing.' He kissed me again just as I saw my song flash on the screen.

'Carol, that's you!' Jim said.

Why had I chosen to murder a song that I liked? I'd never be able to hear it again without remembering this night.

Amy handed me the mic. 'Have fun!' She grinned as she bounced off to refill her wine glass from the bottles on the small table near the door.

I took a swig of my drink as the music started, then

opened my mouth.

By the end of the first line everyone knew it wasn't false modesty that made me say I couldn't sing. It was lack of ability. Talk about unfair. My father sang in front of stadiums full of people. He had Grammy Awards. How could my vocal chords be so unColbertlike?

Glances bounced between Ben's colleagues. I caught his boss sniggering but I couldn't stop or they'd think I was sad as well as musically constipated. I ploughed on through the chorus, sounding like a cat caught in a washing machine.

Suddenly Ben was beside me. Looking into my eyes, he smiled and started singing with me. His voice was nearly as out of tune as mine but the tension eased from everyone's expressions as we murdered the song together. And at that very moment, I knew I was in love with Ben. He'd always watch out for me.

The bartender in Lucky Voice was less romantically inclined than my ice cream server, but she agreed to give Ben the next clue when he arrived. It is, possibly, the most important location in our history together.

You said you loved me and my feelings poured out in a fountain. There you'll find your final clue.

I'd got us tickets for a concert in St Martin-in-the-Fields, the eighteenth-century church just at the edge of Trafalgar Square. Ben loves classical music and Vivaldi is my favourite composer, so when I saw the performance advertised I knew it would be perfect. And it was. The church was lit by candles as The Four Seasons washed over us with beautiful clarity. Neither of us spoke as we meandered outside with the rest of the audience afterwards. It was a crisp, clear night with people streaming through the square. The National Gallery's limestone façade and Doric columns glowed against the night sky and the fountain was bathed in blue light. We walked to the fountain.

'Carol, I want to tell you something.'

He moved a lock of hair from my face.

I waited as tourists snapped photos around us. I wanted to freeze that moment in time.

'I love you.'

My heart tapped a happy tune. 'I love you, too. Oh my God, I've wanted to say it for weeks! I'm so happy, Ben. You make me so happy.'

The wind shifted, sending the fountain's mist sweeping over us. Nearby tourists hurried away, but not us. We were too busy kissing.

There are nearly as many tourists in the square as there were that night. I just hope none of them are police. I'm sure it's a felony to deface a national monument, even for love, even with chalk that will wash off in the next rainstorm. Self-consciously I dig the blue stick from my bag. I have to write it big enough for Ben to see. But not so big that someone will stop me. My heartbeat quickens at the thought of flouting the law. I never do this.

Will I do this? Maybe I should have written another note instead and stashed it somewhere. If I knew when Ben was coming, I could have hidden in the crowd and asked someone to hand him the note. But then we'd be heading to the bar at the same time. I'd have to race him there.

Every time I look around I catch at least one

person's eye. It's a very public place to commit a crime.

But most people glance away as quickly as they look. Except for one small boy, who hasn't yet learned that staring isn't polite. He's about five. His parents are arguing over a map, oblivious to the graffiti artist in their midst. I smile at the boy. His expression doesn't change. I wave my hand to shoo him away. Still he stares. I try my mother's you'd-better-watch-yourself-or-I'm-coming-over-there face. That does the trick and quickly I scribble my message.

Go where it all began.

Without looking up, I hurry away from the fountain. When no one shouts for me to stop, at first I feel relieved, then mildly annoyed that people are so willing to see our national treasures vandalised without lifting a finger to stop it.

If I can get to the pub in the next thirty minutes, I might get a table. Then all that's left to do is to wait for Ben to turn up for our anniversary night.

I grin all the way to the Tube…

… By seven o'clock I'm no longer grinning. Where is Ben?

My hand shakes as I tap his number.

He answers on the fourth ring.

'Ben?'

'Hi, sweetheart, how are you?'

'Where are you?'

'Still at the office. What are you doing?'

I don't answer his question. 'When will you be finished?'

'I shouldn't be more than an hour, but don't wait for me if you've got plans.'

If I've got plans? If I've got plans?! What does he think I'm going to do, take myself out for a romantic anniversary dinner?

He doesn't remember. He doesn't know what today is, despite Marley telling him less than a week ago. Despite having been in this relationship for the past two years. He thinks it's just another day.

'Today's our anniversary, Ben.'

'Shit, of course it is. I'm so sorry, Carol. I'll finish up here and leave in ten minutes, okay? We'll go somewhere nice for dinner. Where would you like to go?'

I'd like to go somewhere that my boyfriend thought of before I reminded him. But that's obviously not going to happen.

'I don't care.'

'Where are you now? Do you want to meet for a drink first? I'm buying the champagne.'

He laughs but I don't join him.

'Let's meet for a drink. I really am so sorry, Carol. I've been so swamped with work that everything else has– It doesn't matter. I'm sorry.'

'I can meet you at the Hope in half an hour,' I tell him. I know he'll work right up until the last minute, so I'm not worried about him coming in early and finding me here. 'See you there. Half an hour, Ben, no later.'

'Thirty minutes. I'm synchronising my watch now.'

I hang up and check the BBC weather forecast. Rain tonight. At least my misdemeanour will be washed away, if not my disappointment.

MICHELE GORMAN

CHAPTER 14

Ben may have a habit of standing me up but he won't dare be late now. That gives my eyes twenty-five minutes to unpuff from the angry tears that have leaked out. I can't believe he's forgotten our anniversary. I feel like such an idiot for wasting the whole afternoon, not to mention the brainpower I spent thinking up the idea in the first place. I could have stayed with Marley and Mum instead of hurrying around London playing Remember When with myself.

I know he's got a lot on his mind. He may not naturally be the most romantic man in the world, but it's not like I sit around all day reading romance novels and thinking up loving gestures to thrill and amaze him.

All this time I've been blaming his case. Maybe I need to look a little closer to home.

My BlackBerry buzzes. Harriet.

'Hi, Harriet.'

'Am I interrupting? No, of course I'm not! You wouldn't answer the phone otherwise. How is everything going? Where are you?'

'At the Hope, waiting for Ben.'

She squeals. 'Does he suspect anything?'

'No,' I say truthfully. 'Not a thing.'

'You are officially the best girlfriend in the world.'

'Thanks, Harriet. Can I call you back later? Ben'll be here any minute.'

'Oh, right, of course. I actually have just a quick question. Is there any chance you're free tomorrow night?'

'I think so, why?'

'Promise you won't get angry with me. I know I'm not supposed to contact the guys off the website myself, but I think you'll agree this is a valid exception. He emailed me first. You were busy today and I didn't want to add to your stress. Carol, wait till you see him. I had to email him back, right? Or he'll think I'm not interested.'

I knew I needn't have worried about Harriet taking Squeaky Pete's rejection to heart. She's back on the horse. Unfortunately, there's no way to know whether she's riding a thoroughbred or an ass.

Far from convincing me that I shouldn't act as Harriet's surrogate again, meeting Pete just proved how much I need to. Harriet said it herself. She might have been more lenient about Pete, and where would that have got her? Probably drugged in the back of a taxi.

'Harriet, I thought we agreed that I'd do all the emailing, just to make sure nothing goes wrong?' I don't want to point out that by 'going wrong' I mean *being too Harriet*. 'What did you say?'

'Oh, I was totally cool. I just thanked him for getting in touch and he emailed right back and, Carol, we've been online nonstop all afternoon! He's dying to meet me. So, I was thinking that you could meet for a quick drink tomorrow… or if you're busy, then I could just go…'

'No! Harriet, what do you know about this guy?'

This is exactly why I'm vetting her dates. She'd run off for the weekend with someone who lets her cut in front of him in the queue at Tesco.

'Well, like I said, we've been emailing all afternoon. We get on so well, and he's articulate and we have a lot in common. I think he's a good one.'

'Okay, I'm happy to check him out, but please don't email him again. Make some excuse. Tell him you're going out. I'll email when I get back tonight and let you know where and when we're meeting tomorrow, okay? I'm sorry but I've got to go,' I say as I see Ben coming through the pub door. 'And Harriet? This is great, but don't get your hopes up too high.'

Fat chance of that. I can tell she's already planning their engagement party.

Ben pulls a beautiful bouquet of pink roses and tulips from behind his back as he bounces over to the table. He looks like he's just come from a relaxing spa day, not a ten-hour stint in the office. Self-consciously I smooth down my hair. 'Happy anniversary, Carol.'

I'm out of my seat before he can finish the sentence. 'They're beautiful. Where did you find them between here and the office? I didn't think there was a garage in Holborn.'

'These are not forecourt flowers! And who says I didn't buy them for you earlier today?'

'Well, given that you didn't know it was our anniversary until half an hour ago, that would have made you remarkably clairvoyant.'

He smiles and my heart melts. 'The Flower Pot around the corner is open late. Do I at least get points for knowing that your favourite flowers are pink?'

I nod. 'Not enough to clear your overdraft, though.'

'Then what if I told you that after we have champagne here, we've got a reservation at Ponte de la Tour, where we'll feed each other delicacies while enjoying the beautiful London skyline.'

'I'd say you must have paid a lot of money to get a reservation at such short notice.'

'Nah, but I owe the guys in the office big time. We've just spent the last–' he looks at his watch '– twenty-two minutes calling every restaurant we could think of to find the perfect table. I really am so sorry I forgot. You must think I'm an arsehole.'

'You've still got a lot of making up to do.'

But he can see from my expression that I'm no longer as angry.

'Let me start making it up to you now. I happen to know they keep a vintage bottle of Taittinger in the fridge for special occasions like today.'

He kisses me again, then rummages for his wallet on the way to the bar.

My head tells me that I should hold tight to my anger. Ben is an utter knob who's forgotten our anniversary. That's grounds for breaking up, really, and yet my heart reminds me that I know how easy it is for things to slip your mind when you're slammed at work. Haven't I spent years making guilt-induced flower apologies to my family? I forgot Dad's birthday and Gran's in the space of six months thanks to having to live, eat, breathe and sleep Green T. Let she without memory lapse cast the first bouquet.

But maybe I'm just making excuses so that I don't have to admit that Harriet is right.

I have become a pushover. And it's not just in this case, or just with Ben, is it? Lately, sometimes I don't even recognise myself. I can see Carol the girlfriend, the sister, daughter, colleague, friend. But I can't see myself any more. How did that happen?

I'm relieved when Ben's return interrupts my train of thought. It's time to put the recriminations away, Carol. They'll be just as fresh tomorrow and there's no sense in cutting off my libido to spite my relationship.

'Here's to us,' Ben says, handing me a sparkling glass of wine. 'And to a great night ahead. Now, since it's our anniversary, we shouldn't talk about anything mundane like our jobs or families. Agreed? Only interesting topics.'

We stare at each other as our champagne fizzes. Will we spend the next four hours in silence?

'I didn't realise how much our jobs dominated our lives,' I finally say. I hope that doesn't go against the spirit of the law.

'Well, I guess it's only natural. We're both driven people and it's what we spend most of our time doing.'

'Still, it shouldn't define us.'

'What should define us?'

I think about that for a minute. When I was at school I had a pretty clear idea about who I was and what I stood for. Being a teen with a cause made that easy. Was that any different than defining myself by my job? Maybe not, but it did feel like my world was bigger then.

Finally I say, 'Our feelings about things define us.

Or at least the way we see the world.'

'You mean like being an optimist or an emotional person? Maybe,' he says. 'But how do you keep from defining yourself against other people or the roles you play in society? You can say you're an optimist or an emotional person when someone asks you to describe yourself but it seems disingenuous not to also mention what you do or who your relationships are with. They're defining features as much as anything else.'

This is one of the things that I found so appealing about Ben when we first met. Discussions with him are like playing all day long in the most fun adventure park in the country. He never tires of exercising his brain.

'But ideally you're more than the sum of your relationships and career aspirations,' I point out.

'What if that's what fulfils you, though? Why shouldn't a mother be content defining herself as a mother if that's what she's happiest doing?'

'Doesn't the world close in if you're only doing one thing?' I'm trying not to think of myself.

'That makes her a specialist instead of a generalist.'

'How did we get on to the topic of mothers?'

'See what fun we can have when we don't talk about work? More champagne?'

We finish the bottle but I hardly notice because we let our debate meander wherever our points and counterpoints take us.

'We'd better be going,' I say when I notice the time. 'I wouldn't want to lose our table when you've had it booked for months.'

'You're going to remember this for a long time, aren't you?'

'Count on it.'

The night is perfectly clear, and we're treated to a panoramic view from the restaurant of the skyline over the Thames. London may not have skyscrapers like New York but its architecture is in some ways more beautiful.

'The lady likes?' Ben says, pulling out my chair.

'The lady loves.' I can feel the tension of the past few months slipping away as I glimpse the old Ben. Relaxed and smiling like this, he really is the perfect boyfriend. Lapses in memory notwithstanding.

'It's not been easy these past few months, has it?' I say, thinking of his case.

He shakes his head. A look of sadness crosses his expression.

'Ben? What is it?'

'It has been hard,' he says, making my tummy clench. 'I won't lie to you. This has been the hardest six months of my life. I didn't expect that. It was so easy to start with, you know?'

I nod, feeling ill. He's talking about us. I had no idea he was unhappy. Maybe he's been a bit distant lately, but that's normal when you're working seven days a week. Even when we find the time to be together, it's hard to find the head space.

'But it's not supposed to be easy, right?' he continues. 'Nobody I know says it is. Look at my parents.'

Ben's parents divorced when he was twelve... No wonder he brought me here tonight. He knows I won't make a scene over the amuse-bouche.

'It took Mum nearly six years to qualify, and Dad says the reason they divorced was because they couldn't find the time to devote to their marriage.'

Wait. What's he talking about? Not breaking up. He's talking about his job.

'But you're so close!' I say. 'As soon as this case is finished you've said yourself that they'll look at moving you up. You're going to get everything you've been working for, you'll see, it's all worth it in the end.'

Relief is making me babble. I don't point out that we're not supposed to be talking about our jobs. It's safer than talking about our relationship.

'I know,' he says. 'I'm doing awesome on this case.'

I should have known he wasn't looking for sympathy. Ben doesn't have crises of confidence. That's one of the things that makes him so appealing. 'So the next time we come here may be to celebrate your promotion.'

He smiles as the waiter arrives to take our order, and the conversation is forgotten. But my feelings aren't.

That fear I felt when I misunderstood Ben was suffocating. Just the idea that we could break up makes me panicky. My last 'important' relationship (with Skate) was four years ago. Even now, all I have to do is recall the conversation that ended it and the feelings flood back. They may not be as instantly fatal as they were, but they still pack a hell of a punch. I don't want to go through that again.

So instead, I do what I do best. I play the perfect girlfriend. I am cool, I am fun, I am relaxed. I am the Carol he loves.

Fast forward twenty-four hours and all the happy serenity I'd manufactured is a fading memory. In front of me (allegedly) stands Harriet's date, Sebastian.

His photos on the website are very clear. They are also very clearly not Sebastian.

I was surprised when this squat, thinning-haired man called Harriet's name as I arrived. I thought it must be a distant friend of hers, mistaking me for her, as had happened before. Then I remembered she'd sent him a photo.

This man with the fleshy lips claims to be Sebastian.

'You didn't have any trouble finding it?' He tips his head in a concerned manner, not unlike a spaniel hearing a whistle.

'Not at all. I've been to South Bank quite a lot. Shall we sit?' As soon as I get home I'm going to use that Google image search to find out whose identity he copied and pasted into his own profile. Until then, I may as well at least try to enjoy the next hour.

That turns out to be easy. Within minutes we're engrossed in a discussion of films, books, favourite London haunts, our conversation galloping along like we're old friends. What a nice surprise this is, after my date with Squeaky Pete, who approached each word as if weighing up the possibility that I'd use it against him in court. And Sebastian hasn't stopped grinning since we sat down. He may have fudged his photos, but he seems to be a nice man, and a true free spirit, perfectly at ease with the world and his place in it.

'You're really interesting,' I tell him after he describes the two years he spent training as a yacht master so he could sail boats to Asia and South America. That was after he bounced around the world's beach resorts teaching diving. 'And what do you do now when you're not delivering yachts for millionaires?'

He grins. 'Want me to show you?'

If he were a puppy he'd wriggle and have a little accident under his chair.

He's holding his inked arm out for my inspection.

'Oh, you're a tattoo artist?' I'm not much for tattoos, I must say. What seems a good idea on a taut body at 20 can look like a landslide at 60.

His good-natured chuckle bubbles forth again. 'I wish I could do this. But no, I make these.'

'You braid bracelets?'

'Not just bracelets. Necklaces, too. There's a very high margin on them. They cost less than a pound and they sell for three. That's a two hundred per cent mark-up. Companies would kill for that.'

'And you sell them? In a shop near here?'

'No, there'd be too much overhead. I busk.'

I think this means he tacks his wares to a piece of cardboard to make it easier to run from the police. 'Oh…'

'Not just on the South Bank, though. I also do the festivals in summer. I have a camper van. Would you like another glass of wine?'

'Sure, but please, let me get this round. Be right back.' My wine alone cost him three bracelets.

Sebastian is interesting, though I'm not sure he'll be Harriet's type. She tends to go for rugged outdoorsy guys. Sebastian looks like he spends most of his free time playing video games in his bedroom.

But you never know where true love will blossom, so maybe I shouldn't automatically dismiss him. He is very nice, and interesting, and he must support himself or he wouldn't be here in London. Unless he lives on a vacant lot in his camper.

'So, you work the festivals in summer, and busk here,' I say when I return with our wine. 'What else?'

'I do some design work for magazines sometimes, but it's just the odd job really, nothing steady. I wouldn't want to do it full time.'

'Oh. Why not?'

'Because I like what I do. So what about you? Why are you on a dating website?' Again, he has the look of a spaniel about him.

'Well, I'm single...' His head is still cocked, so I give him the sanitised version of Harriet's dating history. It makes me uncomfortable to lie so obviously like this, but it is for a good cause. 'So why are you on the website?' I ask him.

'I guess I've been thinking lately that I'd like to settle down. I really like being in a relationship, though I've been happy on my own, too. It's time for me to consider my priorities in life. I've taken stock of what's important to me, and I want to find a woman to share my life with. Are you looking to settle down?'

'Yes, with the right person.'

Am I imagining that this conversation just took a serious turn?

'Do you want children?' He's no longer smiling.

Indeed, quite serious for a first date. 'Um, I'm not sure.'

'Can you have them?'

I've known this man for less than half a bottle of wine. Surely that's the kind of topic you ease into. 'I, erm, yes, in fact, I can.'

'How do you know that when you haven't had any?'

Am I out with Jeremy Paxman? 'Well, because I'm young and healthy and there's no reason to think I can't.'

'But you haven't.'

'But I can.'

'But you haven't.'

'Is this a problem?'

'Well, it's just that I know I want kids, and I don't want to get a couple of years into a relationship before having this discussion and have wasted those years.'

'Well, I'm sure it wouldn't take a couple of years to come up… but a couple of dates, maybe?'

I laugh but he's now decidedly less spaniel-like. More pit bull. With a bone.

'I have to be honest,' he says, like he's been sugar-coating his conversation till now. 'It bothers me that you've been out of uni all this time but haven't yet had children.'

He isn't even from the twenty-first century. 'All this time? I'm twenty-six. It's not exactly too late.'

'Everybody says that.'

'Doesn't your profile say that you don't want to date a woman with children?'

'No, that's right. I don't want to raise someone else's.'

And where, exactly, would he do this? In his camper van? He's seriously pissing me off.

'Then it sounds like you're asking the impossible. You want me to have had children to prove, what? My working womb? But you wouldn't have gone out with me if I'd had them. You do realise that is a double standard, right?'

He shrugs, his grin back. 'Yeah, I guess it is.'

'Also, as we're on the topic of standards, I have to say you look a bit different from your photos.'

He looks surprised.

'I mean, you look nothing like your photos.'

'Well, they were taken a few years ago. They do still look like me, though.'

'Yes, if you squint and look at them in the dark.'

'Listen, I'm going to take off,' he says. 'It was nice talking to you anyway. You seem like a nice woman.'

I *am* a nice woman, I want to shout (while strangling him with his own necklace). He's not looking for a date. All that talk about being easy-going, letting life unfold, is bollocks. He's wombist, that's what he is. He's just looking for functioning ovaries. The irony is, after mentally belittling his career choices, Harriet and I have been judged a poor prospect by a man who sells jewellery on the pavement.

She'll be disappointed not to go out with Sebastian, or whichever boy band lead singer his photo turns out to be. But at least she won't have her reproductive system called into question.

MICHELE GORMAN

CHAPTER 15

It's not even 8 a.m. and I feel like I'm buried under a pile of bricks. I shift my phone to the other ear and reach for my cooling coffee. Ryan taps his wrist, where his watch would be if he didn't use his phone to tell time.

'Yes, Mum, I just told you I would. I've got to go to my meeting now. Tell Gran I said bye, okay?'

I should have known when she snatched the phone from Gran's hand that it was going to be one of those days.

'So I can tell Zoe you'll find something for her?' Mum sounds impatient to end the call. As if she's the one with a colleague making threatening gestures over her head.

'I didn't say I'd find something for her. I don't own the bank, you know. I said I'd talk to HR to see if there are any suitable positions. Now, I've really got to–'

'Well, then, call her and tell her, will you? She must find work soon. This is really bothering her. You know how sensitive she is.'

'Well, it probably wouldn't bother her so much if you hadn't called her a scrounger for living off her parents' money,' I say, immediately regretting it. Now she'll keep me on the phone.

'Carol! You know I'm only concerned for Zoe's well-being. It isn't good for her self-esteem to coast along like this. She's in London now and she should be getting on with her life. Promise me you'll call her. And don't wait until you see her after work. Promise?'

'I promise. I'll call after my meeting. She's still sleeping now anyway. I've got to go, Mum. I'll talk to you later.'

She hangs up without saying goodbye, let alone thanks for sorting out Zoe's life along with everyone else's.

The conference room is full and the traders are more unruly than usual. This sometimes happens when there's uncertainty in the market, and last night the government announced that it was cutting subsidies for onshore wind and solar energy. That means most of my day will be spent on the phone with panicky clients, trying to convince them not to sell their investments.

Derrick raps the table to get everyone's attention. 'Ryan, what's the likely impact of the government's subsidy changes?'

I watch Ryan's eyes widen in fear and even though he is repugnant, I feel a tiny bit of pity mixed with a wave of relief. It could just as easily have been me that Derrick picked on. There's no right answer in a situation like this, because no matter what an analyst says, there are twenty traders in the room waiting to tell them why he doesn't know what he's talking about.

PERFECT GIRL

I can see the traders mentally sharpening their knives as Ryan stutters through a lacklustre answer. Then the room explodes with a cacophony of expletives. Ryan closes his eyes as they batter him.

Derrick lets the verbal brawl carry on for the first half of the meeting. Everyone is shouting to make their point, which means nobody is listening. Then, when he thinks the traders have had enough fun, he calls for their attention again. 'All right. Analysts, the official line is that subsidies aren't being withheld. They're shifting from onshore wind and solar to offshore, therefore our overall portfolios aren't affected. The important thing is to keep the client's money in the funds. I want to know if there'll be an impact on each of your individual companies. By nine o'clock. Send the analysis with headline bullet points to me and your traders. Is that clear?'

It's perfectly clear. I've got a little over an hour to analyse nearly thirty companies, and Joe will be making multimillion pound investment decisions based on my work. So no pressure.

We analysts practically run back to our desks, knowing that every second will count. When Derrick says 9 a.m. he doesn't mean 9.01.

There's not a sound on our side of the floor except for fingers furiously tapping on keyboards. I work through my companies in just under an hour (twenty-three minutes to spare!). Then, to double-check I haven't missed anything, I scan my companies' share price data just as London Stock Exchange trading gets underway.

What the...?! The share price for Green Energy Ltd is down 16% from its closing price last night. The morning's coffee curdles in my tummy. That can't be right. Green Energy is one of the most solid and profitable companies I cover. Their operations are all offshore and there was nothing on the horizon to spook investors. There must be something wrong with the pricing stream. I refresh the page.

Still down 16%.

Then there's something wrong with my computer.

'Ryan? Can you check Green Energy Ltd's price for me?'

'No, I'm working,' he says.

'Come on, it'll take you a second.'

'I don't have time!' His voice hits such a funny octave that he may actually be a stroke risk.

I log on to the London Stock Exchange's website, knowing I have only minutes before Joe sees the price collapse. And I'd better have a good explanation when he does.

Holding my breath I type in the company's ticker… and see a big red –18%.

This is a disaster. My hands shake as I dial the company's head of Investor Relations.

'Sharzad, it's Carol Colbert. I'm watching the share price. What's going on?'

'Carol, hi. We're completely at a loss here. We didn't issue any news yesterday or after the close of trading.'

'Okay, can you please let me know as soon as you figure out what's happening?'

'Of course. We'll put out a statement as soon as we can–'

'But can you–'

'Also call you. Of course. Talk to you soon.'

'Thanks, Sharzad, and I hope it's… well, I hope

there's a simple explanation.'

'Me, too.'

Green Energy Ltd was the first company Derrick gave me to cover, so I've known Sharzad for nearly my entire banking career. And I probably know the company as well as she does. This just doesn't make any sense. A company's share price only falls like this when all its investors turn away from it at once. Barring its CEO being arrested or other major malfeasance, share prices do not move this wildly.

'Colbert, get over here!' shouts Joe. 'What the fuck, Colbert. What's happening?'

It's not hard to rile Joe, but I've learned over the years that his anger doesn't rise in direct proportion to his shouting. So at least when he's screaming like this I know he's not as angry as he could be. Unfortunately, he's also not as angry as he might become when he finds out I don't know what's going on.

'I've just called Sharzad, Joe. They don't know what's happened but she should call me soon.'

'She *should* call you *soon*? Do you think you work at McDonald's or something? *Those fries should be ready soon, sir?* What am I supposed to do in the meantime, sit around while the share price slides further? Is it going to slide further? What the fuck is going on, Carol?'

'I… I don't know, Joe. I'm sorry. There's nothing in the market that should cause this to happen. Sharzad confirmed that.'

'Fucking-c***ing-son-of-a-bitch!' shouts the trader at the desk opposite Joe. 'Ryan!'

As Joe and I watch, Ryan scuttles towards his trader, Kevin. For the second time in a few hours I feel sorry for him. Kevin doesn't have the cheery disposition that

Joe does.

'Octagon Energy is down nineteen per cent,' says Kevin. 'Why?'

'I've got one down twenty– fuck, twenty-one per cent,' Joe says.

I can hear the panic in his voice.

'What's happening, Ryan?' Kevin asks again.

Ryan has gone the colour of this morning's *Financial Times*. 'I'm not... I haven't... I don't know but I'll find out right away.' He runs back to his desk to phone the company.

As we watch the screens, shouts go up around us. It's a blood bath in the green energy sector and nobody knows why.

Traders are skittish animals, especially when they're not running with the rest of the herd. Within minutes rumours are flying. Russia has finally made good its threat and shut off its gas. North Sea oil has run out. But anything like that would be reported in the press. This is like the investors have all phoned each other and together decided that these companies are no longer worth investing in.

'Who's selling these shares?' Joe asks.

I can find that out through our systems. I push Joe away from his keyboard and start typing. It's clear that whoever is selling has jumped on these companies like a pack of hyenas on a limping gazelle. They'll reduce it to bare bones by lunchtime.

To my horror, my eyes begin to sting with tears at the thought of Green Energy Ltd going under. I pinch myself hard on the arm. If I cry in front of these guys, I may as well join that limping gazelle, because I'll be as good as dead.

It's just that I love that company – its ethics and ethos, and the enthusiasm with which its scientists and engineers approach our future. I've often thought that if I left banking I'd try to convince them to hire me–

I don't believe what I'm seeing.

Programmed trading is accounting for the huge declines.

Programs like Green T.

Our bank has sold large positions in Green Energy Ltd… and each of the other struggling companies. In other words, by dumping such big blocks of shares into the market, we're forcing their price lower…

Well, not all of us.

Our bank is a beast with many arms, and it's normal for one department to have no idea what another department is doing. It wasn't any of our traders dumping the stocks. They're still holding their investments, and watching their values plummet as their colleagues sell off.

All eyes on the floor are boring into me.

'That system you built is selling the shit out of those stocks,' Joe says. 'This is your fault, Carol. You wanted to play God with Green T. Well, you got your wish because nobody understands what the fuck it's doing. Why didn't anyone give us a heads-up about the trading, Carol, so we could get out of our positions in time? Who's side are you on?'

'I don't understand it,' I say. 'The government's subsidy shift shouldn't cause such a big sell-off. Joe, these companies are fundamentally sound. There's no good reason to sell.'

'Colbert, my portfolios have just lost nearly a million pounds. Fuck that, I'm selling.'

'You're just contributing to the panic!' I say.

'I'm getting out before I lose the whole position,' he says.

I can't do anything but watch as the traders sell their investments, effectively nailing the lid shut on the companies' coffins. This is the worst day of my career. And it looks like Green T is to blame.

I've got to find out what's going on. I know my system. It isn't designed to react so dramatically.

I run to Derrick's office.

'Not now, Colbert, I'm busy,' he says when he sees me.

'It's important, Derrick. I think there's a problem with Green T. I want to run some tests to make sure it's running properly.'

'You don't have time.'

'Derrick, have you been watching what's going on out there? It's causing a panic. The traders have lost significant positions because Green T triggered a sell-off.'

Derrick smiles. 'Well, maybe now they'll realise that they can't beat the system. Those guys are living in a dream world if they think they're better at predicting the markets than Green T. I've been telling them that all along. It looks like now they know I was right. Aw, Colbert,' he says, noticing my expression. 'Don't be upset. Your system is doing exactly what you designed it to do.'

'But it's not! It's overreacting to minor market news and a bunch of companies may go out of business as a result.'

He shrugs. 'It hasn't overreacted. It has predicted a share price decline and sold off in time. That's brilliant.

I'm just sorry the guys out there weren't smart enough to start using it. If they had, they wouldn't be panicking now.'

'But what about the companies?'

'You know that's how markets work. Companies are commodities. Now get out and leave me alone. You've got work to do.'

Within fifteen minutes it's all over. The traders have all dumped their shares in the stricken companies. They'll know this afternoon when the daily profit and loss position reports are run just how big a loss they've taken.

But it's not over for the companies, is it?

Derrick is right. When we buy and sell those shares, they're just numbers on a screen. It's easy to forget that behind every stock is a company made up of people just like us who go to work every day and do the best they can. If Green Energy's share price gets too low, then the investment community will lose confidence in it and it won't be able to get loans. Without loans, it can't develop the offshore wind farms to fulfil the contracts to its customers, and won't get the revenue it needs to pay its employees. That will put nearly a hundred people out of work.

People, not numbers.

My BlackBerry rings just as I'm returning to my desk.

'What is it, Mum?'

'Zoe says she hasn't heard from you. Have you talked to your company?'

'Mum, I've been busy!'

'Don't take that tone with me. I'm only asking because you promised you would call her. She's waiting.'

'I need to talk to HR first to see if there are even any positions open.'

'And you'll do that now?'

I sigh. She won't give up. 'Yes, I'll call Zoe within the hour.'

'Thank you.'

She ends the call before I can hang up on her.

'Ryan, I'll be back in a few minutes in case anyone needs me.'

'I don't give a shit, Colbert.'

The HR department is only one floor below, but I have to take the lift because they lock the stairwell doors from the inside. I found this out early in my career when I went to visit Zack in IT and ended up having to trigger the emergency exit alarm eighteen floors below. Security was thrilled with me that day.

HR's door is kept locked, allegedly because of the confidential employee files inside but it's also handy for keeping the odd irate banker from rampaging.

Within a few minutes the young woman who invites me inside has a list of available entry-level positions.

'There are several cashier positions,' she says, running her finger down her screen. 'Does your friend have any experience that might be relevant?'

'Erm, probably not,' I say, thinking about Zoe's inability to divide a restaurant bill three ways. 'But she's very bright and willing to learn. She's just graduated with a First.'

The young woman stares at me. 'And she wants to be a cashier?'

'Well, she's looking for work and understands that she'll have to work her way up from any entry-level position. She took her degree in English Literature.'

'Ah, I see.'

The country's Job Centres are full of graduates like Zoe.

'Exactly. So maybe there's something a bit more, I don't know, creative? Maybe something in marketing?'

She doesn't look too sure. 'Why don't I print off all the entry-level positions and your friend can apply for whatever she feels would suit her?'

'Thanks,' I say. At least I'll have something to give Zoe after work. Then I'll just need to write her CV and covering letter.

I need a cigarette.

There are a few familiar faces by the bins but luckily none are traders. I'm always self-conscious about being away from my desk in the daytime. Even going to lunch gives me pangs.

Grinding the butt into the pavement, I ring Zoe. 'Hi, honey, it's me. I didn't wake you, did I?'

'No, no, I've been writing. How are you?'

'It's been a tough morning, actually. Some of the companies we invest in aren't doing well. It caused a bit of a panic.'

'Oh, I'm sorry! Are you okay? Is there anything I can do?'

I smile at the idea. 'No, it's fine now. Mum reminded me to check with HR about possible jobs. I've got a list that we can go through tonight.'

'Oh, thank you, Carol! I've been thinking about the best way to use my skills and thought that maybe I could write for the bank? Are there any jobs like that?'

'You mean like a poet in residence?'

'Yes, exactly,' she says. 'Or maybe not a poet,

because banks may not need poets. But some kind of writing job.'

'You may have to adjust your expectations, Zoe. I think most of the positions are for cashiers.'

'Oh.'

'But we'll look together tonight. Maybe there's something more creative. I'd better get back to the office. I'll see you tonight, okay?'

'Okay, thanks Carol. I'll make dinner for us.'

'Thanks, honey.'

'Can I take some money from the kitchen drawer?'

I keep the cleaner's money there. 'Of course. See you tonight.'

Back upstairs the traders have gone back to their normal abusive ways. It's in their nature to pick themselves back up and move forward quickly. I wish I could say the same about myself. I can't stop thinking about Green T. I know there's something wrong with it.

Last month I'd assumed that the intern, Stephan, was doing something wrong when he ran it, or that the dummy program was corrupted somehow. But what if it isn't the dummy system that's wrong?

It shouldn't take more than five or six hours to test it. I can get a clean copy of the program from Zack and rerun it. If it matches the live results, then… well, at least I'll know who's to blame for putting those companies out of business.

Me.

My BlackBerry rings just after lunch but I haven't got time for Marley right now. I send it to voicemail. It rings again. And again and again until finally I answer it.

'What is it, Marley?'

I keep typing in data. I should be fine as long as Marley doesn't recite any numbers in my ear.

'Hello to you too.'

'I'm very busy right now. A bunch of our companies are in trouble. Can't we talk tonight?'

'Oh, I'm sorry. It's just that I have to have your opinion now. It can't wait because I've found the perfect dress designer, but he only has one-offs. So if we don't decide on one now someone else might buy it, and they are so gorgeous you can't even imagine. Ready? Here's the web address.'

'Hold on, I'm in the middle of something else. I'm not on the internet. What kind of designer only makes one copy of a dress?'

She squeals with excitement. 'He's a Central St Martin's fashion graduate! Ready? Here's the–'

'Wait a minute! Okay, go ahead.'

She gives me the address and within a few seconds a page full of floaty romantic dresses fills my screen. I check quickly over my shoulder to make sure nobody sees it. I once made the mistake of looking on eBay within sight of Derrick and a few of the traders. The next day I found rotten banana mooshed into all the shoes under my desk, with a note that read *You might find some new shoes on ebay.*

'Hmm, they are very pretty.'

'So, I'm thinking of the first one, and the fourth and the fifth. What do you think?'

I feel a cloud pass over me. I don't have to turn around to know Derrick is behind me. I can smell his breath. 'I have to call you back,' I tell Marley, ending the call.

'Online shopping again, are we, Colbert? And there I was thinking that I pay you to work.'

'I am working, Derrick. I was just helping my sister–' But I stop. Struggling is pointless. 'I am working.'

'Are you sure you're not shopping for tarty clothes? Do you like to wear tarty clothes, Colbert, hmm? Maybe a bit of PVC? Leather boots? I'd love to see you in leather boots, Colbert.'

'Me, too,' Ryan says, swivelling around in his chair to enjoy the spectacle.

'Shut up, Ryan,' says Derrick. 'You probably wear nappies and suck your thumb outside the office.'

Ryan's interjection seems to have put Derrick off his train of thought. He ambles back to his office just as my BlackBerry rings again.

'So which one do you like best?' Marley asks, as if I haven't just hung up on her.

More bricks pile up. Something's got to give.

CHAPTER 16

It says something about my life when I find it relaxing to watch Zoe interpretive dance around my flat to a soundtrack of what might be whale noises. But compared to my day, it's as peaceful as an evening at the symphony. Not even Marley's phone call dislodged my equanimity. Not even the fact that Ben hasn't called in two days.

Beautiful cooking smells are wafting through the living room. I have a glass of wine and Zoe is trying to explain her preference for assonance over alliteration in poetry while lurching and jerking across the floor. Her French-accented words wash over me. She may as well be reciting the shipping forecast for all I understand.

'I've also been thinking about jobs I'd like to do for your bank,' she says, waving her arms over her head in some kind of fly-swatting movement.

I love that my whole family calls it my bank, as if I sit in the penthouse boardroom on my throne made of fifty-pound notes directing minions all day.

'Thank you again for getting the list for me. I think maybe the bank is not very used to English Literature graduates, and may not have very many jobs for people like me. But I think I can bring creativity to any work I do. Even as a cashier. So I will apply.'

She performs a passable arabesque in front of the TV.

'They'll be lucky to have you, Zoe. As soon as we've got your CV together, I'll submit it for you. And if it helps, most people have to take the job they can get when they first graduate. Look at me.'

'But I thought you loved your job?'

'I do love the work, but the job isn't ideal. My dream was to work for one of the companies I analyse.'

I feel a pang thinking about Green Energy Ltd. They probably won't be hiring me any time soon.

My BlackBerry rings just as Zoe begins a yogic sun salutation with her arse in the air.

So much for my peaceful evening. 'Hi, Mum.'

The whales are working up to a climax in the background.

'Darling. I have the most wonderful news. It turns out that Dad and I can go away next month after all!'

'I thought Dad had a show that couldn't be moved.'

'They cancelled it!'

'Well, that's not good news, is it? I mean, did Dad want to do the show?'

'Oh, he doesn't mind. And now we can go away like we wanted to.'

Mum has always been lax with her pronouns. Whenever she says we, she means I. 'So we were thinking something at the seaside,' she continues. 'Not that the Cotswolds cottage wasn't lovely last time, but I do think that damp patch in the bedroom was the reason for your father's bronchitis.'

She won't forgive me for Dad's mould-induced lung ailment. Like I had any way to see that from the photos when I booked the cottage for them. 'Where by the seaside are you thinking of booking?'

'I thought maybe something in Cornwall. What was that website you used last year?'

Her question startles me. Is she actually thinking of looking herself? Give a mother a fish and she eats for a week. Give her a fishing pole and she'll book her own bloody holiday.

'It was called English Country Cottages. I think it's all one word with .co.uk at the end.'

'Perfect. Can you look now?'

'Mum, I really don't have time. I've got to work on Zoe's CV with her.'

'But you do research for your job. You can find the perfect place in no time. It would take me ages to find what we're looking for. You know how important these holidays are for your father's health. He works so hard. He needs the break.' She sighs with all the feeling she can muster. 'But if you're too busy to help your parents, then I suppose we'll manage.'

'Fine. The website is EnglishCountryCottages.co.uk. Just filter it for Cornwall, the week you want to go and the price range, and it'll bring up all your options.'

'Wait, wait. Slow down. E. N. G. L. I. S. H. Did you say county?'

'Country. Country Cottages.'

'C. O. U. N. T. R. Y. C. O. T. T. A. G. E. S. That's it?'

'.co.uk.'

'And where do I type this?'

'In the address bar at the top.'

'Where it says Search?'

'No, the address bar. At the top of the screen.'

'There's already something written there. H. T. T. P–'

'Type over it.'

'How do I do that?'

'Mum, you're hopeless! Just highlight it and type over it.'

'How do I highlight it? Carol, I'm sorry but I'm not a computer genius like you are. I don't understand.'

I knew she'd win. 'Fine. I'll do it later this week.'

'We really need to book something quickly, darling. You remember how hard it was to find availability last time.'

I remember that every option I presented to Mum lacked something crucial, and previously undisclosed, in her list of requirements. 'Well, I haven't got time tonight. I'm supposed to go out.'

'Fine, go out and have fun. It's only your father's health.'

'I'll talk to you later. I've got to go. Zoe needs me.'

I hang up before she can pile on any more guilt.

'Was that Madame Colbert?' Zoe asks.

I nod. 'She wants me to book their holiday in Cornwall. But I need to help you with your CV.'

'Did you say you were going out tonight?'

'My friend, Zack from work, has his birthday drinks tonight. But we should get your application in to HR as soon as possible. It can take a while to get an interview.'

'We'll prepare my CV tomorrow after your work, ma

chérie, so you should go out tonight.'

'I can't tomorrow night. I– I've got a work thing in the evening.'

I can't tell her that I'm meeting Harriet's next date tomorrow. He's a speech policy writer for the government and we've been messaging for the past two days. There must not be very many policies for him to spin at the moment because no sooner do I send a message, than he responds. He's clearly very keen to meet Harriet.

His enthusiasm makes him suspect (too good to be true) but I think he's worth a closer look. After the last few dates I thought it best to take over the whole process, which is why I've been the one messaging. That way I can do a little more testing before wasting an hour in a pub with another crazy.

Zoe stomps across the floor and throws herself on the sofa. 'Carol, you must go to your friend's party. Madame Colbert's holiday and my CV can wait. Go, Carol, I will insist on this.'

'But dinner isn't even ready. Can't I eat first?'

She considers my question. 'You may eat, because my cooking is delicious and you should have a full stomach before you drink. And then you must go. First, I'll get you more wine.'

She bounces back to the kitchen to stir her pots, waving her wooden spoon as if to cast a spell on the refrigerator.

The pub is crowded but I spot Zack right away, surrounded by around a dozen friends at a long table. 'Carol, you made it!' he shouts above the pop music pounding from the speakers above his head.

He's squashed in on the far side of the table, making it awkward to properly greet him. I lean over his friends anyway to kiss his cheek. 'Happy birthday!'

The man next to Zack stands up. 'I'm just going to the bar, so you can sit here. Can I get you a drink? It's my round anyway. Sit, please, I insist.'

When Zack makes introductions it takes me a moment to adjust my expectations from the acid-washed-jeans-and-thick-rimmed-glasses-wearing computer boffins I'd imagined, to normal people who probably don't all live in their mothers' spare rooms.

In fact, I have no evidence that Zack's friends even know their way around a keyboard. So I shouldn't judge him by his day job. Besides, he doesn't look like an IT nut either. He looks quite presentable. I'm used to seeing him in a suit, which always seems a little out of place on such a laid-back man. He's clearly much more at home in his jeans, with the sleeves rolled up on a faded stripy green and white collared shirt. He's always got a bit of five o'clock shadow by lunchtime, on account of his dark hair, and now he's quite beardy. He probably goes Yeti after a few days away from the razor.

Whenever I've tried to get Ben to loosen up on his dress sense, he says he's uncomfortable without a jacket. It's become a bit of a trademark look for him, even when he looks like a complete prat. Last summer he turned up to Harriet's BBQ wearing shorts and a blazer, like an overgrown child at prep school.

'Have you eaten?' Zack asks. 'They may still be serving food.'

'No, that's okay. Zoe cooked for us. I'm stuffed.'

'I'm glad Zoe is pulling her weight.'

'She's a great cook.'

'Maybe so, but has she found a job yet?'

'We're working on that.'

'We? Have you taken her on as your pet project as well? You're amazing, Carol. All you do is work and make everybody else's lives easier. ' Hand in hair. 'When do you get to do what you want?'

I laugh, knowing he doesn't mean that I'm amazing in the positive, admiring sense. 'But I do what I want all the time. I'm here now, aren't I?' I don't mention that Zoe had to threaten me first. 'And we've got–' I check my watch. 'Nearly nine hours before I've got to be back in the office.'

Green T barges into my consciousness at the mention of work. I haven't figured out what's going on with it, but I do know that it's using its power for good as well as evil. Yesterday two more of the companies we cover saw dramatic movements in their share prices. Only this time their values skyrocketed, adding millions to their worth. That means a lot of additional research money and some very happy companies, but I still don't know what the hell is going on.

Green T has become the teenager I can no longer control.

Zack and his friends soon pull my thoughts away from the office, though, when I find myself swept up in a debate about which film sequels were as good as their originals. Since none of them has seen *Three Colours: Red*, and I don't like action thrillers, my contribution to the discussion is limited. 'What about the second *Star Wars* film?' I say, mostly because it's the only film I can think of with any fight scenes. I'm playing the odds.

'Yes!' Zack says. 'Definitely better than the first,

where Luke was a whingey little pussy.'

His friends nod appreciatively. I may not know my *Die Hard* from my *Terminator*, but I'm winning kudos around the table.

Before I know it the barman calls last orders, the lights come up and we're hurried towards the door.

'I guess that's it, then,' Zack says to me. 'I'm not tired, though, are you?'

It seems cruel for the poor man to go to bed before his birthday is officially over. 'Not really. It's only eleven. Did you want to go on somewhere else?'

'Do you want to?'

I nod, just catching a yawn as it begins to pry my jaw open.

'Guys, we're going on,' he tells his friends. 'Want to come?'

There's a chorus of nahs and no thanks, making me feel a bit bad for Zack. These are his best mates, and it is his birthday, after all. 'Party poopers,' I say. 'We don't need them to have a good time. Lead the way.'

Just around the corner from the pub is another that's still serving, and it's not too crowded. 'What would you like?' Zack asks as we get to the bar.

'You can't buy drinks on your birthday. What'll you have?'

'A pint of Seafarer's, please. Thank you.'

We find a small round table in the corner with a comfy banquet on one side. A thick red candle has dripped wax all over the scarred table top. It's impossible not to pick at it as Zack throws himself down beside me on the well-worn faux-leather bench. We sit together in comfortable silence staring out at the rest of the bar.

'Do you realise we've never been out together before?' he asks, rolling his head sideways to look at me. His grinning face glows in the flickering candle flame. 'Outside of work hours or after-work drinks with others, I mean. Isn't that weird, in four years?'

'Well, I don't go out all that much outside of work, so I guess it's not that weird.'

'And you spend most of your free time with Ben now.'

I keep looking straight ahead. 'Actually, we don't see each other that much, for two people who are supposed to be in love.'

Where did that come from? I never complain about Ben in public.

'And you're okay with not seeing much of your boyfriend?'

Finally, I have to look at him. 'We do see each other when we have time.'

'Really. So I guess you saw each other last night?'

'No, he had to work late.'

'And the night before?'

'It was his fantasy football night.'

'And the night before that?'

'You don't have to do this, Zack. I'm aware that we're not seeing each other as much as we should.'

'It's not a matter of what you should or shouldn't do. What do you want to do?'

'What difference does it make what I want? It's not that simple.'

'Of course it is, Carol! It's exactly that simple. Why should you bend over for everyone else and not get what you want? That's crazy.'

'Are we arguing? On your birthday?'

'You deserve to be appreciated, that's all. It pisses me off to see everyone taking advantage of you. And before you object, and try to defend Ben, he's the worst. He takes you for granted and you know it. When you tell me everything you do for him, and it's so clear he doesn't give a shit, it makes me sick to watch you.'

That's the truth, isn't it? I can dress it up all I like, or keep making excuses, but the fact is, Ben really doesn't give much of a shit sometimes.

'I'm so tired, Zack. I don't know what else to do. I feel like I'm trying so hard all the time but it's never enough.'

'Why do you have to try so hard?'

I don't know how to answer his question. That's like asking a fish why he swims or a bird why she flies. This is who I am. If I'm not the one who tries hard, then what am I?

'It's what everyone expects.'

'So?' He shrugs. 'Just because something is expected doesn't mean you have to do it. Why don't you try doing what you want for a change? Come on, try it now. If you didn't have to worry about anyone but yourself, what would you want to do at this very second?'

Zack's eyes are full of kindness as he stares into mine.

'At this very second? I'd like to forget that I have to plan my sister's wedding, or my parent's holiday or Zoe's career, or meet another of Harriet's dates tomorrow night. I don't want to think about the fact that Ben hasn't been in touch since the weekend. In fact, right now, this second, I want to forget that Ben exists.'

'Me too,' he murmurs, still staring into my eyes. 'Do you think we could do that?'

We've never been close to the edge like this before. But that doesn't mean the feeling is unwelcome.

I'm enveloped by his warmth. It feels like burrowing under a fluffy duvet after a day out walking. I know the sensation will be fleeting, which only makes me want to hold on tighter.

He leans in, not taking his eyes off me. Fearful of breaking this spell, I don't move. Instead, I close my eyes and savour the feel of his warm lips on mine.

'I've wanted to do that for a while,' he whispers.

'That's funny, because I've never thought about doing it until this second.'

'Are you thinking about it now?'

'I can't really think about anything else.'

This time it's me who leans in. I want to feel his mouth press against mine again.

'I like you so much,' he murmurs.

He looks embarrassed when I end our kiss, a bit like a fart has just slipped out. Should I pretend not to notice his declaration? That's probably the polite thing to do.

But his dark eyes seek mine over the candle's flame. He's not squeamish about his verbal flatulence. 'I like you, Carol. You must have known that already.'

Did I? Not really. We're friends. That's all. We are friends.

What am I doing, kissing my friend?! This isn't 90210. We're adults. We work together. More importantly, it's less than a week after my anniversary with Ben. That's my boyfriend, Ben, by the way, the man I'm supposed to move in with as soon as Zoe leaves. You know; the one I'm building my future with? This is wrong.

'I should probably go,' I say. 'I'll have to be in the office for seven tomorrow. Not like some people who get to stroll in after a leisurely breakfast!'

If he'll joke back with me, then everything will be fine. That's the relationship we've always had. Not this.

Come on, Zack, please joke back with me. Then I'll know everything is back to normal. Please.

He seems to consider his next words carefully while I hold my breath.

'Come on, I'll walk you to the Tube,' he finally says. 'Ben'll kill me if you get mugged on a night out with me.'

There's no censure or awkwardness as he grabs his coat.

'Thanks for coming out tonight. You're a good pal. I like the idea that you'll probably have a hangover tomorrow, too. Misery loves company.' He flashes his usual grin.

It's like the kiss never happened.

Except that it did happen.

And I liked it.

CHAPTER 17

How bloody typical. When Ben finally does deign to see me again, he shows up at the least convenient time imaginable. And I'm supposed to be grateful.

Of course, he doesn't know it's the least convenient time imaginable, and I can't very well tell him that. What would I say? That I appreciate my boyfriend wanting to see me after work, but I've got another date? Can you imagine the look on his face?

'I wanted to surprise you,' he says when we've kissed hello in the lobby of my building. People are streaming around us, toting gym bags and talking into their mobiles. Everyone's in a rush. 'I thought we could get a drink. I've got so much to tell you!'

That would be delightful, if I wasn't due to meet Harriet's date, Nicholas, in thirty minutes. I can't stand him up. He'll think Harriet is terribly rude, and he sounds like he might just be a good one. I can't even text him because I'm not really Harriet. I've got to think fast.

I am curious, though, about Ben's news. Is it related to us?

'Should we go?' Ben asks, shifting from foot to foot.

I can't go with him. I have to make an excuse. But what? Late meeting? No, I told him I was finished for the day when he called upstairs from reception. Plans with Harriet or Marley? That would only make him sniffy. Think, think, think.

I've got it! Shame floods through me at the very thought of what I'm about to do.

Ben has one fear in life, and I'm about to exploit it. 'I'd love to, Ben, but I'm not feeling well.'

'What's wrong with you?'

'I feel really weak. In fact, maybe I should sit down.'

He takes my arm to lead me to one of the black leather sofas that line reception, just as Zack emerges from the lift.

'Hey, Carol!' He hurries over with a curious look on his face. 'Carol? Are you okay?'

This is just what I need now.

'I'm fine, Zack, thanks.'

'I thought you said you didn't feel well?' Ben asks, eying Zack.

'I don't feel well. I just mean… may I sit down, please?' Ben is clasping my arm quite tightly.

'How can I help?' Zack wants to know. 'Do you want some water or something? Do you feel faint? Is it your tummy?'

As his hand reaches for my shoulder I see Ben stiffen.

I've worked with Zack for four years. Four years, and he's never met so much as a casual date. Now, less than twenty-four hours after we kiss, he meets Ben.

Have I offended the cosmos somehow?

I've got to get away from both of them if I'm going to be on time for Nicholas.

'I said I'm fine, Zack! Ben, my boyfriend, Ben, is taking care of me. You're really not needed here.'

I have to ignore the expression on Zack's face or I'll crumble. And I can't do that or Ben will become even more suspicious than he is already.

'Really, I'll be fine,' I say more gently. 'I'm sure it's just a twenty-four-hour bug or something.'

He stares at me for a second too long. 'Okay, fine. I hope you feel better.' He turns towards the door.

There's little chance of that. Now I really do feel terrible.

'Who was that guy?' Ben asks, as I knew he would.

'That's Zack. He does our IT support. I'm sure I've mentioned him. We started at the same time. We go to lunch together sometimes.'

'No, I'd have remembered. He seems awfully chummy for just your IT guy.'

'Well, yes, as I said, I've known him for years.'

'How well do you know him?'

'Are you jealous?'

'Are you surprised? He practically hugged you.'

I roll my eyes. 'He did not. He was just concerned, as any friend would be, because I don't feel well.'

'What's wrong with you anyway?'

'... I think I've caught what one of my colleagues has. He was vomiting in the loo earlier. Nasty thing. He barely made it to the toilet.'

Ben moves away from me so fast that even if I did have germs, they wouldn't catch him. 'You know I can't be ill right now,' he says from a safe distance.

'Not with the case going on.'

I stare at him. 'You're the one who turned up here, Ben. It's not like I've cornered you.'

'Aw, darling, you know I'd take care of you. It's just that I can't afford to get ill. Will you be okay?'

'I guess I'll have to be. I should just go home and rest.' He won't offer to come with me, for fear of contamination.

'I'll get you a taxi. I'm really sorry you don't feel well, darling. I'll call you later though, okay? Here, take twenty quid for the taxi. That's the least I can do.'

Yes, I think as he puts me in a cab and blows a kiss through the closed window. That is the least you can do.

The taxi driver is understandably confused when I ask him to drive around the corner and drop me back at my office five minutes later. I know Ben won't stick around any longer than he has to, lest the galloping lurgy catches him.

And as much as I wish Zack had stuck around so that I could apologise, I know that he too will have hurried away. *Ben, boyfriend, Ben*, I'd said. *You're not needed*. Who can blame him for being mad, when I was such a bitch?

I don't know what to think. When I came in to the office this morning I was sorely tempted to stop by his office. But that wouldn't be fair. I have a boyfriend and that fact won't go away, no matter what feelings Zack's kiss excited in me last night. I can't think about him. It isn't fair to him or to Ben…

But not thinking about him isn't fair to me either, is it?

I'm meeting Harriet's date, Nicholas, at a trendy bar near Liverpool Street and I already know that I like his sense of humour. I'm to look for a man wearing a green overcoat and carrying a copy of *The Spectator*. If he's wearing novelty glasses or a false moustache, though, the joke might be going too far.

It'll be up to me to find him anyway since there still aren't any photos on Harriet's profile. And after my date with Sebastian, the wombist who cruised the site looking for nubile bodies to incubate his offspring, I think we've made the right decision there.

The bar is busy with the typical Wednesday after-work City crowd, who are mostly dressed like me in suits or jackets. When Marley drags me out to trendy spots in Hoxton or Shoreditch I always feel like the uptight aunt amidst all the skinny jeans and facial hair.

There is a man wearing an olive coat at the corner table. It can't be him, though, unless he's *eaten* the real Nicholas. Besides, he's not carrying a... oh, wait. The magazine is in front of him.

'Harriet?' he asks, grinning broadly as I approach him. 'You came!' When he stands to greet me I see he's not as big as he looks sitting down. He's just wearing a very large coat, like he'd dressed up in his dad's going-to-work clothes. The rest of him looks pretty much like his photos – his wavy dark hair is neither too short nor too long and his brown eyes sparkle with laughter.

'Nicholas? Hi, it's nice to meet you.'

He takes my extended hand and pulls me towards him, planting a pepperminty kiss firmly on each cheek. 'I'm so glad you're here! Can I get you a drink? They make a very nice vanilla martini.'

'I think I'd better stick to wine. A glass of Sauvignon

Blanc would be great, thanks. If I had a martini, I'd be under the table.'

I could be wrong, but he might have just said 'Promise?' as he turned to the bar.

Even after just a handful of dates I'm already beginning to dread this process. It seems so false, condensing information into a few hours, like interviewing for a job that you're not confident of getting. And sometimes you realise halfway through that you don't want it.

Nicholas bounds back to the table with a bottle. 'This way we don't have to get up for more wine.' He pours two brimming glasses and slides one towards me.

'Thank you very much,' I say.

'Hmm? Oh, you're very welcome,' he says, glancing up from the briefcase he's been rifling through. 'It's the least I can do when such a beautiful woman agrees to have drinks with me.'

He pulls a few pages from his bag. I can see Harriet's login name at the top, and annotations all over the sheet in black pen.

'I hope you don't find this presumptuous, but I've made a few notes about your profile. It's very interesting. Shall we go through them?'

So it is an interview. If he asks me to give him a urine sample for testing, I'm definitely leaving. 'Erm, well, sure, we can talk about whatever you like. But do you really need the notes?'

'I don't want to miss anything.' He scans his sheet. 'It says here that you like classic books. So do I!'

He clasps his hands together in prayer formation, looks skyward and mouths 'Thank you'. He must really love the classics.

'Which are your favourites?' he asks.

I try to remember any books that Harriet and I have talked about over the years. If he'd asked about celebrity gossip or crappy films, then I'd be spoiled for choice. I'll just have to brief Harriet later in case this comes up again. 'I love anything by Margaret Atwood. They're modern classics, I guess, rather than Shakespeare-esque. I've always found his language impenetrable, though Baz Luhrmann's *Romeo and Juliet* was great because I could see what was happening and the language made more sense to me. Have you seen it?'

He nods briefly. 'Great film. What about Hemingway?'

'Nah, I can't really relate to his characters. I prefer to get more emotionally invested and his writing is so sparse that I don't connect with it.'

'I know exactly what you mean. Wasn't he the one who said "Why use ten words when five will do?"'

'I'm not sure. He did say that there's nothing to writing. All you do is sit down at a typewriter and bleed.'

'I hope it's not that difficult for all writers,' he says.

'Well, you tell me. You're a writer.'

He blushes. 'No, not really. I just write boring government speeches. That doesn't really count. It's not like I can write whatever I want to.'

'Aren't you tempted to spice things up sometimes?' I say in a stage whisper. 'Or make the prime minister say something completely stupid?' I imagine writing speeches for Derrick. I'd choose my moment and make him admit to paedophilia.

'The prime minister doesn't need my help looking

stupid.'

He laughs and I forgive him for taking notes on Harriet. I'm sure he's just nervous. We're getting on like we've known each other for ages. His easy banter reminds me of Zack. Oops, I mean Ben. His easy banter reminds me of my boyfriend. Not Zack. I'm not thinking about Zack.

'Where are your favourite places to travel?' he asks, looking at his notes again. I wish he'd put them away.

'Oh, I mostly do weekend breaks when I can get away. Venice, or the South of France.'

'That sounds very romantic…'

His question is implied. I must remember I'm Harriet. 'I often go away with friends, to the sun in winter, or skiing. Do you ski?'

He nods. 'I love it.'

'Oh? Where are your favourite places?'

'Where are your favourite places?'

'I like France and Italy, mostly for the food.'

'Me, too! It's amazing that we have so much in common.' Again he makes his praise-to-heaven gesture. He's a very grateful man.

'Which resorts do you go to?' I ask, trying to ignore his beatific expression.

'The ones in the Alps. You too?'

'Yes, usually Chamonix or Courmayeur. I don't like anything too difficult. I'm all about the après-ski.'

'There's nothing like a nice drink after a day on the slopes.' He smacks his lips over an imaginary glass of glühwein.

'When were you last skiing?'

'Well, I had a knee operation and haven't skied since.'

'Oh, that's a shame. How long ago was that?'

'I was seventeen.'

According to his profile he's thirty-two. Can one qualify as a skier after fifteen years of non-skiing? 'That's a long time away from the slopes.'

'I know, and I miss it every day.'

'You must have skied a lot as a child, then.'

'No, only a few times in Scotland. But I loved it. Like you do. Once it's in your blood, it doesn't leave. You know the feeling... Hey, I've got an idea. This will be fun. If you could plan the perfect romantic weekend away for us, where would we go? What would we do?'

I'm not sure what to say to this. We've known each other for less than an hour. A tiny alarm bell rings. 'It's a little early to imagine weekends away together, don't you think?'

'Well, I just thought that, as we're getting on so well... But you're right. Besides, we should have more time to think about it. Maybe we can each write out our perfect weekend later, and compare notes the next time we see each other.'

Again with the notes. 'I don't usually prepare homework for dates.'

'It's just that I like you so much.'

His face suddenly goes... oh, I recognise that look. It's desperation. Ryan makes the same face when Derrick rejects him.

'We can see each other again, can't we? Please say we can.'

He grasps my hand.

'Nicholas, you're making me feel a little uncomfortable. Can't we just chat and see how we feel later?'

'But I already know how I feel,' he says. 'I'm sorry, but I haven't felt a connection like this in a long time. I want to see you again. Are you free tomorrow? I could take you to a nice restaurant for dinner. Or lunch, or breakfast, or even a coffee. Anywhere you want. I'm buying, of course.'

Fantastic. Now I'm going to have to get away from this guy and then I'll be guilt-ridden for a week. Gently, I pull my hand from his sweaty mitt. 'It's just that you're coming on a bit strong, that's all. I am having a nice time talking to you, but I'm not sure if I feel as strongly as you seem to.'

'Are you breaking up with me?'

What did I miss?

'I wasn't aware we were going out. Isn't this only our first date?'

'Yes, but we've got such a connection. I felt it when you first emailed me back. We may have only seen each other once, but we've written eleven times. You can't deny that there's something here.'

There's something here, all right. It's called a lost cause. I gather my coat and bag.

'Thanks very much for the wine and conversation but, Nicholas, you're really making me uncomfortable, so I think I'm going to go now.'

'But what about our connection? We have so much in common. The wine, and books, and skiing and our love of travel.'

As I think about it, I don't know much about him at all. He's just agreed with everything I've said. 'Sorry, Nicholas.'

'Fine, I understand,' he says. 'This always happens to me. I meet a woman I could happily settle down with and she's not interested.'

He downs his wine in one go.

'I'm sure if you just relaxed a little bit, and maybe took things a bit more slowly, then you'd have better luck.'

'If I relax, will you see me again?'

'No, I don't mean you'll have better luck with me. I mean other women. Thanks again for the wine.'

I leave him sitting at the table in his too-big coat, and I feel so sad for him. Desperation like that will never let him see where he's going wrong, which will only make him more desperate to please.

I shudder to think what Harriet would have thought of Nicholas. She'd be ringing wedding venues for availability by their second date, not realising that she hadn't fallen for a man, but a mirror.

My phone buzzes with a message from the dating site just as I get to the Tube station. *Are you always this beautiful or was I just lucky to see you tonight? xxxxxxxxxxxxxxxx Nicholas*

Nicholas, I message back. *Please do yourself a favour and learn to take no for an answer. Harriet*

Just as I'm sliding my BlackBerry back into my bag, it rings.

'Hi, Mum.'

'Hello, darling. Have you had any luck finding cottages for Dad and me?'

'I sent you a bunch by email. Did you check those?'

She sighs. 'I did, but they're not really right for us.'

'But they're all two-bedroom cottages in Dorset with fireplaces, carpet in the bedroom but not the living room or bathroom, and within a mile of a village with a pub.'

'They just don't have the right look. We'd like something with a lovely garden, and old. Some of the ones you sent were pebble-dashed. Ghastly. Can you look again now?'

'No, I'm not near a computer now, Mum. I'm out.'

'Well, when you get home, then.'

'I really don't have time.'

'You don't have time to help your mother? You know we need to get away. Your poor father is working so hard, and I've already told Mrs Latham that we'll be away. She's been bothering me all week to know where we're going.'

Her words press into me like something I've knelt on in the carpet. It's too much. It's all too much. Everyone expects a piece of me. There are no pieces left to give.

The anger wells up so fast that I've got no chance of stopping it.

'You know what, Mum? I don't give a flying fuck about Mrs Latham. If she's so worried about your holiday, then let her book the damn thing herself. I don't care. I don't care if you go away to an old cottage or a pebble-dashed one or if you stay home and stare at each other for a week. I've given you reasonable choices based on what you told me you wanted. It's not enough. It's never going to be enough, is it? Well, this time, Mum, I get to decide what's enough, not you. I'm ending this call now, Mum, and this time, I'm getting the last word. Goodbye.'

Then I do something I hardly ever do. I turn off my BlackBerry.

PART TWO

CHAPTER 18

Mum hasn't spoken to me directly in nearly a month. I should be more upset about this, but it turns out I've only got so much worry to go around and at the moment it's spread pretty thinly over the rest of my life.

Zoe is watching me carefully for signs of a breakdown, but actually I feel lighter without Mum's steady stream of demands. I've always wanted her praise more than anything. I didn't realise that getting it meant carrying so much weight. I know we'll talk again eventually, but I'm not anxious to go back to the way things were.

She's not going out of her way to forgive me either.

'Colbert, meeting in ten minutes,' Derrick shouts through a mouth full of cronut. They've become his breakfast food of choice, so his odds in the heart attack pool make him hardly worth betting on any more.

'Me too?' Ryan asks.

'Yes, you too, Ryan. It's mandatory.'

Derrick stomps off to spray cronut over the rest of our colleagues.

An impromptu, mandatory meeting can't be good. There've been too many closed-door meetings lately. In the banking world that means one of two things: we're either being taken over or closed down.

'Hi, Granny, can you talk?' Our daily phone calls have become even more important lately.

'If you mean is your mum safely out of earshot, then yes, doll. How are you this morning?'

'I'm okay. I've got a meeting in a few minutes but just wanted to say hi.'

'You sound down. You're not letting your mum get to you, are you?'

'I haven't talked to her, Granny.'

'I know, doll. That's what I mean. Can't you patch things up? She's really upset, you know.'

'Funny, she doesn't sound upset when she makes Marley pass on her bad daughter accusations.'

'She doesn't mean it. She was just surprised by your reaction, that's all. If you ask me, it's good for her. She can be such a bossy boots.'

'Anyway, how are you? How's Dad?'

'He's fine. He's ducking your mother's slings and arrows as usual. I hear you've been seeing him in London.'

Dad called me soon after my blow-up with Mum to ask me to lunch, and we've been meeting at least once a week. Mum is starting to suspect he's having an affair.

'Just because Mum and I aren't talking doesn't mean I can't talk to Dad or you.'

'I know that, doll. And nothing in the world would make me stop talking to you anyway. I miss you, though. Don't stay away just to spite your mother, okay? Justifiable anger is okay. Don't let it go on too long or it will turn into something else. Come back to us as soon as you feel able.'

'I will. I love you, Granny.'

'Right back at you, doll. Have a good day. Give 'em hell, okay?'

'I will. I've gotta go now, Granny. I'll talk to you tomorrow.'

I grab my coffee cup to top up. You never know with Derrick's meetings. They could go on for a minute or an hour.

As I round the corner from the kitchen towards Stephan's desk, I notice two of the guards from downstairs. He hands his pass to one of them.

'Stephan? What's going on?'

'See you, Carol. Thanks for everything.'

'Where are you going? We have a meeting now. It's mandatory.'

'Not for me. I'm leaving.'

He shoves a few papers into his bag.

'Sorry, mate, you can't take those,' says one of the guards. 'Personal items only.'

'But why, Stephan?!' His contract isn't up for another month. 'Are you working somewhere else?'

'Not likely,' he says sadly. 'I'll see you around.'

He doesn't look back as the guards escort him to the lift.

I try not to run to the conference room. 'Ryan,' I whisper as soon as I sit down. 'They just took Stephan away. What the hell is going on?'

'What do you mean, they took him away?' His pale blue eyes dart to the doorway like he expects snipers to be there. 'As in: he's been thrown out?'

I nod. 'I have a bad feeling about this meeting.'

The traders aren't any happier about being called away from their desks when trading opens in less than an hour. All indications are bad.

Derrick clears his throat. 'I'll keep this short because you're all busy. There've been some irregularities and the Financial Conduct Authority is investigating. They should have their findings ready in two weeks and I expect everyone to give them their full cooperation. Is that clear?'

'Is Stephan involved in this?' I ask.

'That's none of your business and I can't go into details at this stage anyway. It should go without saying that this meeting is off the record. Way off the record. As far as anyone outside this room is concerned, there is no investigation, there is no Financial fucking Conduct Authority. Got it?'

The room erupts in conversation. The traders are shouting at Derrick, who remains impassive.

'We need to know if this is going to affect our clients,' Joe says. 'Derrick, we're going to look like right arseholes if it gets out to them before we can tell them.'

But Derrick won't be drawn into conversation about it. He just keeps saying there's nothing to worry about. He only told us, he says, because the investigators are in the building now and might want to talk to some of us.

Of course I don't believe him. He'd lie on his mother's life.

This must be related to Stephan. If only I'd known him a bit better, then I'd have his mobile number. Not that he'd answer my call but at least I could try.

But that's the thing about banking. When you leave, they cut you away so cleanly that there's not even a scar left. Your memory is erased from the collective conscience as quickly as your phone number and email address is from the system. I won't hear from, or about, Stephan again. He may as well have never worked here.

* * * * *

Leave it to Harriet to know more than me about the investigation in my own bank. She rang my landline at home at the crack of dawn this morning (it's been so long since I've heard it that at first I didn't realise what it was).

'Meet me for lunch at Luigi's,' she said. 'But don't tell anyone.'

She might be completely hopeless when it comes to men but she's a sharp cookie in all things conspiratorial. Like an idiot savant, her powers are sometimes jaw-dropping.

Speaking of idiot men, I've got to tell her that I'm bowing out as her surrogate. I don't mind the boring dates so much. At least they're harmless and usually give me a few minutes to zone out with my own thoughts while they drone on about their divorces or cars or obsessive love for Scunthorpe United football. It's the other ones I object to, the ones who shave off a little piece of my soul with each encounter. Needy Nicholas didn't give up as easily as I'd hoped after our date. His messages became increasingly argumentative, as if bullying is really the way to a woman's heart. We finally had to have him blocked on the website.

The others weren't as bad but they weren't the pleasant diversion I'd imagined when first agreeing to help Harriet. The ukulele-playing primary school teacher with advanced halitosis wasn't so much a soul-stripper as a sympathy-sucker. The dear, stammering man pulled at my heart strings even as he assaulted my senses.

Harriet has already found us a table at the back of the restaurant. She's not wearing a wig or dark glasses, I'm glad to see. She is, however, wearing a very serious expression.

'Sit down,' she says.

As if I planned to eat standing up. 'What's wrong with you?'

'Do you want a glass of wine?'

'Harriet, you're scaring me.'

'I wish I had better news, but things don't look good in your office.'

'Well, I know that. The financial police are there, remember?'

'Yes, they're there, and they're investigating Green T.'

She searches my face for a reaction as a chill dribbles down my spine.

I feel ill but I'm not surprised. At some unconscious level I must have known this was happening when Derrick told us about the investigation. The suspicious programmed trades last month, Stephan's abrupt departure at the hands of security guards. My gut instinct already knew what my brain wouldn't piece together.

'How is Stephan involved?'

'The intern? It was his father who tipped off the regulators. Stephan knew something was wrong with the way Green T was working. He told his father and they went to the FCA.'

'What are they accusing Green T of doing, though? If it's not working right, then we'll fix it. I'll fix it.'

There has to be a way to make things okay again.

'They say it's illegally manipulating share prices.'

I don't ask how she knows this when she doesn't even work for my bank. 'Illegally? Is that the word being used?'

She nods. 'You know, don't you, that Derrick isn't going to take the blame for this?'

Of course I know that. There isn't a less loyal industry on the planet than banking, except maybe mercenaries, and sometimes even they have hearts. 'There's nothing wrong with my system, Harriet. I tested it for nearly a year. I can't explain why it behaved the way it did before, but I didn't programme it to do that.'

'You might have to prove that, sweetheart. Are you prepared?'

I shake my head. I am definitely not prepared to defend myself against the charge of illegal manipulation of the world's stock markets. There are people in prison for doing that kind of thing.

'I haven't done anything wrong,' I whisper.

Harriet, bless her, tries her best over lunch to distract me from her news, but of course I can't concentrate on anything now. If the regulators do find that Green T is behaving badly, how am I supposed to prove that I'm not an accomplice? There's only one person who might be able to help, and he's not willingly speaking to me.

Zack totally took to heart my behaviour in the lobby that day when Ben surprised me. He's not openly rude to me (he never would be) but we haven't had lunch together either, and he doesn't stop by my desk anymore, even when he's on the floor.

And every time he ignores me, a little voice on my shoulder whispers *You've hurt your friend and now he's ignoring you and you deserve to feel like a little hole is being bored into your heart with a dull corkscrew.* And that smarts. I mean, it really smarts, because bound up with all the guilt is the realisation that my feelings for Zack aren't strictly platonic. Leaving the fact that I have a boyfriend aside for a moment, I've ruined not only my friendship but any possibility of more with Zack.

'Come on,' Harriet says after lunch, dragging me by the hand through the maze of shops beneath our office buildings. It's a fully-formed subterranean world, a high street that never sees daylight. The corridors are lined with sandwich shops, restaurants, clothing shops, dry cleaners and newsagents. It's got everything that a busy executive could need down here, except vitamin D.

'I want your opinion,' she says. 'As my dating consultant, you need to tell me if you think this guy is as perfect as I think he is. We've been flirting like crazy since last week when I went into his shop to get a card for Dad. Carol, wait till you see him. He's beyond gorgeous, and so funny!'

'You've kept that quiet! All this time online and you've found one right under your feet? Literally?'

'I know, wouldn't it be the way, though? And before you judge him for being a lowly clerk, he owns the shop.' She steers me inside. 'There he is!'

Standing next to the till is not a man, but a god. Tall, with broad shoulders and the most perfectly formed biceps I've ever seen. His black tee shirt hugs his torso so perfectly that I can see the muscles in his back flex as he bends to get a bag for the customer he's helping. He's laughing easily with her, flashing beautiful teeth framed by full, sensuous lips.

'What do you think?' Harriet whispers. 'Isn't he perfect?'

'Is he stupid?'

She shakes her head, pretending interest in the rack of Get Well Soon cards in front of us. 'He did Philosophy at Durham. And no,' she continues, cutting me off, 'he's not boring. He's very funny and likes film and theatre and going clubbing.'

At that moment he glances over, sees Harriet and waves.

'Come on, let's talk to him!' She grabs my hand and pulls me along to the front of the shop.

'Hi! Busy day?'

'Not too bad,' he says, catching me in the beam of his smile. 'Did your Dad have a nice birthday?'

As Harriet gives him the highlights of her father's celebration, I watch him carefully. He certainly is very tactile, reaching out to touch her arm whenever he makes a point. In fact, his hands don't stop moving, flapping here and there as he talks. When he makes a heart with his fingers over her new handbag, I bite down a grin.

'So if you ever want to check out a club,' she says. 'I go quite a lot.'

'I would L-O-V-E that! We get so bored of the same places in Soho.'

'Me too! Here's my mobile.' She scribbles her number on top of the stack of bags on the counter. 'Call me!'

With a flick of her hair, she turns and bolts from the shop as I try to keep up.

'Oh, my God, isn't he the most gorgeous thing?!'

'Yes, but–'

'And he'll definitely call me. There were practically sparks flying between us.'

'Harriet, he's gay.'

'He is not!'

'He told you where he goes for waxing.'

'I like a groomed man.'

'He's wearing a rainbow pride bracelet. Honey, give it up. He's more camp than the accommodation at Glastonbury. Can't you see that?'

She shakes her head with a look of utter disappointment upon her face. 'I just thought he was gorgeous and friendly and well-groomed.'

So much for me giving up my post as Harriet's dating scout. She needs me more than I need my free time.

'Try not to let it get you down,' I tell her. 'There are more fish in the sea, and some of them even like women. There was one interesting email from the site today. Did you see it? He sounds promising. I can email him tonight.'

'I didn't see it. What does he look like?'

'He doesn't have any photos either, but he sounds great.'

'I've been thinking about the photo question and maybe we should put mine back on the profile. I bet some guys aren't getting in touch because they assume

I'm minging.'

'But you don't want your colleagues to see you on there, do you?'

'No,' she sighs. 'I guess not. So you'll email this guy back? What's his name?'

'LoveHandles86. I assume he's being ironic.'

She looks as unsure as I feel about this being true.

CHAPTER 19

From: LoveHandles86
To: HarrietLikesWine

Hi Harriet! It sounds like we've got so much in common that it'd be sin not to meet, don't you think? Preferably somewhere where we can drink a nice bottle of rosé. In fact if you added in an old film and a Labrador to the date, I think I might get down on one knee ☺ Let's plan something soon, Jack

From: HarrietLikesWine
To: LoveHandles86

Well, Jack, I'm not sure we'd find a cinema in London who'll welcome dogs so you may have to settle for a bar. Somewhere in Soho maybe? Harriet

From: LoveHandles86
To: HarrietLikesWine

Does that mean no dog either? Our chances of matrimonial bliss are dwindling with each message. I'm not a fan of Soho but I know of a great little pub in Farringdon called The Jerusalem. It's tiny, hidden on a back street. Do you know it? Jack x

From: HarrietLikesWine
To: LoveHandles86

That sounds like something Jack the Ripper should say… wait a minute! Jack, is that you? ☺ I just googled it and it looks great. Would Thursday work? x Harriet

From: LoveHandles86
To: HarrietLikesWine

I'm afraid I'm not that interesting. Hope you're not disappointed by the lack of danger and intrigue. If it makes you feel better I could probably murder a few glasses of rosé. Would seven work on Thursday? I can message you when I get there so you don't have to arrive first. Jack x

Even without photos, I know that LoveHandles86 is a promising prospect for Harriet. After two days straight of back-and-forth messaging, we're at ease with each other. He hasn't asked after the state of my ovaries, or suggested any romantic homework assignments or hinted that he occasionally drugs his dates. Thanks to the men I've met lately, I should now at least be equipped to work out such warning signs in print.

There's no way, of course, to know what he looks like but he did promise that far from hiding his face in shame, he's actually considered by some to be easy on the eye. He just doesn't want any of his colleagues to see him online and, as I look around my office, I don't blame him one bit. Tomorrow night will be the moment of truth, when I'll find out whether his caution is sensible or delusional.

But first I have to explain to one of Joe's clients why we've lost him a few hundred thousand pounds. It's all in a day's work.

'Come on,' says Joe as he passes my desk.

'I'll be back in a few hours,' I tell Ryan.

'Don't care.'

'Just in case anyone wants to know where I am.'

'They don't care either, Colbert.'

I don't bother talking to Joe as we take the taxi to the client's offices. He's never in a good mood but he's been especially foul since Derrick announced the investigation. The rumours are now rife, and all pointing towards Green T. Joe hated it before he suspected it was screwing over his clients. There aren't enough expletives to describe how he feels now that he's got to have meetings like the one we're going to.

As we sign in at reception and get our paper badges, Joe finally breaks the silence. 'I don't think we can save this account but I want you to do everything you can, and I mean everything, to try to convince them that our portfolio is solid. Can you do that?'

'Of course, Joe. Our portfolio is solid. We both know there was no good reason for investors to dump those stocks.'

Green Energy Ltd has managed to stay in business so far, despite the pounding it took on the stock market. Its share price has started to recover, too, and I know Joe bought back a lot of shares at nearly the lowest point, so at least he's making some money for our clients again. But he also lost a lot for them, so I'm not holding out hope either about today's meeting.

Ostensibly we're taking the client to lunch. It's all jovial back-slapping but in reality we're grovelling to keep his business. My job is to convince him that we're still worth our trading fees.

The client's name is Jack. He couldn't be LoveHandles86, though, right? Even though I notice he's not wearing a wedding band. That would be too big a coincidence. He does look around the same age. He probably wouldn't want colleagues to know he was dating online and he is indeed easy on the eye, with his floppy public school haircut and easy smile.

No, it can't be. But if date-Jack is half as nice as client-Jack, Harriet will be a lucky girl. In fact, most of our clients are perfectly nice, courteous men. I just usually have to go out with the spittle-flinging creeps like Trevor.

At least lunch is good, although Joe is right. We never really had a chance of salvaging the client relationship. Jack was ever so nice about it, but he'll be moving his money to another manager.

Joe is in an even fouler mood by the time we hail a cab back to the office.

'I'm sorry, Joe, I did the best I could.'

'It's a little late for that,' he mutters, staring out the window at the sandstone and marble facades along the Mayfair road. 'If you hadn't created that fucking system in the first place, we'd still have our clients.'

'I said I was sorry,' I whisper. I know he's just saying what all the traders are thinking. I'd much rather be told by someone other than Joe, even though they wouldn't pull punches like Joe is doing.

'It's not good enough, Carol, is it? You've ruined people's lives, do you realise that? You played God, being the *clever girl*, and you've ruined people.'

Yes, this *is* Joe pulling his punches. 'Sorry just isn't enough,' he continues. 'Tell that to the people who are losing their jobs because of you. Tell that to my wife when she wonders why we can't afford the mortgage and the school fees because I'm losing my commission every time a client leaves us.'

I feel my eyes sting with tears. 'Joe, I swear, there's nothing wrong with the system I created. I know there isn't. I spent a year creating it. Green T is solid.'

'Excuse me for not crumbling in sympathy at your tears. That system is fucked up, and you made it. Therefore, you fucked up, Carol. Why can't you just admit that? You're going to have to anyway, once the FCA follows the source of this stinking shit back to the arse who's responsible for it. Do you realise you could go to prison over this? If I were you, I'd start figuring out a defence that doesn't involve bursting into tears and whining *I didn't do it*.'

He's right. He's totally right. I know how these things work. When the regulators find fault, everyone points fingers away from themselves. I need help.

My tummy lurches as I knock on the IT office door. 'Zack? Can I talk to you for a minute, please?'

As soon as he sees it's me he turns back to his monitor and lets his fingers fly over the keyboard. 'I'm kind of busy now, Carol. Can it wait till later?'

'I'm so sorry, Zack, but it can't really. Can we go get a coffee?'

His colleagues are watching me curiously. I know he

hasn't said anything to them about our… what shall we call it? Indiscretion? So I must look unusually worried to prise their attention from their screens.

With a sigh Zack grabs his wallet from his desk. 'I'll be back in ten minutes.'

I'm lucky I'm getting that long. The clock starts, now.

'I'll get it,' I say at the café across the road as he takes his wallet out to pay for our coffees. 'Do you want a croissant? It's the least I can do when I'm dragging you away from your desk.'

He doesn't argue with my generosity or my statement as we sit down. 'I want to ask you something, but first I need to apologise for being such an arsehole to you.'

He's not objecting to that either, I notice.

'I was rude when I was with Ben in the lobby that day, and there was no reason for that. I'm really sorry.'

'Actually, I think there was a reason for it. Clearly you were telling me where your loyalty lies, and it's not with me. That's fine, I get it. I'm just sorry you felt you needed to treat me like that in front of Ben. If you don't mind, I'd rather not talk about it. If we're going to keep being friends, the less said about it the better, I think.'

'Are we still friends?'

He shrugs. 'Yeah, I guess, Carol, but I can't pretend I wasn't hurt. I liked you. A lot, if you must know. That night at the pub wasn't just a spur-of-the-moment decision for me. But you don't have to worry. I won't be overstepping any bounds again.' He glances at his phone. 'Back to business. You had something else to ask?'

I can handle his anger (after all, I've had enough practice with Ben), but not the hurt look he's giving me. I've completely screwed up our friendship. And now I have to ask him for a huge favour. I'm such a dick.

'How much have you heard about the FCA's investigation?'

He spins his paper cup between his fingers before he answers. Spin, spin, spin, three at a time, rest, then three more, again and again. I don't think he's going to answer me.

'They've interviewed my boss and asked for reams of documentation,' he finally says, looking relieved to be back on work topics.

'You know they're looking at Green T.'

He nods.

'And you know they'll be looking at my involvement shortly, if they aren't already. I need you to find out why Green T is behaving like this.'

'Whoa, Carol, wait a minute. I'm just a programmer. I don't know enough about the system design to do that.'

'But I do, and I can help you. Zack, something weird is going on and I have to know what it is. Otherwise you know as well as I do that they're going to blame me.'

'I hate to be the one to break it to you but Derrick is going to blame you anyway.'

'And that's why I need you to help me be ready for him. Can you help me?'

I wonder if he knows he's holding my future in his hands. I wonder if he cares. I have no right to ask this of him. He'll be risking his own job by getting involved.

At first I think my tummy's free-fall is because of Green T. The idea of going to prison is enough to put anyone off their croissant. But then I realise it's also because of Zack. I might not have thought of him romantically before our kiss, but I've definitely thought of him that way since. I'm not in love with him like I am with Ben, but there must be something there for me to feel like this. Or there was something there. I crushed it with one selfish, flippant retort. In that one irretrievable moment, I hurt my friend and threw away any chance of more with him. Way to go, Carol, nice one-two punch.

Zack sips his coffee, staring at me over the lip of his cup for what seems like a million years. 'Of course I'll help. Tell me what you need.'

I need nothing short of a miracle.

I don't deserve it, but I'm so very grateful that Zack will at least give me the chance..

CHAPTER 20

I dress extra carefully for Harriet's date the next night. We've agreed that I'll only wear black (all the better to pass Harriet off as me later, should I ever meet someone who doesn't need psychological evaluation or a restraining order). It's easy to do my hair like hers, with a deeper side part than I usually wear, but it feels odd. I have to resist the urge to flip my hair back into place.

And the pièce de résistance, the clincher in this doppelganger stakes, is Harriet's necklace. I gave it to her for her birthday years ago. It's what the jeweller called a *statement* piece. The white and yellow gold swallow sails gently across my collarbone, suspended by a delicate yellow chain.

I feel like the odds are stacked in Harriet's favour now. Surely there are only so many frogs one can pucker up to before a prince emerges. I've had fantasies about double dating with her ever since we began this charade. I only hope I won't have to do it with an electronic bracelet around my ankle. *We'll take the early reservation so I can be back by curfew.*

Zack and I have hatched a plan to keep me out of the magistrate's court, but neither of us is sure we can do it. First, I have to figure out exactly how, and most importantly, why the system that the bank is running is overreacting to market news. That means testing every one of Green T's functions with every conceivable scenario, and comparing the results with the original system I designed.

Zack has bootlegged Green T for me, which is an immediately sackable offence. And he's given me one of the bank's most powerful laptops to use at home. Zack needs the laptop back by Thursday to give to the trader who's waiting for it. Which means all I have to do is condense a year's worth of testing into a few days and nights.

I started as soon as I got home from work last night, stopping for two hours to sleep around 4 a.m. As soon as I've met LoveHandles and then have a quick wedding-strategy dinner with Marley, I can return to the laptop for another night of testing.

Every time I think about failing, such a feeling of dread rises up from my gut that it becomes hard to breathe. It's a panic attack, I know. I've seen enough of them at the bank, usually when interns or new analysts get so overwhelmed by the volume of work and the constant shouting that they have to be walked (or carried) to the in-house nurse for a dose of gentle nurturing and a mild sedative.

I don't have the luxury of an in-house nurse at home, and I haven't told anyone in the family about the investigation. Imagine how that conversation would go.

Actually, Mum, it's funny, I'd say. *Remember all those times when you were proud of me? Well, it turns out that I'm a First-Class, Grade-A screw-up. So sorry, you've been backing the wrong horse all these years.*

Whenever the tearing, ripping, hollow terror fills me, I have a shower. I sit on the cold bathtub floor, let the hot water run over me, and I do something I would never do in public. I sob until I can breathe again. I'm so afraid. I'm afraid of not finding the error. I'm afraid of finding it but not being able to prove it wasn't mine. I'm afraid it won't matter what I find or don't find because my career at the bank will be finished anyway. But mostly, I'm afraid of what everyone will think when they find out.

Perhaps this isn't the ideal mindset to have when going on a date, but I feel strangely calm. There's nothing like a real crisis to put the minor ups and downs into perspective. I just hope that LoveHandles isn't awful.

The pub is only a few minutes' walk from the Tube. I message Jack through the website as I leave the train. *Just leaving the Tube. Harriet x*

I'm here, front right-hand table as you walk in. See you in a minute. Jackxx

Despite everything else that's whirling through my head, I'm excited to meet him. Something about the way he writes tells me he's the kind of guy Harriet will love. If I'm honest, he might be the kind of guy I'd love if I weren't with Ben. He's certainly smart and funny and a little bit of a smart-arse. Granted, I don't know what he looks like, but it would be a very bold statement to claim beauty when he's really uglier than a baboon's arse.

Mentally I slap myself as I walk slowly up the narrow lane, careful not to break a sweat. (*She was fun*, noted LoveHandles in his feedback form, *but she had a manly sheen.*) This is for Harriet, I remind myself, because she hasn't had a decent boyfriend, well, ever. If LoveHandles is as funny and smart and normal as I hope he'll be, then Harriet will be a lucky woman and we'll get to double date and have fun with our respective funny, smart, normal boyfriends. Ben might even grow to love Harriet like I do if we all go out. He can talk football or whatever instead of always going out with me alone. Everybody wins.

The pub is tiny, its façade no more than twenty feet wide, and charming. LoveHandles scores his first points. There's a small crowd milling outside in the mild weather, most with pints in their hands, a few with cigarettes that excite my craving.

There's no time to smoke now, though. I push through the door into the crowded room, and glance left at what might be Harriet's future husband.

'Ben?'

Hearing his name makes him smile as he looks up from his phone. Then he stares at me.

'What are you doing here?'

Near simultaneous thoughts are pinging through my brain. *I'm not supposed to be here... Ben's just caught me on a date... How am I going to explain this... Why is he here? Sitting at the table where Jack said he'd be... Are they friends?*

'Ben?' I say again. This time the single word demands a response. I want to hear him give me a perfectly reasonable explanation that we'll both laugh about, because my brain is giving me a very unreasonable one right now.

'What are you doing here?' I ask.

'I could ask you the same question.'

For a split second I think about lying. But then I remember that I'm not technically doing anything wrong. I'm simply helping Harriet. 'I'm here to meet someone for Harriet.'

I can see it in his eyes when he hears her name. Confirmation of everything I didn't know I was afraid of until a minute ago.

'And you're here to meet Harriet, aren't you?' I say. The rushing sound I hear is my relationship crashing at about a hundred miles an hour into a concrete wall. There are no survivors.

He's not going to lie, he's too proud. I've literally caught him in the act.

'I don't really know what to say.'

'Well, then, listen to me,' I begin, as a rage so red, so fast and monumental swells up inside me that I feel like I might explode into a thousand little pieces. I'm surprised by its intensity, so many years have I lived with only a pale, middling feeling of disappointment. This anger bursts upon me in glorious high-definition. I can see every pixel.

I don't recognise my own voice as the words fly out. 'Listen to me, you lying son of a bitch! All these months, while I've been bending and bending and BENDING to your needs, your schedule, your goddamn MOODS, you've been cheating on me?!'

'Shh, Carol, please keep your voice down. Come on, let's go somewhere to talk.'

He stands up.

I shove him with all my might back into his chair while the whole room seems to go silent. Maybe it really does go silent at the crazy woman in their midst. I couldn't give one half of one shit right now.

'Why go somewhere else to talk, when we can talk right here? After all, this is where you came to meet the woman you planned to seduce tonight. Tell me, Ben, do you come here often? Maybe I should ask the barman. Does he come here often, or is this the first time you've seen this lying, cheating bastard in here? Is it the first time, Ben? Is that what you'll try to claim? That you made a mistake and this has never happened before? That you're so sorry, DARLING, and promise never to do it again because you love me so much? Is that what you'll CLAIM? Well, why don't we find out? Sit the fuck down you pencil-dicked weasel!'

I pull my BlackBerry from my bag as two men move closer to us. I seem to have the bar on my side now.

'Harriet?' I say as soon as she answers. 'Oh, yes, he's here all right. I'll give you the details later. PUT THAT PHONE DOWN!' I shout at Ben as he fiddles with his iPhone. 'Harriet, I need you to do something for me right now. Go on the website to LoveHandles' profile and screen-print the whole thing. Every single page and everything you can find on there about him. I'll explain later. No, I'm not okay. But I will be. I'll talk to you later.'

'Carol, you've gone mental, really. You're making a fool of yourself.'

'No, Ben, you've made a fool of me. How many months have I waited for your bloody case to be finished? Just a little longer, darling, I promise, and then we'll get our lives back. Well, you know what, Ben? I'm getting my life back RIGHT THIS SECOND. I have spent months... no, I've spent

YEARS doing what you want, what everybody wants, and for what? To be shit on, Ben, that's what. To be shit on by you in a bar.'

'Please,' he calls to the barman. 'I think my girlfriend is having some sort of episode. Can you call the police, please, before she hurts someone?'

'Don't touch that phone! I'm not having an episode, but if you want me to explain to everyone what's going on, then I'm more than happy to.'

I turn to the room, keeping an eye on Ben in case he tries to do a runner.

'You see, Ben Thomson, my boyfriend here, has joined a dating site. Only it wasn't to meet me, it was to meet random women. He didn't give his real name, oh no, he calls himself Jack, everyone. As in jack-off. Jack, here, or BEN THOMSON, who works at the solicitors CAYMAN CAYMAN WIBBLE AND WISE, by the way, if anyone wants to LINK-IN with him, set up a fake profile with a fake name on a very real website. And this is the great part. Are you ready for the REALLY FUNNY part? He emailed my best friend Harriet! Oh, he was smooth. What was that you said, darling boyfriend? That it would be a SIN if we didn't meet? Well, Harriet was hooked. But you see, Harriet has very bad taste in men. She has a very bad track history when it comes to affairs of the heart. So I've been helping her, vetting her dates for potential psychos. And guess WHAT? I've hit the jackpot. Because you're not only a psycho, you're a lying, cheating, using, selfish, whoring bastard.'

I turn to the barman. 'You're not calling the police, are you?'

He shakes his head slowly.

'Good, because I'm nearly finished. I've got a question, Ben, while I have your attention. Why did you say you wanted to live with me?'

He is silent.

'WHY, BEN?'

He shrugs. 'It would have been easier than having to find time for you. You can be quite demanding, you know, Carol.'

'I'm demanding? Really? Because from what I can tell, I'm the only one in my life who isn't demanding. If it's not you with your long hours and conditional love, it's my boss or my sister or my mother. But not me, Ben, it's never been me, and as I think about it, that's exactly what my problem has been all along. Well, guess what? Those days are over. So all that remains is for me to say a huge FUCK YOU for the last two years of my life that I've wasted. I don't ever want to see you, or hear from you, or hear about you or think about you again. If you so much as walk on my side of the road, I swear to god I will make you sorry to be alive.'

I lean very close to my now-ex-boyfriend, and whisper into his face, 'In fact, you're going to be very sorry you've done this anyway.'

I barely hear the claps and cheers as I leave the bar, because I'm distracted by the odd sensation coursing through me.

It's not a sense of dread, embarrassment or regret over what I've just done, or even anger or sadness. It's more the *absence* of something, like after taking strong pain medication for a blinding headache or twisting period cramps. One minute it hurts and the next it doesn't. It doesn't hurt.

I'd forgotten what it's like to live pain-free.

I just ended a two-year relationship with a man I imagined spending the rest of my life with. You'd think that would warrant a snivelling breakdown at the very least. But I have no tears to shed. I am completely, utterly unmoved by what I've just done. Am I in shock? As I examine every edge of my consciousness for signs of denial, a feeling does start to wash over me.

What is that?

It's not something I've got very much experience with. Why, I do believe it's self-respect!

Is that why I'm not crying? Because, regardless of what I just gave up, I know I'm gaining more? After all, I'm getting me back.

The feeling grows as I take the Tube to meet Marley. I've got something to say to her now.

She's already at the table when I arrive at the busy restaurant.

'I've got so much to tell you!' she gushes as we hug and kiss hello. 'I may have found a venue for the wedding and the reception… it's in Scotland!'

'Oh, good,' I say, just knowing she's going to expect me to travel north to see the venue. 'But there's something I need to tell you first.'

She frowns. 'Carol, why can't you let me have my moment? Didn't you hear me? This is exciting news. I may have found a venue.'

'I just broke up with Ben.'

'What?! What happened?'

She is silent when I tell her the whole story, only breaking eye contact with me to point out a bottle of wine to the waiter and make sure my glass is filled quickly.

'It doesn't sound like you're very upset,' she says

when I've finished. 'How do you feel? I'd be devastated if I broke up with Jez. Do you remember when we went through that rough patch? God, just thinking about it makes me feel like crying. '

Sure enough, there are tears in her eyes. Tears for herself.

'But as long as you're okay with it, then that's good. Now can I tell you about the venue?'

'You know what, Marley? I don't really care very much about your wedding right now. I am sorry about that, because I know I'm supposed to be living and breathing your nuptials every day of my life, but I really don't give much of a crap at this very moment. I'm sure I'll feel differently in a little while but right now, this is about me, not you.'

Tears fill her eyes again. 'I know it's about ou. Didn't I just say so? Jesus Christ, I'm trying to empathise and you accuse me of being selfish. That's just shitty, Carol. You should think more of me.'

Talking to Marley is like throwing a boomerang. It always comes back to the same spot.

'You've done it again. For fuck sake, Marley, listen to yourself. Every single time I tell you how I feel you turn it back to yourself. I'm begging you; for once let this be about me, okay? I've been the one who's had to listen for such a very long time. Between you and Mum and everyone else, I have been taking it and taking it and taking it, and I'm finished taking it. No more. No. More.' I shake my head. 'I feel like I've woken from a nightmare, Marley, where I've been the main actor, though it's one of those dreams where you know it's supposed to be you, but you know it isn't really. You don't recognise yourself.' I run my hands through my hair and realise it's still styled like Harriet's. For some reason this strikes me as hilariously funny.

'Are you okay?' Marley asks when my laughter shows no sign of abating.

I nod. 'I need a cigarette. I need a fag and then I need to go.'

'Since when do you smoke?' She looks appalled. 'That's a terrible habit.'

'Since college, Marley, since college. And yes, it's a terrible, filthy, deadly habit. But it's my habit. So I'm just going to go outside now and light up, and then I'm going home. I've got a lot to take care of. For myself.'

I throw a twenty-pound note on the table to cover the wine, and head for the door. I'm getting quite good at dramatic exits.

I'm wide awake now from the deep, dreamless slumber of the past few years, and I'm not going back to sleep. Like drifting off at night, I've got no recollection of the moment I first dozed. One minute I was conscious, the next I was drooling into my pillow. The alarm clock in my life has finally rung, loud and clear, and I'm not going back to bed.

CHAPTER 21

Marley has been trying to convince me all weekend that we're not angry with each other (despite me telling her that we're not angry with each other). I just don't have the bandwidth to deal with her or the wedding right now. But she won't accept my answer. So she keeps calling. And I keep telling her. Eventually she'll either get the message or her mobile minutes will run out.

I was sure that my girl-power high from the night of Ben's betrayal would be short-lived, that I'd sober up, as it were, and then have to deal with the emotional hangover of a failed relationship. It's the end of a way of life for me. I'm no longer Ben's girlfriend, potential future wife and mother to his children. That should hurt.

But it doesn't. When I peer into the big dark hole where my feelings dwell, I see anger instead of sadness staring me down. So maybe I was so busy trying to keep everyone else happy that I didn't notice I no longer loved the arrogant prick who was taking me for granted.

There's something else inside me too, something I didn't expect. I may not know what my life holds for me in the future, but I know exactly how I'm going to live it. Whoever that pushover was that sat at my desk and kowtowed to my family is gone. It's about time I look out for myself for a change.

* * * * *

As soon as I get back from lunch on Monday afternoon I know something is wrong. The traders are loitering in small groups, talking quietly. There's a lot wrong with this scene. First, they aren't shouting. That's as suspicious as when a child suddenly goes quiet in the other room. Second, they're in groups. This isn't unusual behaviour in a normal office, but traders are the leopards of the corporate world. They like the solitude of their own territory and aren't often seen together, unless it's at the local watering hole.

Heads turn as I walk to my desk. I'd like to think it's because they're admiring my new silk print dress but the pit of my stomach tells a different story.

Derrick's head pops out of his doorway. 'Carol? Can I see you?'

I begin to shake as I walk the twenty feet to his office. I've sometimes watched those epic films set in medieval Britain or France, where someone who has displeased the king is led to his own beheading. I always wonder what they must be feeling, to know the exact moment of their own death.

Now I know.

A man in a suit and two police officers are standing

in front of the low table where Derrick keeps his tombstones. I resist the urge to giggle. Tombstones are the little glass trophies that companies give out when they issue a new bond or share deal. They're a bit like shrunken heads for bankers.

I guess this is gallows humour.

'Carol. We need to talk to you.' Derrick is all business. You'd never know he was probably licking tequila shots off a pole dancer's cleavage last weekend. 'This is Richard Bean, the FCA investigator.'

'Hi, Carol.' Richard strides forward to shake my hand. 'As you know, we've been called in to investigate some trading irregularities, and our team has been here for the past two weeks collecting information.'

I notice he doesn't say evidence.

'We've pinpointed the source of the irregularity now, and want to talk to you about it.'

'Am I the source of the irregularity?' I only just keep my fingers from making the ditto sign.

'The problem seems to be Green T,' Derrick says.

'Yes, I know. It's overreacting.'

'You know about this?' asks Richard.

I nod. 'Last month, when several of our companies lost significant share value, I noticed that its programmed trades had kicked in.'

'You noticed?' He glances at Derrick. 'So you're saying you didn't know about it before that? Before you noticed?'

'Well, how could I? Up to that point it was acting correctly.'

'Are you aware that the bank holds significant proprietary positions in those companies?'

That's banker-speak for investments that the bank

owns directly. It also means that if our system is manipulating the stock market, we are insider trading.

'No, they don't.'

'Carol, you don't have to lie,' Derrick says. 'They've seen the bank's portfolio.'

'Why would I lie? As far as I know, only our clients hold those shares. They're the only ones using Green T. You said so at the launch.'

Derrick sighs. 'Carol, it's all right. They know.'

'But I don't know! What are you talking about, Derrick? Green T is supposed to be for our clients only. If the bank is also using it, then that has nothing to do with me.'

Richard produces a sheet of paper. 'Do you remember getting this email?'

I quickly scan the page. Then I read it more carefully. It's from Derrick to me, talking about the bank's proprietary trading position in our green companies. The last line reads: *No pressure, Colbert, but your system is going to be used for our prop trading, so don't fuck it up.*

'I've never seen this email,' I say, as my face begins to sweat.

Richard brandishes another page. 'Then why did you respond?'

I'm looking at my reply: *Don't worry, Derrick, I won't.*

'I didn't write that.'

'Carol, they got it off our system.'

I want to slap that fake look of pity right off Derrick's face.

'I didn't write it! Go look at my email. I don't know where those came from but I swear I never saw Derrick's email, so I couldn't have responded to it.'

'Unfortunately, Carol, we have the evidence that says you did. We also have the evidence that you manipulated Green T to benefit the bank's own investments.'

In other words: insider trading. I notice that now he's using the word evidence.

'We're going to need you to come with us, please. We have some more questions.'

My voice wavers as I ask the next question. 'Am I being arrested?'

'We need to ask you some more questions,' Richard says. 'You'll want to grab your things.'

'Can I use the loo?' I think I might vomit.

'Of course. We'll see you by the lifts, okay?'

He smiles reassuringly.

I definitely might vomit.

Everyone stares at me as I walk on shaking legs to the loo.

What am I going to do? I've never seen that email and I certainly didn't respond to something that didn't exist. They think I designed Green T to exploit the market. When I think about the last few nights in front of the laptop going through the system with a fine-tooth comb… ugh, what a waste of insomnia when they already know the system is manipulating the market.

The problem is, they think I'm the architect of that manipulation.

And why do they think that? Because that's what Derrick has told them.

Of course my boss is setting me up. Why didn't I see this coming? His moral compass swings between his crotch and his wallet. Though even if I was bonking him on the boardroom table each afternoon, I doubt there'd be any way to save myself now.

Carefully, I wipe my eyes, reapply my make-up, then take a deep, steadying breath and prepare to be taken in for questioning.

The flashes start as soon as I stumble through the revolving door. Ping, ping, ping. Little white boxes burning across my vision.

'Look here! Hey, this way! Darlin', over here!'

Someone tipped off the media. I could turn away, try to hide my face like the A-listers do, but that'd seem a bit pretentious for someone so far down the popularity alphabet. There are at least a dozen photographers flanking us. I'll have to go down the steps. Even if there was another way out, they'd probably find it. I'm surprised so many are bothering with us. This isn't Boujis and I'm not exactly with Prince Harry.

We're attracting quite a bit of attention now. More and more people are holding their phones up, trying to snatch something worth tweeting. They have no idea who we are. They're just hoping to capture the photo that'll catapult them towards viral Instagram fame.

At least I got to touch up my lipstick before we left. There's nothing worse than those unguarded photos of a woman tumbling from a nightclub with the smudged smile of a psychotic clown. Well, okay, of course there's worse, but I am wearing knickers and my skirt's not too short.

I can see the car now. It's ticking over beside the kerb in a double red zone. Rock Star parking.

As he opens the passenger door (courteous to the

end) I think about how far I've come. I can even point to where it started, with Dad's party. Has my life really changed so completely in six months? Time sure does fly.

'Mind your head,' he says as he gently pushes me into the police car. He joins the other Met officer in front as the reporters aim their cameras into the windows and howl like a pack of overexcited hounds.

'Why did you do it, Carol?'

'Are you sorry?'

Over and over they repeat their questions, like there's a simple answer.

At least they don't turn on the lights as we pull away. After all, there's no need to rush now.

* * * * *

Harriet leaps up from one of the grey plastic chairs in the strip-lit reception area when I emerge four hours later from the police questioning room. Her eyes are rimmed red. They spill over when she hugs me.

'Are you okay?' she whispers.

'I'm supposed to be the one who's crying, not you. Please, let's get out of here.'

She nods. 'Do you want to go home?'

Ugh, the very idea of having to tell Zoe what happened. 'No, I'm hungry. Can we get some dinner? And wine. I need wine.'

We're quiet on the taxi ride into Soho as I try to make sense of what just happened. I, Carol Colbert, pillar of society, have been arrested. They haven't charged me with anything, but does getting arrested mean I now have a record? Will I be denied entry to the US, like Nigella Lawson, forevermore barred from the New York sales?

My hand drifts to my BlackBerry. Force of habit.

'They let you keep your phone?' she asks.

Grimly I nod. 'They can get all the records anyway.'

The screen is filled with the usual messages: afternoon briefing notes and meeting minutes, a warning from HR that if we keep leaving the kitchen in a mess they're going to take away our privileges. Like it's a privilege to drink bitter, tepid coffee from a sachet forced through a machine. My eyes scan the inbox. There's nothing from anyone about my arrest. No *Are you okays*. No *Sorry to see you led away by the police*. Not so much as a *Did they cuff you?* from Ryan. Have I already been cut away from the collective conscience?

I'm unsure what happens next. Richard and the police asked the same question every way they could think to pose it: Did you build the system to manipulate the markets so that the bank could cash in? No, no, and no again, I told them. I can't explain the email Derrick produced, or my response, because I can't explain something that didn't happen.

'Do you want to talk about it?' Harriet asks when we've squeezed into a spot at the bar at crowded Barrafina.

'I guess I'm allowed to talk about it. They didn't tell me I couldn't… Everything is such a disaster.'

'You mean your life in general?'

'No, Harriet, I mean Green T in particular, but thank you for pointing out that my whole life sucks.'

'Sorry! And it doesn't really suck. It's just that you've had a lot going on lately, between your mother and Ben and now this. Were the police able to tell you any more about their suspicions?'

'Oh, yes, quite a bit, actually. Derrick is saying I misunderstood his email and took it upon myself to tweak the system so that it inflates market movements. Essentially, that I've purposely created a system that manipulates the London Stock Exchange.'

'But that's not true!'

At her protest, faces turn curiously towards us.

'I know,' I say. 'Whatever Green T is programmed to do now has nothing to do with me. Harriet, I swear I didn't build it to manipulate anything.'

She grabs my hand and squeezes till I feel the bones grind. 'Carol, you don't ever, ever have to say that to me. You're my best friend. I know you wouldn't do this.'

'Thanks, but as of now, nobody else believes me and I can't prove that their suspicions aren't founded. It's my word against Derrick's, and he's got those fake emails on his side.'

'How would he be able to fake emails? All they have to do is look at your account and see that you didn't send it.'

'They're saying I deleted everything. The system backs up every night. They say I deleted the emails in-between the backups.'

'But they can't prove that.'

'No, but I can't prove I didn't, either.'

When the waiter appears I fumble for the menu.

But Harriet speaks before I've even scanned the starters. 'We'll have the prawn and pepper tortilla, sardines a la plancha, ham croquettes and the chorizo.' She looks at me. 'You've had enough to worry about without deciding dinner, too. We'll also have a bottle of this, please.' She points to the wine list. 'Thank you.'

She's right. I don't think I can take in any more information. My hard drive is full and I keep crashing.

'What am I supposed to do tomorrow? Do I show up for work? Am I even allowed to?'

'You haven't been charged with anything, Carol. You still have your job. Of course you should show up. You know they'll tear you apart if you show any weakness. You have to go on like nothing has happened.'

I don't relish the idea of facing Derrick, pretending like everything is fine and he isn't trying to frame me.

But then again, I didn't think I'd have the guts to stand up to Ben, and look what happened there. I'm stronger than I thought.

'You're right. I'm going in tomorrow. If Derrick has a problem with that, well, fuck him.'

She looks at me. 'You're taking this amazingly well. I'd be having a breakdown.'

I probably should be clutching my knees and rocking in a corner, but something in me wants to fight. For the first time since I can remember, I want to come out swinging in my own defence. It felt so good standing up to Ben instead of ingratiating myself like some stiletto-wearing Sméagol in my own Lord of the Rings drama.

'I don't have time for a breakdown. I've got too much life laundry to do.'

'I'm proud of you,' she says. 'And don't worry about going on my dates any more either. Jesus, what are the chances you'd catch Ben in the act like that?'

'Judging by his profile, they were pretty good odds. Thanks for screen printing everything out before he deleted his profile. I knew he would, but we've got the evidence. Did you notice how many "likes" he had?'

She shakes her head. 'As in Facebook likes?'

'Something like that. It's weird that a dating site would have them, but I guess they want to show how popular their members are. Over 200 women liked him.'

'Maybe he's rigged the system. You know, getting friends to vote for him like people do when they enter their ugly babies into photo contests.'

'Or maybe he's gone out with a lot of women.'

Anger wells up from the seemingly endless supply I've enjoyed lately. I have plans for my ex-boyfriend. Oh, yes, I have plans. But that's for another day.

'You did mention one more guy from the website you think you might be interested in,' I say. 'I may as well meet him and then it's probably best for you to take over. After all, I might be a felon soon so impersonating you won't go over well with my parole officer.'

'Very funny.'

I wish I was joking.

CHAPTER 22

By the time I push through the bank's revolving door the next morning, my tummy is churning breakfast like an aggressive spin cycle. I can feel sweat trickling between my shoulder blades. This was a stupid idea.

It doesn't matter that I still technically have my job. My colleagues rip me apart for getting a new hair cut (*You can try, Carol, but you still look like you've got a pole up your arse*) or being five minutes late (*Did you lose track of the time jerking off your boyfriend in the shower this morning?*). They're not about to let something like my arrest pass without comment.

It isn't until after I've swiped my card through the turnstile that I think about the bank turning off my access. They would have done that if I wasn't supposed to turn up for work, right? So at least I know I won't be ushered off the floor by security this morning.

Just as the disembodied lift lady's voice purrs that the doors are about to close, I see one of Zack's colleagues hurrying towards us. He recognises me as the doors slide shut.

'All right?' he manages as his eyes slide away from mine.

He must have heard what happened. Does everyone in the lift with us know? I nod and count the seconds until we reach my floor. At this point, the less said the better.

My tummy might be dodgy but my stride is assured as I make my way to my desk. If you can't make it, fake it.

Just as I wonder if my torture will start immediately, I see that I won't be disappointed.

A large plastic ball and chain sits in the middle of my desk.

'Very funny,' I mutter, sweeping it into the bin.

'Have a good evening, Colbert?' Ryan asks, looking over the partition that separates us.

'Not bad, thanks, Ryan. I got a bite to eat with my friend.'

I won't give him the satisfaction of mentioning the police. If he wants it, he'll have to work for it.

My computers whir to life.

'Anything interesting?' he asks.

'No, just tapas.'

I smirk as he sits down again. If that's their worst then I'll be okay.

I have to laugh when I open my drawer to find a book I didn't put there. Someone has taped a full colour printed cover over a Windows for Dummies manual: *How to Survive Prison*. Beneath it is another Do-It-Yourself title: *How To Pick Up Chicks: A Lesbian Guide to Girl-on-Girl Action*. Excavating deeper into the drawer, between the company brochures, I see a stack of porn magazines.

'New book, Colbert?' Derrick asks as he approaches my desk.

'Just having a look at some suggested reading, Derrick.'

I could ask the IT department to trace the printed documents to the user's computer, but what's the point? Then I'd be crucified for grassing them up as well as manipulating the markets. The former is worse than the latter in our world.

'Oh, good. Well, read up, Colbert. You never know what you might find useful. Don't be late for the meeting.' He ambles back to his office.

I have to hand it to Derrick. I wouldn't have the chutzpah to be so casual with the person I was framing. But then I'm not a sociopath.

No matter how cool I play this, and I am playing it extremely cool, the tension is gnawing at my insides by the time everyone makes their way to the conference room for the morning meeting. I don't bother trying to make small talk when I sit next to Ryan. He ignored me before I was less popular than a leper at a finger buffet.

There's only one person in the whole room whose opinion I really care about. 'Morning, Joe,' I say.

He nods, but says nothing. I can't read him. He's often gruff. Is this normal gruffness, or I-hate-you-Carol gruffness? I think I know the answer. Tears threaten to corrode my entire façade but I hold it together through the meeting. Somehow, I talk my way through it like it's just a regular briefing. I talk as if I didn't spend last evening in police custody and my colleagues haven't stuffed my desk with porn.

'One last thing,' Derrick says as we get up to leave.

'I want to know why Carol is still here.'

Everyone stops talking so they don't miss a word.

My face burns as I consider my next move. How I answer will decide whether I keep my job. Aside from whether the FCA presses charges, even though I'm not guilty of anything, despite being a damn good analyst even if I don't get any credit for it, my future really comes down to just a few words.

Derrick's eyes are filled with malicious glee. He's enjoying himself.

I think about how many years I've spent manufacturing Carol Colbert. No one could fault the blueprints. The execution was nearly flawless and the result calibrated to perfection. The reviews poured in – *5 stars! So useful… Does all that's promised and more! Everything I could want in a daughter, sister, friend, girlfriend, colleague, no complaints here.*

How deluded I've been to believe that everyone else's praise is the same thing as liking myself. I don't want to be on a pedestal if it means giving everyone else what they want while I feed off nothing but their compliments. I wish it hadn't taken a police investigation and a cheating boyfriend to realise that, but better late than never. I'm climbing down from that plinth and doing what I should have done long ago.

'Derrick, I want you to listen very carefully to what I'm about to say. I did not build Green T to manipulate the markets. I built it to accurately predict share price movements. I'm not guilty of any wrongdoing, and I have every right to be here to do my job. So you can just piss off and let me get on with it. Are we clear? No, you look a bit confused, so let me put it simply for you. Stop bullying me, you bloody shit of an arsehole, and fuck off. I'm not your punching bag, your prostitute or your indentured servant. I'm your employee, so grow up and start treating me like one. If you can't do that, then that's your failure, Derrick, not mine.'

I haven't often seen Derrick shocked. Once, when he got punched in the mouth at happy hour for sticking his hand up a woman's skirt, he looked momentarily taken aback. But then he was more surprised by the strength of the slight woman's right hook than at the sentiment of her action.

'You know I could fire you right now for talking to me like that.'

'That's bullshit. You'd have to fire every trader in this room, because they've all called you an arsehole.'

'That's because you are an arsehole, Derrick,' one of the traders says.

Derrick shrugs. 'And that's why women want to bed me and men want to be me. All right, gentlemen, back to work.'

I push past Ryan and the traders and walk through the conference room door with my back straight and an incredible feeling of lightness for someone who just told her boss to fuck off.

* * * * *

I found it. I FOUND IT! After only fifty hours of testing Green T, till it felt like my eyes were bleeding, I've found the error. Just to make sure, I've run the scenario two dozen times and there is definitely a glitch in the bank's version. I can prove that it isn't in the version I submitted to the programming team. All Zack has to do is find out who did make the changes.

It's nearly midnight when I ring him from my landline. I'd use my BlackBerry but I'm sure it's being monitored and I'd rather not get Zack fired if I can help it. So normal workday calls aren't an option.

I can't keep the excitement from rattling my voice. 'I'm really sorry to call so late, Zack, but I've found something. I'm guessing you'd rather hear from me now, not at six o'clock before I leave for work.'

'Correct assumption.'

He listens as I describe where the discrepancy between Green T and its evil twin seems to be occurring. 'Can you look there?'

'Uh-huh, now that I know where to look, it's a bit easier.'

'A lot easier?'

He chuckles. 'No, only a tiny bit easier. I have to compare each line of code between the systems. There are hundreds of thousands of lines of code. It could be in about a hundred different places. Even if I can find the difference, I might not know who made the changes.'

'But you'll try?' I'm fighting the urge to cry. I thought it'd be simple to find the difference once he knew what to look for. I didn't realise he was searching for a needle in a field of haystacks. My only hope relies on a run of luck so improbable that I wouldn't bet on us even with the best odds in the world.

'Of course I'll try. I'll go as fast as I can but it'll take a while. You owe me, big time.'

'I'll owe you my life, Zack.'

I do use my BlackBerry to make a call the next day. After all, there's nothing secret about what I'm about to do.

'Hi, Jim?' I say when Ben's receptionist puts me through to his colleague. 'How are you?'

'I'm fine, Carol, how are you? We haven't seen you lately. Have you been extra busy?'

So Ben hasn't mentioned that we're no longer together. Of course he hasn't, otherwise he'd have to admit that we broke up, and why.

'Yes, I have been pretty busy lately.'

'Are you after Ben?'

'No! I called you, though, because I did want to talk about him.'

'Are you planning a party or something?'

Or something.

'Actually, we broke up.'

He's quiet for a moment, probably trying to figure out whether he should be speaking with me. 'I'm really sorry to hear that. Are you okay?'

'Yes, I am, thanks, I'm just fine… I don't really know how to approach this, so I'm just going to come out with it.'

I tell him the whole story, about my surrogacy dates for Harriet, LoveHandles86's interest in her and our final confrontation in The Jerusalem.

'Wow, that doesn't sound at all like Ben. Could it have been a one-off? Not that that excuses him.'

'His profile had over two hundred "likes". He probably hasn't had two hundred dates but I doubt it was a one-off.'

A hot flush of shame creeps across me whenever I think about Ben. The things I put up with! What was I thinking?

'I don't know what to say, except I'm sorry that this

happened. He never let on and you two seemed so solid. Is there anything I can do?'

'Thanks but not really. It's definitely completely over between us. I guess I just want to make sure someone in his world knows the real story in case it ever comes up. He doesn't seem like the type to lie about it, but then again, I didn't think he was the type to cheat either. So now you know what he's really like. Do what you will with that information.'

'I understand, Carol. Thanks for telling me. Take care of yourself, will you? And for the record, I always thought you were too good for Ben.'

I laugh. 'Thanks, Jim. Do you know what? I finally think the very same thing.'

My next call is to *The Evening Standard*.

'Hello, Advertising, this is Charlie,' says an efficient-sounding woman.

'Hi, Charlie, I'd like to talk about placing an advert with you.'

'Sure, I can help you with that.'

As I explain what I want, she laughs. 'We can definitely do that. It could go in the day after tomorrow, in time for the evening commuters.'

Perfect.

The week's activity has put me in no mood to make small talk with Harriet's latest internet date. On the other hand, my bullshit detector is fully charged and working perfectly, so this shouldn't take long.

He's called Tom (allegedly, but I might ask to see his passport for identification purposes. You can't be too careful these days). He and Harriet emailed only a few times before he suggested meeting for a drink. This could mean that he's desperate, or it might mean that he doesn't want to get caught up with a time-waster. Lots of people are on the site just to boost their egos, trading internet banter without ever intending to meet in person.

I see him straight away, sitting on one end of a small sofa tucked into a snug corner of the bar.

He raises his eyebrows when he sees me. It's a common look amongst Harriet's dates when I approach. I could be their date. I could be the waitress coming to offer a drink. That's the downside of not having Harriet's photo on her profile. The upside, of course, is that I can make an anonymous getaway if I ever decide to abort the mission.

'Harriet? It's so nice to meet you. Is this okay here? We can move to a table if you want but I thought this might be more comfortable.'

'This is fine, thanks,' I say, lowering myself on to the leather cushion.

He looks exactly like his photo, with thick, medium brown, longish hair that stands up a bit to keep it from looking too neat. His blue eyes are crinkled at the edges and there's a definite kink in his nose where it must have been broken.

'Thank you for meeting me,' he says. 'What would you like to drink?'

'I'll have some wine but please, let me get it. What would you like?'

'That's very kind, thanks. I'll have a pint of IPA, please.'

As I make my way to the bar, I search my instincts for any signs of trouble. He's neither overly friendly nor standoffish. He hasn't misrepresented himself in his profile photos and is quite handsome in real life. Harriet forwarded me their messages and he sounds like a normal person.

'Was it a pain taking the Tube here during rush hour?' he asks when I return to the sofa. 'I generally ride my bike where I can. I'm not crazy about crowds.'

'Oh, no, I'm used to it.' Then I remember Harriet's complaints. 'But I hate crowds as well. I'm a country girl at heart. I was raised in Gloucestershire, in Chipping Norton.'

'I'm from Cirencester,' he says. 'It's a beautiful part of the country.'

'Do you think you'll go back there some day?'

'I do get back regularly to see my parents, but I don't think I'll live there again. I love London, and there isn't much pathology lab work in Cirencester.'

'I guess if you did work there, you'd know all of your neighbours' medical complaints.'

'That might be uncomfortable for Mrs Wiggins at the village fête.'

His whole face lights up when he laughs. I think Harriet's going to like him.

'In London you probably walk by your bowel complaint, diabetic and pregnant patients every day and don't even know it.'

'Hopefully that's not all that same patient,' he says. 'What do you do?'

'I work in Canary Wharf as an– in events management for a bank.' This is dangerous. Tom has put me completely at ease in about three minutes. I must remember that I'm Harriet tonight.

'It's a great job. I get to plan events for the bankers and, while they're not always fun, the work is varied.'

'It does sound fun. The one thing I'd change about my job would be the social element. I spend a lot of time alone with my microscope. It'd be nice to work in an office environment.'

'Are you very social, then?'

'I'd say that I'm medium-social. I love being out with my mates but don't mind being alone either.'

It's only been twenty minutes and already I know this is the kind of man that Harriet should be dating. When he tells me about the two long-term relationships he's had (unafraid to commit), which ended amicably because they weren't enough in love with each other (no obsessive exes), I have to fight the urge to call Harriet then and there.

She'll meet him soon enough.

I'm sorry that I have to stick to our one-hour rule because I could talk to Tom all evening. Despite the events of the past few weeks, I don't wish a plague of locusts upon all men. Only lying, cheating, rat-bags who use dating sites to cheat on their girlfriends.

Harriet's number comes up on my phone just as Tom and I part on the pavement.

'How was my date?' she asks.

'Wait until you meet him!' I whisper. 'You're going to love him.'

'So he's good, then? Woo hoo, that's fantastic! Tell me everything.'

'Let's meet for a quick drink. This deserves a face-to-face meeting. I can be at Oxford Circus in twenty minutes. Meet you there?'

'I'm leaving the flat now!'

I smile all the way to the Tube. Finally, Harriet is going to get the chance to go out with a nice guy. All we have to do is convince Tom that she's me, or that I was her. That can't be very hard, right?

CHAPTER 23

'Carol, *please* let me in!'

I hurry to the door before Marley bangs it down. She's carrying on like I've spitefully locked her out (she has a key).

'Marley, there's no need to shout.'

Mrs Gaynor will not be pleased by the noise.

'Well, you weren't answering me.'

'I was on the loo, if you must know. Do you need a more detailed explanation?'

'Can I come in?'

'I'm really rather busy at the moment.'

'This'll only take a minute. Please, Carol.'

Zoe opens her bedroom door just as we reach the living room. She's got her enormous retro earphones on.

'Marley!' She runs to my sister for kisses. 'How wonderful for you to visit. Isn't it wonderful, Carol?'

'I'm over the moon,' I say.

Zoe has been trying to mend the Colbert fences

since I blew up at Mum. As much as I'd like to make her feel better, my days of worrying about other people are over.

Marley settles herself on the sofa like we're about to enjoy a bottle of wine together. 'Did you repaint the walls?'

'No.'

'It looks nice.'

'What can I do for you, Marley?'

She snatches my hand before I can pull it away from the back of the sofa. 'I owe you the biggest apology on the planet, Carol. I'm so sorry about the way I've been behaving. I've been a shitty sister. I'm sorry.'

I glance at the tears in her eyes, but find myself unmoved by them.

'It's not just about the wedding you know. You've taken me for granted my whole life. You and Mum.'

'I know! I'm sorry, Carol. I can't change what's happened, but I promise I won't ever do it again. I didn't take advantage of you on purpose, you know. What I mean is, I didn't set out to take advantage. You seemed to really want to help out all the time, so I let you. Then I guess I got lazy, knowing you'd always take care of everything. So I assumed you always would, but I swear if I knew how you felt, I wouldn't have asked. You're my sister and I love you. I don't want to see you upset.'

In a way she's right, but just because I never objected doesn't mean it was all right to take advantage. 'I should have said something sooner but you shouldn't have been so demanding, even if you knew I'd do what you wanted. That wasn't fair.'

'I know. I'm sorry. Can we please move on from

here? I'm going to be a better sister, I promise. You probably need help as much as I do, and I'm going to be there for you.'

'Like if I needed someone to help Zoe with her job search, for instance?'

'Absolutely.' She turns to Zoe, who's been hovering by the kitchen door. 'Zoe, just let me know when you're free and I can help. There, what else?'

'You need to let Jez's cousins come to the wedding. I'm running out of excuses to satisfy Isabel and I'm tired of running interference for you. Either deal with her yourself, or let them come.'

I can tell she really wants to fight me on this, but eventually she says, 'Fine, they can come. I'll tell Isabel.'

'No way, Marley. I've had to give her bad news for six months. I get to give her the good news, thanks. And one more thing. Mum and Dad need to find a holiday house in Dorset.'

'Already taken care of. We found a great cottage in Poole last week. They're all booked.'

Well, I'll be damned. My family is capable of taking care of themselves.

'Don't count on Mum being happy with it.'

'You'll have to talk to her eventually, you know. You have to tell her what you've just told me.'

'I know. There are a few things I need to take care of first.'

'Promise you will talk to her, though?'

'I promise.'

'Do you love each other again?' Zoe asks.

'We've always loved each other,' I say. 'We just don't always like each other.'

'I am so happy to have my family back together.'

She envelops us with her skinny arms. 'Well, nearly. I do not like when the Colberts are unhappy. Let's open wine to celebrate.'

She's a hopeless romantic but I am glad Marley and I are good again. Now I just have to have it out with Mum.

Zack drops a note on my desk as he walks by the next morning. He's not exactly James Bond. I feel more like I'm in primary school, and half expect to see *Do you like me? Yes/No* written on the balled-up bit of paper.

As if it would say that after the way I treated him in the lobby that day with Ben. I'm lucky he's even agreed to be my friend, or to help me. I'm very lucky for that.

The note says I'm to meet him at the Corney & Barrow in ten minutes. It's barely eleven o'clock. He must have found something.

'Want a drink?' he says when I get there, all casual, like my future doesn't lie in his next words.

How can he be calm at a time like this? 'It depends on what you're about to tell me. Do I need something alcoholic?'

He's enjoying torturing me. 'I'll have an orange juice and lemonade,' he tells the young bartender.

'Me, too, please.'

We carry our drinks to a table away from the large front windows, where the sun is streaming in, warming the coarse wooden table tops. No sun for us though. We're under cover, apparently.

'I can hardly believe what I've found,' Zack says. 'I mean, really, I wasn't sure I'd see anything at all, and then when I did, well… We've got all the proof you could want that you weren't the one who changed the system.' He starts pulling sheets of paper out of his courier bag.

'Does that mean you know who did?' My heart is doing a salsa against my ribcage.

He nods. 'I'd better start from the beginning. When you told me which scenarios were making Green T go out of sync with your prototype, I had to scour all the code that might relate to that scenario. Luckily, I was able to write a little program to help me and eventually I found the exceptions.'

He takes a long, long, *long* sip of his drink.

'Someone rewrote part of the coding to make Green T overreact to negative news.'

'Which caused it to sell off shares, which drove down the prices of those companies. To put them out of business?'

He shakes his head. 'To make money for the bank. Every company whose share price fell had short sell options written against them.'

My mind races to catch up with what he's saying. It boils down to the bank having investments that get a huge sum of money when a company's share price falls, like an insurance policy where I get paid if you crash your car. It's bad news for you, but great news for me. The more bad news, the better.

'Like I said, I checked our trading positions,' he says. 'Every one of those companies has an option against it, Carol. That can't be coincidence. Our traders are good but they're not that good.'

My head begins to spin.

The system that I built to help environmental companies has been the engineer of their downfall. Green T is purposely putting companies out of business so that the bank can cash in on their demise.

Those are the same companies that I'm supposed to be helping.

'Are you all right? Here, drink this. You look like you've seen a ghost.'

'That's appropriate, since I've killed those companies.'

'You haven't done anything, Carol. I told you. The system was tampered with.'

'That won't matter to the companies, though, will it? They've still lost millions off their share price. Some are close to bankruptcy.'

Joe was right when he said I'd enjoyed playing God, thinking I could build something that was smarter than the traders. I was a fool.

'Listen to this punchline,' says Zack. 'As I suspected, there wasn't any way to see in the code itself who'd made the changes, but I could see when it was last changed. So I figured that whoever rewrote that code must have been told to do it by someone in the bank. After all, the bank is profiting, right? They'd be stupid to keep emails in their inboxes, but the changes were substantial enough that there had to be a written record somewhere. So I went to the system backups prior to the last change to Green T. I went through each of the coders' emails. And I found this.'

He pushes a slender stack of paper towards me.

One name jumped out again and again as I scanned the pages.

'Derrick?'

He nods. 'It's all there. Derrick was working with one of our coders to alter Green T. It doesn't look from this like the coder knew he was doing anything wrong. He was just following orders from one of the business heads, just like the coder who built Green T in the first place.'

'But Derrick knew what he was doing.'

'Definitely. And he tried to cover his tracks. I checked his email and he has deleted all these. But the coder didn't know he was doing anything wrong so he didn't delete Derrick's emails. They're all here because the regulators make us keep everything.'

'Yay for the regulators,' I say faintly.

'It gets worse. Or better, as long as you're not Derrick…'

When Zack checked into the bank's short-selling options, those contracts that pay out when a company's share price falls, he found that they all came from one of the traders just a few days before the companies' share prices tanked. In other words, Green T was set to force the entire ethical investment market into liquidation. Those contracts were just sitting there, waiting to be exercised at the first whiff of bad company news. Each bad earnings announcement, every government flip-flop on its green policy, meant another nail in the coffin for an ethical company.

'But why this sector? Why not oil and gas, or tobacco or arms or something that isn't…'

Something that isn't good, I was about to say.

'I guess it's because it's still small, and its volatility makes it easier to manipulate.'

I think back to the media launch.

'Derrick said when we launched Green T that the bank wasn't using it.'

'He wasn't lying, technically. Green T isn't managing any of the bank's investments. But it is managing its clients' investments. So when it dumps a stock, there's so much money moving away from it that it that forces the price down and the option contract kicks in, paying the bank.'

He sits back in his chair, clearly pleased with himself. 'You've got everything you need to clear yourself, Carol. Is there anything else I can do?'

I look at my friend. We've known each other for four years, yet I feel more distant from him than I ever have. 'Can you forgive me for my behaviour, Zack? I was such an arsehole.'

'You were an arsehole, but I forgive you. We're friends again. Just friends, though. I'm sorry to say that you've blown any chance of ever getting a piece of this.' He gestures to his midsection. 'Go on, admit it. You're a little disappointed now, aren't you?'

Actually, I am, a little bit. But then, that's probably just my ego talking. As great as Zack is, and as good a friend as he's been, until he kissed me it had never occurred to me to want more. I was single for nearly two years between Skate and Ben, years when Zack and I could easily have gotten together, but we didn't. I guess that tells me something.

'I'm gutted,' I tell him. 'But I'll have to learn to live with it. Are you ready to go back? I've got to call Harriet. Then I'm calling the FCA.'

When I tell Richard Bean what Zack has found, he says he can be at Canary Wharf within the hour. Zack and I return to the Corney & Barrow to fill him in.

They wait until I get back to my desk before approaching Derrick. Once again, the police flank Richard as he makes his way to Derrick's office.

'What the fuck?' says Ryan over the partition.

'What's happening?'

'Don't care, Ryan,' I say, not looking away from my screens.

'Are they after Derrick?'

'Don't know. Don't care.'

'Don't be a bitch.'

'Don't be a wanker.'

He stands up. 'Is something wrong, Colbert?'

'No, why?'

'You seem different.'

'Get used to it.'

The press is waiting for Derrick when he emerges from the building with the police. I made sure of that when I called Harriet. I slipped out not long after Richard went into Derrick's office with the police. He'd told me there was no need for me to be with them, since it was Zack who'd uncovered all the evidence, and it was right there on the bank's computers for the FCA to confirm.

So I took a little walk. I didn't go far. Just to the pillar next to the building, where I'd have the best view.

As I stand here watching the journalists gabble to each other and the cameramen set up their equipment, I search my conscience for any sign of guilt at what I've done. There isn't any. Here is a man who has humiliated me for four years. He's framed me, dangled me as bait for lecherous clients and taken credit for my achievements. He's put good companies out of business just to feather his master's nest. One short burst of unwanted publicity doesn't even come close to making up for that.

He looks bewildered as he's led through the doors. I wonder, briefly, how I'll feel if he sees me. He'll know by now, or at least strongly suspect, that I was the one who gave the evidence to the FCA.

But he's too focussed on all the journalists who are about to make him a headline to look for me. Besides, something tells me that if he did catch my eye, it wouldn't be anger that I'd see. Derrick has always had a soft spot for merciless self-preservation.

The journalists are baying for blood. I can't make out what they're shouting at him as they snap their photos and get their footage for the six o'clock news. *Head of Trading Arrested for Market Manipulation. Details after the break.*

He's not hanging around for photo ops and the whole scene is over within minutes. The police car pulls slowly around the corner. The journalists are soon lost amongst the early afternoon suits.

I'll watch it on the news tonight, even though I know the whole story. I don't think I'll be completely at ease until he's convicted and I know he can't get to me.

I don't plan to let anyone get to me like that again.

Good riddance to Carol the pushover. I've got control of my own life now.

CHAPTER 24

Now that Marley and I are back on sisterly terms, she's ringing again every day. There is a crucial difference, though. Instead of requesting some feat of bridesmaid derring-do, she just tells me what's happening in her life. So she's still completely self-absorbed but at least she's not demanding. Baby steps.

'It's Jez's birthday on Thursday,' she says as I sit at my desk scanning one of my company's investment reports. I'm having a hard time caring about these reports just now, given that the future of the whole department is in doubt.

Our clients are understandably upset that the money they've lost thanks to Green T was the result of fraud. Lawsuits are probably popping up faster than spots on a teenager.

Only Joe and one or two of the other traders are in a position to gloat over everyone else. Their mistrust of the programmed trading system was justified, though that will be cold comfort if they lose their jobs with the rest of us.

Derrick's departure hardly made a ripple on the floor. The trader who helped him was suspended as well and one of the other business heads stepped in to take charge until our future is decided. Compared to Derrick, he practically wraps us in cotton wool. I never imagined a world where workdays didn't involve shouting or tears.

Of course, the bank is now in serious trouble with the FCA for manipulating the world's stock markets, but they'll take it in their stride. They've got teams of lawyers and PR bods mobilised to limit the damage. In a world where people are surprised when a bank does something right, this will be yesterday's news by next week.

'Can you come for drinks?' Marley continues. 'There's someone I want you to meet. It's Jez's best friend. We'll be there until late so you can come any time.'

'Okay, I'll probably get there around nine. Haven't I met Jez's best friend already?'

'Erm, no. But you'll meet him on Thursday!'

'What's he like?'

'He's great. Wait and see.'

He can't be that great if I've not met him in the five years Jez and Marley have been going out.

'Hey, Carol? I'm glad everything is back to normal.'

Well, not quite everything. I still need to talk to Mum. Just not yet.

The bank decided our future today. It's not as bad as it could have been. The FCA won't close us down because as far as they can prove, Derrick and his puppet trader acted alone. The poor programmer who made the changes to Green T nearly had a heart attack when he found out that he was an accessory to the fraud. They had to take him to the nurse, and the regulators are satisfied that his shock is genuine.

But it means the death of Green T. I felt sick when the interim manager told us that too much reputational damage has been done to bother resurrecting it.

It won't take long for everyone to forget Green T ever existed. Traders will gladly forget it once their losses have been taken and their clients are happy again. The analysts have so much new information pushed into their brains every day that they'll gladly let go of the details of the past month. Clients will move on to the next hot investment as easily as a popular boy changes girlfriends.

But I won't forget this. I despise Derrick for perverting something that was harmless at worst and helpful at best.

Still, at least I've got my job and I'll work as hard as I possibly can to make sure the companies that Derrick plundered get every chance to rebuild their business. I didn't set out to create a monster, but that's what Green T became. This Dr Frankenstein owes the villagers a fresh start.

It's just after eight when I leave the office for Jez's drinks. I'm not overly anxious to go but there is something I want to see on the way over.

I hope it's something that a lot of people will see, but as I get to the Tube station I know I'm too late. There's no mountain of free commuter papers. *The Evening Standard* man has gone and the box that holds his paper is empty.

I guess Harriet may have one.

I type a quick text to send to her once I'm above ground again, and hurry into the carriage to nab one of the last empty seats. Just as the doors close I spot a woman further down the carriage reading *The Evening Standard*.

She doesn't look up as I approach.

'Excuse me. Could I look at your paper quickly?'

She's staring at me like I've just asked to take a poo in her handbag.

'Please? There's something in there I need to see. In fact, you may want to see it too.'

A flicker of interest passes over her expression. 'What is it?'

'Oh, it's an advert.'

I've got to hook my arm around the central pole to keep from falling over in the moving train as I quickly flip the pages. Weather, Jeremy Clarkson in another scandal, boring advert, boring advert, boring advert.

Finally, near the back, I see it. The photo is just the tiniest bit out of focus but it's one of the few where he's grinning and I don't look like I've had a stroke. It's about four inches square, and anyone who's ever met him will recognise him. That's what I'm counting on.

Underneath, in a big, bold, headline font, is my letter to Ben.

Dear LoveHandles86 on Dates.com,

If you wanted to date other women, you probably should have told them about me first. I'm sure not all of them would have minded that you've had a girlfriend for two years.

**Sincerely,
Your (now ex-) girlfriend,
Carol**

'Have a look,' I tell the woman who's paper I've stolen.

'You're Carol?'

'Yep.'

She points at Ben's nose. 'And that's LoveHandles? What's his real name?'

'It doesn't matter. It's a nice clear photo.'

'What an arsehole,' she says. 'Was it worth it? That advert must have cost you a fortune.'

'It's the best £800 I've ever spent.'

As I walk to the bar to meet Marley and Jez, I wonder if that advert means that I'm a psycho. Or have I just enacted every girl's perfect revenge fantasy?

You know what? For once I don't care what other people think. And that feels great.

When I see how packed the bar is, I'm in half a mind to turn around. If I say a quick hello to Jez and Marley, I can be on my sofa in time for the ten o'clock news.

A few of Marley's friends are near the bar, but there's no one that I know well. There is one tall, lanky man who looks familiar. Do I know him? He glances in my direction and I find myself smiling. He grins in return.

'Carol, hey!' says Jez, suddenly at my elbow. 'I think Marley's just gone to the loo if you want to join her.'

'Why would I want to join her in the loo?' I ask, kissing him hello. 'I'll get a drink and mingle. Are you having a good birthday?'

'It's great,' he says. 'Everyone's here. Oh, look, there's Marley. Do you want to go say hello?'

'I will in a minute. I'll just get a drink first.'

'Are you sure?'

'Jez, what is wrong with you? You're acting weird.'

'Nothing! I just thought that since you didn't know anyone, you'd want to find Marley.'

'I promise I'll go find Marley after I get a drink. Okay?'

'Sure, fine.' He looks like he's about to say more, but instead he just watches me head for the spot next to the tall smiling man.

'Do we know each other?' he says as I wait for the barman to serve me.

'I wondered the same thing, but I don't think so.'

Suddenly, I remember *The Evening Standard* advert. While I was gloating over exposing Ben, I never stopped to think that now about a million people have seen my photo, too.

'I'm Robert. Do you know Jez?'

'Marley is my sister. I'm Carol.'

'Oh, of course. Maybe that's why you look familiar. I'm Jez's mate. It's nice to meet you.'

So this must be Jez's best friend. On looks alone I can see why Marley wanted me to meet him. He's got friendly yet bashful deep blue eyes that are stirring something up in my tummy.

'How long have you known Jez?' I ask.

'Not as long as you've known Marley, but we were in primary school together, so I've got a fair amount of blackmail material on him.'

'That'll come in handy if he ever runs for

Parliament.'

'On the contrary, bad behaviour is a prerequisite for our politicians. If you can't come up with at least one indiscretion for the membership form, they won't let you into the party.'

'Are you political?'

He shrugs. 'Not really, I'm just an interested member of the public who likes to keep an eye on our public servants.'

'I see you two have met.'

Marley staggers a bit as she leans in for a kiss.

'I'm glad you came, Carol. Jez is having an awesome night.'

'You're pissed.'

She sniggers. 'I am! Jez and I shared a bottle of fizz before we came. Oh, you'll never guess what… I only went and found the perfect wedding venue, in Scotland!'

She catches Robert scanning the room over her head. 'Robert, pay attention. As our best man, this involves you, too.'

'So I guess we'll be spending some more time together,' he says to me.

'I guess we will.' I pull my eyes away from his. 'When are you going to see it, Marley? Do you need me to come with you?'

'No, thank you. I've already booked the train for Saturday. Jez and I are going up and we'll stay the night there.'

So my sister can stand on her own two feet when she wants to. Miracles will never cease.

'Ooh I love this song!' she shouts as a Black-Eyed Peas song comes on. 'I'm going to make Jez dance with me.'

She weaves off into the crowd.

'Your sister is one of a kind. Jez is nuts about her.'

'Sometimes I think Jez is nuts to be with her, so it must be true love.'

'Ah, true love, that elusive Holy Grail.'

I can't help but stare at his lips as he takes a sip of his beer.

'They're proof that it does happen, though.'

Do I still believe in true love? I'm not sure, and not just because Ben is an arse. Maybe it only happens for a lucky few people who manage to meet their soulmate at the right time. I was convinced that Skate and I were destined to be together, and yet whatever we had wasn't strong enough to last out in the real world after university. If someone had asked me a year ago whether Ben and I would be together forever, I'd have said yes, of course. But he obviously had other ideas. So I'm not quite sure what I believe any more, but I'm willing to keep an open mind.

He taps my wine glass with his bottle. 'Well, here's to true love.'

I haven't even finished my drink and already I feel a bit spinny-headed. My tummy is rolling over on itself. I had sushi for lunch. I hope it wasn't off…

Wait a minute. That's not bad sushi.

It's lust.

My tummy confirms it when I look at his lips again.

Definitely lust.

Well, at least I'm not dead inside.

Within a few minutes, Robert and I are chatting like Skate and I used to. Not in bone-shattering confidences, but with an easy repartee.

I'm not at all surprised when he asks for my number. If he hadn't, I'd have asked for his. Whether lust or bad sushi, I want to see this man again.

CHAPTER 25

'But I cannot. *Je suis désolée.*'

I'm *désolée* too, and Marley looks like she's about to cry.

'You have to come, Zoe, you're part of the family. My wedding won't be the same if you're not there.'

At her words, a tear rolls down Zoe's cheek. 'But I cannot miss my mother's birthday, Marley. It is her fiftieth and it's expected that I am there. Please say that you understand. I cannot be in two places at once.'

I have to give Marley credit where it's due. Not only did she find a possible venue, she dragged Jez all the way to Scotland to see it, and decided to book it without my help. The only problem is that it won't simply be a matter of hopping on the Tube or sharing a taxi to get there. My sister has officially booked a destination event. Unfortunately, so has Zoe's mother.

'Maybe you could fly out to meet your family after my wedding. Then you'd only be two days late. You said they were staying until the first–'

Seriously?

'Marley, Zoe is going to Thailand, not Brighton. That'd mean her flying thirteen hours for a four-day holiday, missing Christmas, and her mother's birthday, just so you can have her at your wedding, which is about a million miles away from any airport all the way in Scotland. Stop being so selfish.'

Marley's tears miraculously evaporate. 'I'm only saying that she knew we were going to be married in December and she could have factored that into her plans.'

'You're right, what was she thinking? The audacity to have a mother who was born fifty years before the day you decide to get married. Zoe, don't listen to her.' I put my arms around her. 'You should be there to celebrate your mum's birthday. We'll take lots of photos and we'll all get together to tell you every detail as soon as Marley and Jez get back from their honeymoon. Marley will be fine with you going to your family.'

'Stop speaking for me, Carol!'

'I'll stop speaking for you when you stop speaking for Zoe.'

She glares at me. 'You know what? I don't like this new you very much.'

'Well, you'd better get used to her because I like her quite a lot and she's not going anywhere.'

Zoe backs out of the room to check on dinner. 'I'm sorry I'm causing such a fuss,' she says as she goes.

'You're not! It's Marley that's being unreasonable.'

The doorbell cuts my sister off mid-insult.

It's nice to be back to normal.

'That'll be Harriet, so can we all please behave?' By

all, I mean Marley.

She'll have forgotten all about Zoe by tomorrow. As much as she loves wallowing in drama, she can only hold on to each crisis for a few hours before the next emergency captures her attention.

'Harriet, tell me everything!' I shout as I open the door. She went out with Tom, from the dating website, last night.

'Erm, Carol, look who's here,' she says, stepping aside.

Mum.

She sweeps into the flat, kissing my cheeks as she passes. 'Hello, darling. Have you had the place painted? Where's Zoe? I've brought wine!'

My mother hasn't been in the flat since soon after I moved in.

'To what do we owe this pleasure?' I ask.

I catch Zoe's glance at Marley.

I've been set up. I knew this day would come. I just hoped to be the one to decide when it did. Standing up to my boss and the police and the FCA is one thing, but do I really have the courage to stand up to my mother? I'm about to find out.

'Well,' says Zoe. 'I was cooking and I thought it would be nice to have Madame Colbert here too. Since I am cooking.'

'You look tired, darling,' Mum says to me. 'Is everything okay?'

'I've had a lot on my mind lately.'

'Anything you want to talk about?' She sips her wine, then hands me a glass. 'Maybe I can help?'

Here is the woman I've been desperate to please all my life. I wonder how it started. Did she hold back her affection at some failure of mine? Or did I get addicted to the heaps of praise she gave me when I excelled? I don't know. I'll probably never know, but something occurs to me as I stare into her concerned face. It doesn't really matter. Marley had the exact same upbringing as I did and she couldn't be less of a people-pleaser. This isn't something Mum has done to me. It's something I did to myself.

And that means I can undo it.

'Well, in fact, something did happen at work, starting a few months ago. Marley?' I call into the kitchen. 'Can you bring that bottle of wine in here?'

She doesn't interrupt as I tell her the whole Green T saga, ending with Derrick's arrest. She just drinks her wine with her eyes trained on mine. Every so often she reaches over to touch my hand or my leg.

'You shouldn't have kept something like this to yourself, Carol. You'd have felt better telling us, don't you think?'

'Maybe, but I had enough to worry about keeping myself from freaking out. I didn't want to have to worry about you, too.'

'I understand, but I wish you hadn't gone through that alone.'

'I wasn't alone.'

'No, you had Ben, I suppose, but that's not the same.'

Harriet squirms on the sofa, staring into her wine glass.

'Well, actually, about Ben…'

Marley and Zoe sit down on each side of Harriet.

'We broke up.'

'What did you do?' she cries. 'I know he's been

working a lot but Carol, you've got to be supportive of his work. It's not forever and he'd do the same for you.'

This is exactly why I didn't rush to tell her.

'Mum, she didn't do anything,' Marley says. 'He was the arsehole, not her! God, you can really be impossible sometimes!'

My sister might feel she has every right to attack me, but nobody else had better try it.

'He was cheating on me, Mum, so I broke up with him.'

That stops her indignant huffing. As the wife of a touring musician, she's extra-sensitive to infidelity. Not that Dad has ever cheated. He wouldn't dare.

'Oh, well, I'm sorry to hear that, darling. Is it definitely over?'

I think *The Evening Standard* advert made sure of that. I nod.

Marley starts to grin. 'But you have met someone, haven't you, Carol?' she sings.

'Yes, but we haven't even gone out yet so it's nothing. We're having dinner together on Friday.'

Robert texted me before I'd even got home from Jez's drinks and we've been in touch constantly since then. I don't want to get ahead of myself (or jinx things) but I haven't felt this much excitement in a long time.

Zoe's hands fly to her heart. 'Maybe you will fall in love and have a double wedding with Marley.'

As if Marley would ever share the limelight on her wedding day. 'Let's just see how the date goes first, okay?'

'Well, if it's anything like mine was,' Harriet says

through her enormous smile, 'you and I might have a double wedding. Carol, you were right, he's amazing!'

Marley looks confused. 'You know Harriet's date? Is he with the bank?'

'Well, I don't exactly know him,' I say. 'I mean, I only met him once.'

'I'm hopeless at judging men, so Carol has been going on my internet dates.' Harriet announces this without an ounce of embarrassment. 'Carol has been my dating surrogate!'

'That's nice,' says Marley. 'You haven't had time to help me with my wedding but you've had time to go on dates for Harriet?'

'Don't get your knickers in a twist. I've done plenty for your wedding and you know it.'

'Don't twist your knickers, Marley,' Zoe says.

'Go check on dinner, will you?'

'Tom and I stayed out till after three and even then we didn't want the date to end,' Harriet says. 'We've got so much to talk about and we're going out again tomorrow. I think I'm going to invite him to my birthday party.'

'Okay,' I say diplomatically. 'But that's still a month away.'

She shrugs. 'I've just got a good feeling about him. You did too, right? He doesn't seem like a weirdo.'

'No, on the contrary, he seemed great!' The last thing I want to do is put a doubt in Harriet's mind. He did seem great. 'And he never suspected that it wasn't you on the first date?'

'Actually, he said I looked even more beautiful than the first time we met.' She's blushing. 'Sorry, Carol.'

'Yes, well, I can't really be upset that my best

friend's new boyfriend thinks she's prettier than me, can I? Come here you lucky, lucky girl!'

She throws herself into my arms.

'It's all thanks to you, Carol. You are the most amazing friend.'

'And amazing sister,' says Zoe, raising her glass along with Marley.

'And daughter. Darling,' Mum whispers. 'Does this mean that you and I are okay? Are you still angry with me?'

I'm not sure if I was ever really angry with her. I was certainly angry with myself.

'No, I'm really not, Mum, I promise. Look, we don't have to have a big talk about this.'

She looks relieved.

'Just know that I've spent too long trying to be perfect in everyone else's eyes. I thought that made me happy, too, but it didn't. It made me miserable. So I'm not doing it any more. That might come across as selfish but…' I shrug. 'Well, maybe sometimes it is, and I'll have to find a balance somehow. So if you can be patient with me and know that I'm not trying to be mean or malicious, I feel like I can be happy. You'll do that for me, right?'

'We'll do anything for you, Carol,' she says. 'We love you.'

I know I can't change them, or make them less self-serving. All I can do is not let them bully me.

That's the thing with the real world. It's never going to be perfect, and I don't have control over that. But I can control how I behave in it, and how I let things affect me. I can choose to be perfect in my own way without having to be perfect in everyone else's eyes.

Relying on other people to reflect my worth back to me is a fool's errand. I need to stare directly at it.

CHAPTER 26

I've taken so much care over my appearance that I could stroll down the runway at London Fashion Week and it'd probably be at least two minutes before the front row realised I was an imposter. Then, of course, I'd be dragged off by security and thrown in jail, and would miss my date with Robert tonight.

He hasn't been far from my thoughts all week. We've been texting and emailing like school kids, minus the half-naked selfies and LOLs. How can I feel this already for someone I've barely met? We're building a relationship around words, and can't possibly live up to each other's expectations. Can we? I'm excited by the possibilities.

Ben barges his way into my head as I walk from the Tube to the restaurant in Farringdon where Robert has booked us a table. There's a tiny kernel of doubt that my mind keeps rubbing against. I know (I know!) his cheating was in no way caused by me. But you hear it all the time, don't you? He slept with the neighbour because his wife let herself go after the children or didn't pay him enough attention. She ran off with the plumber because her other half always worked late or was too clingy.

I know that's a stinking fresh pile of poo. It's not the cheatee's fault. Ever. On an intellectual level I know that, yet when I let my guard down my mind slides towards the sticky tar pit where his betrayal wallows.

I won't let myself be drawn in there. Just because he's a bloated tick on the belly of humankind doesn't mean that all men are. If I'm wrong, and Robert turns out to be a rat, then that's because Robert is a rat, not because of his gender or anything I do.

Besides, tummy flutters like this don't come along every day, and I'm not about to dampen them down.

He's already at the table when I arrive.

'Hi, you look great,' he says, leaning in to kiss my cheek. The little bit of stubble I feel against my skin sends my gut into joyous spasms.

'Thank you. I'm not late, am I?'

'No, you're perfectly on time.'

He pulls my chair out for me.

'Good, because I hate being late. I've been called obsessive over it, actually.'

Why am I confessing faults before we've even sat down?

'Now that I know you're a stickler for time I can tell you that I find habitually late people really rude. Their time is no more important than mine and yet they're happy to make me wait around because they're busy doing something else.' He suddenly grins. 'I'm sorry. I don't mean to rant on our first date.'

'You usually like to save your tirades for the second date?'

'Yeah, I like a rant right after coffee,' he says. 'You never get a second chance to make a first impression.' He grimaces. 'I sound like a wanker, sorry. I don't know why I'm so nervous when we've been emailing all week. That's been great. I feel like I know you already.'

'Have you been looking through my curtains with binoculars?'

'How can I when your curtains are always closed?' He laughs. 'Your curtains aren't really always closed, are they?'

I shake my head.

'That's good, because otherwise my attempt at a funny quip might have come across as grounds for notifying the police. I promise I haven't been spying through your curtains.'

The waiter hands us our menus. The dishes seem to consist mainly of entrails.

'This is offal!' I say.

'Oh, it's not that bad,' he deadpans. 'Nose-to-tail dining. Will you have the bone marrow or the trotter pie?'

'Bone marrow is a treatment for leukaemia, and I make it a rule never to eat meat with toenails attached. I think I'll have the roast beef.'

'You're living dangerously.'

'I'm playing fast and loose with the horseradish, though.'

His laugh is rich and warm and makes me think of cosy jumpers and wine by an open fire. What's happening to me? It took nearly two years to work up the courage to mention living together to Ben and here

I am imagining weekends away with Robert before we've even held hands. I seem to have left inertia behind and run headlong into impulsiveness. Steady on, girl.

Our conversation bounces along through the meal as the restaurant chatters and crashes around us. Everything about the night is comfortable. The rough wooden tables, casual waiters, open kitchen and general air of controlled chaos. It's all much more fun than the creeping deference of the Michelin-star restaurants I've been to with clients.

Before the main course plates are cleared I find myself telling Robert the whole story of Ben and me. It's only when I see his eyes widen at *The Evening Standard* advertisement that I think about tempering my enthusiasm. But then it's too late.

He's probably wondering how to escape the date without risking an exposé in tomorrow's papers.

'I'd have done exactly the same thing,' he finally says. 'Ben sounds like an arsehole. Why did you stay with him for so long when it was clear he was just using you?' He looks embarrassed. 'I'm sorry. I didn't mean for that to sound judgmental.'

'That's okay. It wasn't always bad, but then he got his case, he's a trainee solicitor, and had to spend more time at the office and things just... you know what? Forget I said that. I'm so used to making excuses for him that sometimes I forget I don't have to anymore. He is an arsehole. And he expected me to be the one to always give in and make everything nice. Some of that was my fault. I made it easy for everyone. That's who I was for a long time. It's natural for people to eventually get used to that and come to expect it, but that's all changed now. Now I don't make it easy for anyone. Just so you know.'

He takes my hand across the table. His is large and warm and gives me wintertime musings again.

'Easy or hard, Carol, I think you're pretty incredible, and I can't wait to get to know you better.'

Wow. Just... wow. He talks like an adult.

'I think this is where we kiss,' he says.

The table between us doesn't stop him. He stands up so he can lean across. When his lips meet mine I feel as if we're losing altitude at 30,000 feet.

'That's my reward for telling you about my rotten ex? I wonder what I'll get when you hear about my boss.'

We split the bill and walk, hand in hand now, into the cool night. I have no destination in mind and, it seems, neither does he. As we wander, I tell Robert everything. My whole life comes tumbling, unedited, from my lips. As I listen to myself talk about Derrick and my lecherous clients, the strip club and daily humiliations, it doesn't sound like it could be true.

'It sounds pretty dire, doesn't it?' I say as St Paul's cathedral comes into view. 'If someone had just told me that story, I'd have told her not to bother with Human Resources but go to the police instead.'

I should probably feel self-conscious telling Robert just what a pushover I've been. Instead, the words keep coming like they can't get to him fast enough.

'It's always easier to see things clearly from the outside,' he says when I tell him about Derrick's arrest. 'And now that you're outside it, so to speak, because you're not putting up with anyone's shit, it looks bad. It was bad, Carol. You're a very strong person to have been able to deal with all that.'

He draws me to him as we stand in the shadow of St Paul's, and we kiss. I can't think of anywhere I'd rather be at this very moment.

'Well, I don't have to deal with it any more,' I say. 'I've stripped out everything in my life that isn't exactly the way I want it. I might not have had any control over my life before, but I do now.'

His eyes search mine. 'Is control very important?'

'Oh, yes,' I laugh. 'I thought I had everything under control before, but actually, it was everyone else who had the control because I was reliant on their good opinion of me for my opinion of myself. How crazy was that?'

'Not crazy. It's common. We all want to know we're liked, admired, whatever, right? I think it's normal.'

'But not to this extreme. Anyway, it was like I was shaken awake one day by the truth. Other people don't make me happy. I make me happy. Now that I realise it, I'm making my life just the way I want it. I can make my life perfect for me so I don't have to worry about being perfect to everyone else.'

I might be babbling. 'Am I making any sense?'

'Perfect sense.' His dark blue eyes crinkle.

When he kisses me again, I lean in to his body. I could do this all night.

'I'm not sure how I measure up in your perfect life,' he whispers. 'But I'd love to see you again.'

I can't think of anything I'd rather do than see this man again. Tomorrow, and the next day and the next...

CHAPTER 27

… And the next day and the next day and the next. Robert and I have barely spent an evening apart in the past three weeks. I did wonder if it would start to grate after barely seeing Ben for so long, but I love it. There's no guessing, no wondering and not one jot of will-he-won't-he uncertainty. He will!

I've never been a big romantic, even as a teen when Skate and I were together. I sometimes made romantic gestures, but that's not the same thing as *being* romantic.

These days I'm practically farting rose petals.

The more I see Robert, the more I want to see him. It's an easy exploration with little drama and I often find myself wanting to cook him candlelit dinners and surprise him with flowers. I'm a step away from sending him a giant cookie heart with *Carol likes Robert* iced on it.

The best part is: he happens to think I'm the best thing since five-a-side football.

As I get to my desk on the morning of Harriet's birthday party, I see something on my chair. It's an A4-sized white envelope with my name written neatly across the front.

It could, of course, be some new porn to top up the collection in my drawer. But unless someone went to the effort of cutting out individual images – and here I envision a potpourri of pneumatic breasts and labial close-ups fluttering around me as I open the envelope – it's too thin.

My heart stutters as I go to chuck my (absent) gym bag under the desk. I also panicked at the Tube turnstile, then as I left the carriage at Canary Wharf. I reached for it when I slid my pass through the reader at reception and in the lift on the way up. But it's finally time to drop the pretence. I'm no gym bunny and I'm not going to haul a useless bag around. So shoot me.

I peek inside the envelope. It's just my review.

That's odd. Derrick gave me my review more than six months ago. It said that I was a barely acceptable employee.

Just as I'm about to chuck it into my drawer, something catches my eye.

REVISED is typed in one of the boxes.

As I flip through the pages, REVISED is typed in several more boxes. In fact, it's everywhere that Derrick rated me poorly.

There's a handwritten note from our interim boss stuck to the last page.

Come see me when you've had a chance to read this.

I knock on his open door. 'You wanted to see me?'

He doesn't bother saying anything, just waves me in. He's a no-nonsense guy, and nearly as gruff as the rest of our department, but he lacks that bullying meanness that Derrick so successfully cultivated. I'm slowly getting used to the idea that going to work doesn't have to mean daily humiliation.

'You've read your review?'

I nod.

'Good. We've amended it in light of circumstances. You're happy with it?'

Again, I nod.

'Good. You can go.'

'Can I ask you something?'

He peers over his reading glasses.

'Why did you change it?'

'One of your colleagues brought it to my attention that it may reflect Derrick's views more than your actual performance. I checked into it and based on the feedback, we changed it. Anything else?'

'Just, thanks.'

He looks over his glasses again. 'You're welcome. Get back to work.'

I go straight to the IT department. I could kiss Zack.

'Hi,' I say when I get to his desk. 'Busy?'

He's tapping away at his keyboard and squinting at his screen. 'Yep. I'm trying to get some coding done. What's up?'

'Can I buy you a coffee?'

'Sure, thanks. Double espresso, please.'

'I meant can I take you out for a coffee.'

'Oh, no, sorry, I've really got to do this.'

'Zack, you're not making it easy to thank you.'

'Thank me for what?'

I smile. 'You know.'

He shakes his head. 'Sorry, Carol, I really don't.'

'My review?'

I can see from his expression that he doesn't know what I'm talking about.

'They changed my review, Zack. Someone flagged up the fact that Derrick is a biased arse. It doesn't mean I'll get a bonus or anything. All the lawsuits from Green T will probably suck the bonus pool dry. But at least I'm getting a fair chance now.'

'I'd love to take the credit, but I can't. I can take you for drinks, though, if you don't mind a couple of my friends being there, too. You met them at my birthday.'

'I can't tonight. I'm taking Robert to Harriet's birthday party.'

'Well, afterwards, then. You've been going on about Robert for weeks, you know. You'll have to introduce me to him some time. It may as well be tonight, when we can celebrate.'

'I'm not sure if Harriet will need me later. I'll text you, okay? I've got to go talk to someone right now.'

I leave him squinting at his code and return to my floor.

I can see that Joe is on his phone as I approach. He holds up a finger.

I'm grinning like a lunatic.

'What?' he says when he ends the call.

'I just wanted to say thanks.'

'What for?'

'For getting my review changed. It was really nice of you.'

'Yeah, well don't let that get around. You'll ruin my reputation.'

'Why'd you do it?'

'Moment of weakness.' He shrugs. 'Look, I'm not

about to claim to be some hero who—'

'I never said you were a hero.'

The tiniest smile pulls at his mouth. 'I genuinely don't give a shit what happens to everyone here, but some things are just wrong. I didn't have to go out of my way to say something, so I did. That's all.'

But he did go out of his way. Nobody else bothered to say anything, even when they knew what Derrick was like. He is sort of a hero in my eyes. I'd never tell him that, of course. He'd hate it.

'Thanks, Joe.'

'Don't mention it. And I mean that, Carol, don't mention it again. Most of us around here are arseholes. You're one of the good ones. God knows why you want to work in a place like this. You must be sadistic. But you're not dirty. You shouldn't have been the fall guy for Derrick.'

He swings around in his chair as his phone rings.

I grin all the way back to my desk.

Robert is waiting for me at the Tube station with a gorgeous bouquet of purple flowers for Harriet. 'Am I late?' I ask.

It's been our greeting since our first date. I love that we have in jokes.

'Perfectly on time.' He wraps his arms around me and kisses me. 'Did you have a good day?'

'It was unbelievable, actually.' I tell him about my review, and Joe's hand in it. 'I always thought I was a barely tolerated necessity to the traders. I'd never say it to Joe because he'd deny it, but it seems that he might actually like me a bit.'

'You work in a weird place.'

'Not all of us are lucky enough to work in an office where the bosses buy Krispy Kremes just to say thanks.'

When he first told me that he gets to sit on beanbags in meetings and play table tennis in the office, I didn't believe him. He makes it sound like he works for Google, not a marketing firm in Notting Hill.

'Maybe I'll bring Krispy Kremes to your office one day,' he says.

'You'd be set upon by a pack of hyenas if you did. They'd devour the doughnuts and then probably take out your entrails.'

'Why do you stay?' he asks as we walk towards Harriet's flat.

That's a reasonable question, given events. 'I stay because my motivation for taking the job in the first place is the same. I know I can make a bigger difference to green energy this way. If I worked as an engineer for one company, if I'm very lucky I might come up with a design that revolutionises how we use our natural resources. But if I can help green companies get the money for investment, then there are hundreds, maybe thousands of engineers getting the chance to make a difference. I'd rather have loads of smart people working on the problem. Plus, I really love the work and things are changing now with the new boss. I don't expect Krispy Kremes but I do expect to be rewarded for doing my job, not bullied.'

'I admire you.'

'Thanks, I'm trying.'

Harriet's flat is packed when we arrive. Her casual approach to tidiness and wide array of friends makes the place look like a cross between a rave and a car boot sale.

'So,' I murmur to Robert. 'Harriet is the one in the pale blue dress and red hat, and that's her new boyfriend, Tom, next to her.'

'Do you think he'll recognise you?'

Of course I told Robert about my recent role in Harriet's love life. Luckily, Harriet also told Tom.

'He knows about me. Harriet didn't want to take the chance that he'd be angry if he caught on later. He thinks it's hilarious, and he's happy with his choice.'

'As happy as I am with mine?'

I snuggle into him. 'And as happy as I am with mine.'

'Carol!' Harriet swoops over. 'Here, have some Prosecco. And you're Robert?' she says, handing him a glass. 'I've heard so much about you!'

He kisses her cheek and hands her the bouquet. 'Carol talks about you all the time,' he says. 'It's great to meet you. And you're Tom?' He shakes Tom's hand. 'Nice to meet you.'

'I'm having such a nice day,' Harriet says. 'Tom surprised me with a spa afternoon. He even cleared it with work first. Then we had lunch at the Oxo Tower, and now this. I'm a lucky girl.'

'And she doesn't look a day over twenty-one,' Tom says. 'It's nice to see you again, Carol.'

'You too, Tom. And I am sorry about the earlier ruse.'

He waves away my apology. 'When Harriet told me about some of the guys she's gone out with, I understood completely. You are a very good friend.'

A woman hurries in from the kitchen. 'Do you want

me to run to Tesco to get some more ice?'

'Oh, yes, please,' says Harriet. 'And I'd better get the canapés in the oven.'

'I'll help you,' says Tom, grabbing her hand.

Two hours later the flat is close to bursting with Harriet's well-wishers and we can hardly hear each other above the R&B and happy chatter. I glance at my BlackBerry. 'We should go soon if we're going to meet Zack.'

'Do you want to find Harriet?'

'I feel guilty leaving. It is her birthday. Maybe we should just stay. She might need me.'

'Need you for what?' Harriet asks, grabbing my shoulders from behind.

'I was just saying that Zack has offered to meet us for a drink tonight, to meet Robert.'

She smiles. 'Everybody is dying to meet the lovely Robert.' She leans close to him. 'And you do seem very lovely. You're a very lucky man to have someone like Carol. And I think she's a lucky girl, too.'

'Thanks, Harriet. I just hope I can live up to her expectations.'

'That won't be easy,' Harriet says.

'Hey!'

'Well, it's not easy living up to perfection.'

'Tell me about it,' I say. 'Anyway, we don't have to meet Zack tonight. We can do it another time.'

'You should go meet Zack.'

'But you might want help later cleaning up or throwing out the drunks or something. I feel bad that I haven't done anything at all for this party.'

'Carol, I know old habits die hard but you don't have to help me anymore, remember? Those days are over, and it's time you do the things that make you happy, don't you think?'

She's right. It's going to take me a while longer to get used to the idea that my days of being perfect in everyone else's eyes are over.

'I'll call you tomorrow then,' I say. 'Happy birthday, Harriet. You're my best friend in the world and I love you.'

'I love you, too. Just the way you are. Now go, get on with your own life. The rest of us are just fine.'

Smiling, I take Robert's hand, and we walk out together into the warm night.

THE END

Every time you write a review, an author gets a cupcake, so if you enjoyed *Perfect Girl*, please take a minute to share your thoughts on your favorite book websites.

ABOUT THE AUTHOR

Michele Gorman is the USA TODAY bestselling author of seven romantic comedies. Born and raised in the US, Michele has lived in London for 16 years. She is very fond of naps, ice cream and Richard Curtis films but objects to spiders and the word "portion".

Twitter: @MicheleGormanUK
Facebook: MicheleGormanBooks

Find out what's next for Carol in the sequel, *Christmas Carol*, a novella of approximately 100 pages. *Christmas Carol* is available in paperback and all eBook formats globally.

One winter wedding, two happy couples, three ex-boyfriends. And a very uncomfortable weekend

Meet Britain's Worst Innkeeper

The Reluctant Elf

Single mother and extremely undomestic goddess, Lottie, has five days to become the ultimate B&B hostess to save her beloved Aunt Kate's livelihood.

When Aunt Kate ends up in the hospital, Lottie and her seven-year-old daughter are called to rural Wales to stand in at the B&B. Without the faintest idea how to run a hotel (she can barely run her own life), Lottie must impress the picky hotel reviewer and his dysfunctional family who are coming to stay over Christmas. Without the rating only he can bestow, Aunt Kate will lose her livelihood.

But will Danny, the local taxi driver who she hires to help her, really be Santa's little helper, or the Grinch who stole Christmas?

Available as a **Kindle Single** on Amazon (also in paperback)

Where Confidence is the New Black

The Curvy Girls Club

Fed up with always struggling to lose weight, best friends Katie, Ellie, Pixie and Jane start a social club where size doesn't matter. It soon grows into London's most popular club - a place to have fun instead of counting carbs - and the women find their lives changing in ways they never imagined.

But outside the club, life isn't as rosy.

"This is a delightful book of friendship, acceptance, and belonging for anyone who has ever wondered: "What if?"" **Publishers Weekly**

PERFECT GIRL

Printed in Great Britain
by Amazon